THE
HOMEMAKER

BOOKS BY SHARI J. RYAN

The Bookseller of Dachau

The Doctor's Daughter

The Lieutenant's Girl

The Maid's Secret

The Stolen Twins

LAST WORDS

The Girl with the Diary

The Prison Child

The Soldier's Letters

THE
HOMEMAKER

SHARI J. RYAN

bookouture

Published by Bookouture in 2023

An imprint of Storyfire Ltd.
Carmelite House
50 Victoria Embankment
London EC4Y 0DZ

www.bookouture.com

ISBN: 978-1-83790-505-8
eBook ISBN: 978-1-83790-504-1

This book is a work of fiction. Whilst some characters and circumstances portrayed by the author are based on real people and historical fact, references to real people, events, establishments, organizations or locales are intended only to provide a sense of authenticity and are used fictitiously. All other characters and all incidents and dialogue are drawn from the author's imagination and are not to be construed as real.

To my neighbors who have proven the true meaning of friendship...
Don't worry. This story takes place in a different neighborhood.

PREFACE

There are certain things one can expect to learn about their spouse in the first year together. Oliver and I have been together for just over three years. One year as boyfriend and girlfriend, the second year as fiancées, and the third as newlyweds, soon-to-be-parents, and now...this. For the time we've been together and everything we've been through as a couple, I must know an awful lot about him. Yet, here we are, Oliver and me, face to face in the same dingy room my mother and I sat in yesterday when she asked me if I was the cause of my son's death. I'm not sure how it's possible, but I almost don't recognize the man sitting across from me.

PROLOGUE

The act of watching someone die provokes an abundance of contemplation. I keep asking myself if this was truly necessary, but I've stirred over the plan a thousand times. There was no other way around this roadblock. It's all come down to a choice —him or me. In a world where we all act so upstanding in the eyes of others, I know I'm not the only one who would pick my well-being over someone else's.

Perhaps I should feel some remorse. However, since I don't feel an ounce of regret, it's easier to convince myself I've made the right decision.

He's staring at me pointedly, his tawny eyes round and large like buttons sewn onto the face of a plush toy—the expression intended to appear endearing and delightful. Except, on a person, the look says: I'm choking.

He's not choking. If he was choking, his chance of survival might have been higher, but then this all would have been for nothing.

Maybe he's wondering what's happening to him...or if I'm going to become distressed and jump up to call for emergency assistance.

The right thing for me to do would be to call for help, but people who are in a state of distress, like me, forget to do the simple things that should be considered common sense.

Still, it's difficult watching the color drain from his face. I've seen people become pale many times before but I'm always sure the blood will eventually rush back through their cheeks when the moment of weakness passes. I don't think that will be the case here, tonight.

"Can I take a guess at what you might be thinking?" I ask with a sigh singing out a note of boredom. It isn't easy watching his chest rise and fall much too fast for someone who is in a resting position. These passing seconds feel like hours.

His eyes still have a bit of life left in them as he peers over to me while I patiently kneel by his side. "Why would she do this to me? I'd be asking the same."

A groan or a moan, maybe just an utter, rattles around in his wet throat. It sounds like he's trying to respond, but words aren't forming on his tongue. He's a fighter. I admire that in a person.

"I wish I could offer the answer you're probably looking for right now. I'm so sorry." I'm not sorry. I run my fingers through his dark, damp wavy hair. "We all have a time and a place, and none of us know when or where that is until the moment it happens." I pull my hand away from his head and dry my palm off on my pant leg. "In fact, I'm a bit jealous of you because wherever you're going has got to be better than this place."

The rattle I heard a moment ago returns and grows louder as if it's coming from deep within his chest like he's trying to breathe underwater. Everyone knows you can't breathe under water, yet so many people die from drowning in their own bodily fluids.

I take his heavy hand in mine and press my fingers to the artery within his wrist, feeling the slow, weak beat of a pulse. "Do you see a light anywhere? I know everyone talks about it... there has to be one." Unless everyone is lying about that too.

I wonder what determines whether a person's eyes stay open or close when they die. If they do close, maybe it's a sign that he passed away peacefully. On the other hand, if his eyes stay open, it could mean he suffered a miserable death filled with shock, and pain, all from within the confines of his terrified mind.

"I guess your eyes will be remain open forever," I confirm, feeling the weight of his arm grow a bit heavier.

I close my eyes, waiting for another tick of his pulse, then slide my fingers around in a small circle in case I mistakenly moved them out of place.

"Be still...your poor heart." I brush my hand over his eyelids, finding it surprisingly easy to slide them down to a final rest. "You know, this wasn't about you, right? It really wasn't. But at the same time, we all have a purpose in life, and sometimes that purpose can be a roadblock for someone else's purpose."

His hand becomes lifeless in mine, and I rest it down on his chest. He looks like he has peacefully fallen asleep after a long day.

"I'll be right back, okay?"

ONE

JENNA | NOW

The front door groans with a complaint of grief, sweeping over the welcome mat that dons the greeting, *Hello Sunshine,* in brush script lettering. A gentle spring breeze nudges the door open wider and carries in the aroma of tulips budding in the front garden beds. Then Oliver steps around the corner into the living room. He isn't often caught in a sweatshirt and jogging pants, but life came to a screeching halt a few days ago, so the laundry is overdue, and we've been spending more time in the house than outside. It's obvious that our appearances aren't at the front of our mind. Oliver's beard is at least four days old, the longest I've ever seen.

He's stiff as he steps over the threshold, clutching the doorknob with a white-knuckled grip. Each of his movements is rigid but foggy. He hasn't realized I'm awake. Although, it doesn't take long for him to notice I'm upright on the couch as I stare at him through the haze taking over my mind.

"You're awake?" he asks. I squirm around, trying to find a more comfortable position within the arch of cushions. "I had to run a few quick errands. Did I worry you?" His expression warms, his gray-blue eyes open wider, and the corners of his lips sink into a slight grimace.

"I woke up a few minutes ago. I'm fine." My answer isn't true. I'm not okay—I can't keep my eyes open. The doctor and nurses warned me I would feel depleted of energy during the first several days of motherhood, but I didn't expect to have this much trouble staying alert.

I place my hand on the side of the infant rocker and pull the bunched up knit blanket over it. A smile touches my lips in response to the plush texture, recalling how many hours I spent in the yarn aisle searching for the perfect shade of blue. I didn't have a clue how to knit or crochet but felt determined to make River his first blanket. It took several video tutorials, but I crocheted a one-of-a-kind blanket for my little boy.

"I know it hurts, I know," Oliver says, watching as I wince at the persistent discomfort swelling along my lower stomach. The pain isn't too bad. I'm just trying to adjust. Oliver's gaze shifts between the rocker and me, then to the white tray resting on the plush heather-gray ottoman. "Oh, here, let me refill your glass of water and bring you a snack." He disappears into the kitchen for a moment. "Remember, you're supposed to stay hydrated."

As Oliver rushes past me toward the kitchen, I twist my head to the side to steal a glimpse of the cherry blossoms sprouting along the tree branches outside the window. Each pink flower sways like silk ribbons against the gentle breeze, hypnotizing me into another wave of drowsiness. If only the peaceful sight could distract a new mom from her relentless worries. Days ago, the world revolved around only Oliver and me, but now there is an entire universe to protect. Yet, all I can manage to do is sleep.

"This won't be easy, but we'll get there," Oliver says. He shuffles his feet against the hardwood floor with a bowl of trail mix in one hand, and a full glass of water in the other.

"Are the neighbors eager to come over?" I ask as he places

the glass on the tray, forcing me to face my blurry, distorted reflection.

"Yeah, the texts have been nonstop for days," he says while reaching over the rocker to hand me the snack bowl.

I push myself into a better sitting position. "Hold on a second. River must be starving. I can't eat before he does. I don't even know how many hours it's been since he's eaten last. Do you?" I tug the rocker closer and take a moment to glance at my perfect little boy.

The knit blanket takes up the entire seat. It's suffocating him. I gasp and claw at the blanket. The hint of lavender from the baby detergent wafts around me as I pull it off. As I dig the tips of my fingers against the base of the seat, I'm dumbstruck. "River?" Sweat lines my forehead and my limbs turn to ice, becoming numb. "Wh-where—where is he?" Hysteria laces my words as panic consumes me.

"Jenna..."

"Oh my God," I gasp as if the wind has been knocked out of me. "Oliver, no, no, no. Oh my—where is he? Where is River? My baby!" I can't blink. I can only stare into the fleece fabric of the hollow seat. While trying to stand, the room spins around me and gravity holds me hostage, forcing me to take a hold of the couch's armrest.

"Jenna, Jenna, it's okay, it's okay," he tries to hush me. "Come on, take a deep breath with me."

My breaths lodge in my throat and stomach acid rises, burning the back of my tongue. My unblinking stare bolts from Oliver's pale complexion to the blanket strewn across the floor. "Tell me," I shout so loud my voice sounds rough like it's scraping across sandpaper.

"Okay, okay, shh, shh. It's okay, just breathe. You shouldn't be getting this distraught. You're going to end up in more pain," Oliver says, reaching for the empty baby seat. I put my hand on the rocker's handle to prevent him from taking the carrier away from me. "Jenna, please." My head is heavy, my neck so weak it feels like melting wax. I wouldn't be surprised if it rolled off my shoulders.

I'm unable to fight against his strength, not with the crippling weakness weighing me down. He moves the rocker out of view.

"Why—why—won't you tell me where he is?" I scream at the top of my lungs, my voice cracking halfway through my question. "Why, Oliver? Why?"

I ease back onto the couch, knowing I can't hold up my weight any longer. I fold my arms over my chest and rock back and forth against the pit stretching within my stomach.

"There you go. Just take a few deep breaths," he says.

"Is he upstairs in his crib? Did I sleep through his last feeding? Is that why?" I'm counting the breaths of silence between us. Oliver is too calm for the explanation to be more than River simply being asleep upstairs.

"Please, Jenna, you're going to have another panic attack." He sits beside me on the couch and reaches for my water glass, handing it to me as if I just asked for a drink instead of my newborn. My heart thuds like the roll of a snare drum—it might give out. Flashes of dark and light spots flicker within my eyes as chills skate across my skin.

"Drink, drink some water," Oliver asserts, placing the glass in front of me.

"Where—"

"Just relax, sweetie."

I lean forward, lift the glass, and throw it across the room, watching the glass shatter against the wall, along with my distorted reflection.

TWO

GINGER | LAST YEAR

I lean against the windowpane from the corner of my living room, my gaze set on the pearl-white Land Rover as it glides up the driveway of the property across the street that has been vacant for the last month. The overhanging newly blossoming tree stamps a reflection against the tinted windows, obscuring the identities of whoever is inside. The midday summer sun blazes through the window, casting a glare I struggle to see through.

House number two-forty-two on Sapphire Road should stay empty for the time being.

A young couple steps out of the Land Rover. Both are in professional attire and sunglasses, and they have expressionless faces, and sharp postures. The young woman's hand catches my eye, a diamond stealing a ray of sun with each subtle swing of her arm. I wonder what brings them to this tiny little town of Lakespur in Delaware? They could be relatives who aren't aware that their family have moved out.

On the other hand, maybe they aren't a couple. They could be undercover investigators, but it's been over a couple of weeks since we last saw police on the property.

The man places his arm in front of the woman, forcing her to pause in her steps up the driveway. He holds up his other hand, as he backs away from the house and reaches into his coat pocket, retrieving his phone. The woman turns her back to the front door and offers him a wide smile, altering her stiff persona. He holds up a finger and joins her for a selfie with the house in the background. I'm tempted to go outside and ask them what they think they're doing. The house is still private property.

I lose sight of them as they walk closer to the white-trimmed farmer's porch, so I lunge for my phone, resting beside my laptop on the coffee table, and open the doorbell camera app. By the time the camera focuses on the front door across the street, I catch the tail end of the man carrying the woman over the threshold. Then the door closes, and the story is over.

I've been checking daily to see if the house has gone on the market. As of an hour ago, it hadn't. There haven't been any showings or any realtors. Yet somehow it looks like they have sold the house? I drop into the chair at the kitchen table and scroll down the list of properties for sale in the town. With a brief pause on each listing, I make sure I didn't miss something earlier.

Maybe Joel would know. I tap on his contact in my phone and touch the speaker button. One ring, two rings...the chances of him answering decrease with each passing second.

"Mom, hey, is everything okay? Did you hear something about Dad?" It's the first question he asks me every time we talk. I feel like I'm letting him down each time I call without the news he wants to hear.

"Joel, hi, honey. Everything is fine. No, there's nothing new to report, I'm sorry. I just have a question for you."

"Okay, can it wait? I'm with a client right now." He's always so quick to get me off the phone. He was never like this before. Joel is the talker, the one who always told me every detail about his life, until things changed.

"Of course, no problem. I didn't mean to stress you out."

"I'm not stressed out. I have to go."

He speaks quickly, his words crashing together. "All right then. Talk later. I love you."

"Talk soon," he says just before ending the call. I can't help but wonder what it would take for him to give me the time of day. If I was, God forbid, sick or injured, I hope he'd put his busy life on pause for me.

The doorbell chimes a hollow digital rendition of ding-dong on my phone and from the alarm system speakers. I drop my phone, fisting the linen fabric of my blouse against my chest. *It's just the doorbell*, I remind myself. He wouldn't ring the bell if he came back. I snatch my phone up from the floor, praying the screen hasn't cracked, and kiss it when I see I've gotten away without a scratch. I hold the phone up and switch the camera views to see who's at the front door. I close my eyes and for a quick moment, wish to find James standing there, but as I open my eyes, I find Peyton instead, biting her lip as she bounces up and down on her toes. I wish I didn't find her to be so bothersome. Perhaps if she came over for any other reason but to ask for something, I might not mind her as much.

This will be the third time this week she will need to "borrow" an item she forgot to pick up at the store—usually something she can't return.

With a glance in the foyer mirror, I tuck my short coppery strands behind my ears, finally growing out the pixie-cut style I was sure I'd love, and adjust the peach linen blouse over my lean frame. I don't need Peyton or anyone else seeing me frazzled or unkempt. I think it makes me look guilty of the rumors spreading about me. So, I compose myself with a deep inhale, and twist the oval knob to release the deadbolt. A metal clink follows.

I remind myself to smile when I greet her. "Peyton, what a surprise," I say, sounding like a punctured tire. "How is my wonderful neighbor?" Peyton, Perfect Peyton. The gorgeous blonde-haired, green-eyed doe with a flawless figure and legs for days steps into view. I have never met anyone who tries so hard to make it look like she makes no effort when it must take hours to look as good as she does, even in jogging wear and a messy ponytail. People don't wake up with a fresh dewy glow on their pink pinched cheeks. Even from a few steps away on the front porch, her signature citrus-floral blend of essential oils seeps into my house. Peyton might look like she has it all together, but she's made it clear she has no clue how to take care of a house or a husband, which is why she's likely standing here. It's been almost two years since she and her husband, Lincoln, moved into two-forty-three Sapphire Road, right next door.

Peyton chews on the corner of her bottom lip. She isn't embarrassed to be standing here, not like her cute expression says. I wonder if she bites on her lip out of habit or if it's with intention. I sweep my top teeth across my bottom lip, curious if it feels attractive. It doesn't.

"I am sorry to be here again this week. I'm ashamed because I went to the store and got all the ingredients to make my meat-loaf. Except, I forgot the eggs, again. The next time I go, I'll buy you a new carton, I swear." She curls her fists into the long sleeves of her sweatshirt and presses them beneath her chin. "I'm a train wreck, I know. Last night, I made shepherd's pie because it's Lincoln's favorite, and I think I put too many peas in because the potatoes turned green. I don't know why it's just so hard to be someone's wife." She juts out her bottom lip and huffs, whooshing the loose wisps of hair that frame her face.

Shepherd's pie is not Lincoln's favorite meal. She told me once before that he didn't like it, but she was trying to find a good recipe to change his mind. *I'm sure it is hard to be some-one's wife when all you think about is yourself.* "Oh, you're fine. Like I told you before, with Carter in college now and out of the house like the rest of the boys, I have an oversupply of eggs." I can't seem to remember to stop myself from buying so many when I'm at the store. Cue the tiny violin. I promised I would not suffer from empty nest syndrome because I have been successful in raising four sons. Even though I seem to be the bane of their existence, I'm proud that two have stable careers and the other two are living their best lives in college. It's just so quiet in the house all day after spending most of my life being a stay-at-home-mom.

Peyton places her sweatshirt covered hand over her mouth and her shoulders falter. "You poor thing," she says, clicking her tongue against the roof of her mouth. "I know. You should come over to our house for dinner sometime. Lincoln and I would be happy to have you over. We can keep you company whenever you'd like." *I'm not sure I could eat anything served at her house...* "Or you can just come over for tea or coffee and we can chat. I know you might think you're the best listener on this street, but I'm not so bad."

She must know pity rarely makes anyone feel better. "What a nice offer," I reply. *Nice try.* My gaze drifts from the luminous shimmer on the tip of Peyton's nose, past her shoulder toward the Land Rover. "Did the house sell, or—" I point to Luanne's former house as if I need to clarify my question. No one has put their home up for sale in our neighborhood in over a year or two.

Peyton glances over her shoulder and furrows her brow. "Is the property for sale yet? I haven't seen a sign or anything?" She presses her fingertip against her lips, forging whatever thought she's about to share. "Luanne mentioned nothing about a sale, but I haven't spoken to her in a couple of days—since the moving truck came and went."

"Neither have I." Luanne hasn't returned any of my phone calls. It's clear she doesn't want to talk.

I'm sure there would have been an update on the real estate brokerage list if the house went on the market, but Peyton doesn't need to know how often I check for new listings.

"Well, I know real estate postings have been so secretive lately because of the speed they're flying off the market. Maybe it was a private sale?" A private sale doesn't sound like something Luanne would have considered in her condition. Although desperation always seems to present itself in unique ways.

"Maybe," I sigh, pinching at the cuff of my sleeves, wishing they were long enough to cover my knuckles too. "I'll grab the egg for you. Just one?"

"Two if you can spare them," she says with a giddy giggle.

I flap my hand in the air, underlining how easygoing I am. I should start knocking on her door whenever I'm low on toilet paper.

With one hand on the fridge door and the other grabbing the eggs, I peek over my shoulder, making sure she hasn't followed me into the house again like she did once before. After that incident, I made it clear she needs to stay on the front step and not come in any further.

"All set with the eggs." I step out of the kitchen, thankfully finding her still on the front porch, and exchange the eggs from my hands to hers.

"Thanks again," she says. "Have a good night."

"You too," I sing out, then close the front door and secure the locks before placing another call to Luanne. If she doesn't answer the call this time, I'll take the hint.

Three long rings drawl and my heart flutters in my chest, knowing I'm about to hear the automated voice message.

But then Luanne answers. "Hi, Ginger," she says, her words a mere whisper. "Sorry, I know I haven't called you back. I've been—"

"No need for explanations. It's understandable," I say.

"Is everything okay? Are you just calling to—"

"Yes, everything is fine. I didn't know you sold the house so quickly..."

A sniffle comes across the line like static. "Yup," she sobs. "It's out of my hands now. I couldn't bear to be in there another minute anyway. That house is anything but a home now."

"I understand perfectly well," I say.

"Everything happens so quickly these days, doesn't it?" she cries into the phone. "It's there one day and gone the next, right?"

"Oh, Luanne... I know, I understand completely."

"Do you, though?" she asks. "Look, Ginger, I can't talk right now. I need to go."

I know well how fast life can change. Happiness and certainty once filled my days but now my life is like an incomplete story, its pages shredded and scattering in the wind.

THREE

JENNA | LAST YEAR

People don't buy a house without checking it out first. It was a gamble, all our chips on a random odd number in the color red. With an offer of the asking price and supposedly a few other competing offers on the table, I didn't think the odds were in our favor. Yet, here we are, new homeowners of this charming colonial, nestled in a picture-perfect suburban community in Lakespur, Delaware. I have had my eye on the properties in this neighborhood for over a year, even before we were ready to start looking for houses, but not one house had gone on the market here until this past month.

"This is unreal," Oliver says. He spins around the living room like a child visiting a larger-than-life toy store for the first time. He's scouring every nook and cranny while taking in an exaggerated inhale of the fresh paint and lemon-infused floor polish adding a slight sheen to the walnut brown wooden panels. The walls are a shade of sea-glass teal with satin white trim and crown-molding. The coloring offers a beachy feel, especially with long and wide paneled windows on almost every wall. The open floor concept will make for the perfect breezeway, and a breeze would be nice right about now.

I gather my hair together at the base of my neck and secure it with an elastic. Hopefully the central air works. It's only June, but the summer heat has set in and the house feels like the inside of an oven.

"It's by far the dumbest thing we've ever done," I remind him.

The moment Oliver received notice about a property on this street, he jumped at the opportunity, especially since we had been house hunting for months, knowing our apartment lease was coming to an end next month. The timing couldn't have been better, but still—it all happened so fast. My strangled attempt to laugh is transparent.

Oliver sighs. I haven't been short on commentary on the speed of our purchase, but he did ask me if we should back out before signing the offer letter, and I said no. My desires supersede my intelligence.

"The surveyor said there were no issues. What more could we ask?"

Oliver took the lead on the entire purchasing process, which didn't leave me much time to consider that he should have asked for a background check on the surveyor, references, thoughts from the neighbors, something more than the few recent reviews we found online.

I wish the realtor had sent us pictures from inside the house, but she said no images had been taken and her hands were tied because of specific requests from the previous owners. That's when the purchase became a giant wager. Still, we were on board to make an offer.

I have seen enough interior photos from the real estate archives of other homes on this street. They all look similar, cookie-cutter. If I had to weigh the options of losses, we could be stuck painting and refinishing the floors. On the contrary, the house could have sold out from beneath us if we had requested a tour. Who knows how long we'd have to wait before another property in this community became available?

"There isn't much we need to change," he says. I continue through the living room, which flows into the dining room. I find Oliver brushing his fingers along the bright white wainscoting along the bottom half of the walls—the top half is the same color as the living room, which I like since the rooms aren't separated by more than small sections of walls and pillars. I love being able to see into part of the kitchen and the family room enclosed with glass sliding doors.

As I stare up at the unlit golden chandelier with crystal rods poking out like white seeds of a dandelion, I can't imagine why someone would desert such a unique piece. It must have cost a fortune.

"The realtor never ended up mentioning a word about the previous owners?" I ask.

Everything happened so fast with the sale and purchase, leaving us to stir over our impulsive decision for almost three weeks until the closing this morning.

Oliver rubs the tip of his thumbnail over a dull mark on the wall. "It's clear they were in a rush to sell. One of them might have received a job offer in another state."

"A job transfer would make sense for how quickly it came together." So would many other circumstances.

I continue along the flow through the house, making my way into the kitchen but Oliver seems more excited about checking out the second floor as I hear him jetting up the stairs.

After admiring the canvas of stainless-steel appliances between frosty granite countertops and a matching island, I stop to inspect the interior of the white cabinets, then the mostly empty fridge. I squint at a decaying, flimsy bouquet of white roses wrapped with a gray lace ribbon sitting along the top shelf. A bad floral perfume assaults my nose. They must have forgotten them. I lift the stems and place the wilting array on the counter. A small card beneath the ribbon catches my eye. I don't think anyone is returning to claim the dead flowers, so I pluck it off the stems and flip it, finding a simple note:

We send our deepest condolences
The darkest of nights might seem blue
But the sun will again rise
Unless it's you...
the cause of his demise.

As I take in the words, the oatmeal I scarfed down for breakfast gurgles in my stomach.

"Babe, come up here for a minute," Oliver hollers from upstairs. I slip the card into my back pocket, leaving the dead flowers out so I can toss them away before we leave.

Trying to find Oliver, I scale the long, straight stairway made up of wide wooden planks with a matching handrail. The wall on the right side will be perfect for hanging pictures. I reach the top landing and peer in each direction. There are four bedrooms—two on each side of the hallway, and a bathroom across the hall. Each space is decorated much like the kitchen, with an abundance of white, with dark contrasting fixtures and golden hardware.

The first room might be great for my home office as I could have a clear view of the front yard. It's always nice to know what's happening outside even if I'm busy working indoors. As I arrive at the next room at the end of the hallway, I find Oliver leaning against the wall between the two six-pane windows. "This will be the nursery," he says, trying to contain his smile.

He says all the right things—everything I want to hear. I want kids; a big family, the whole package. I had my wedding planned out before I got into middle school and my kids' names picked out by the end of ninth grade. Then, when I started college, I found out what it would take to be a young successful attorney.

"Oliver," I groan. We've talked about having children so many times. He knows how badly I want them.

"I didn't say it has to be our baby's room this very minute," he mumbles.

"Well, good...because that would be inconceivable since I'm not pregnant. We agreed to wait, remember?" I don't know if we'll hold out for three years as we discussed, but my career is not ready for that next step yet. After four years of working toward my undergraduate degree then three more years for my law degree, and another year working as an intern while preparing for the bar exam, I was lucky enough to acquire a position at a well-known local law firm with an impeccable reputation I'm honored to represent. I pretty much missed out on most of my twenties as I committed myself to working as many hours as possible, knowing it would be the only way to make a name for myself in a cut-throat career. I've been with the same firm for five years now and my hope is to become a partner within the next few years. If we have a baby right now, I'm not sure that career goal will ever come to fruition. This is the part about being an adult I hate the most. I want it all, right now.

"What if you become a partner before the end of the year?" So does Oliver.

We've had this rhetorical conversation a dozen times. I have no idea when or if the promotion will happen. "That would be amazing, but if I become pregnant within months of accepting a share in the firm, it wouldn't shine a good light on me." This is where our unrivaled argument with a list of *what ifs* begins. "We're young. We don't need to be in a rush," I say, making my way toward him. I've had to convince myself of this enough times as it is. It's much harder to look my husband in the face and try to convince him of the same.

"You're young. I'm almost forty-one. Those ten years make a big difference." He drops his gaze down, trying to drive his point home.

I place my palms on his cheeks and straighten his head. "You're not the one carrying the baby in your body. Forty-one is the new thirty-one, which makes my thirty-one the new twenty-one."

"I hope your arguments are better in court than with me." He furrows his brow and pecks a soft kiss against my lips.

I smile in response to his playful joke and try to offer some understanding for the way he feels. "Someday this will be our son or daughter's room. I'm sure of it."

"Fine," he laments. A jolt fires through his body as if something zapped him. He pulls his phone out of his back pocket, checks the screen, silences the call and slips the phone back into his pocket.

"Who was that?" For someone as nosy as he is when my phone buzzes, he should expect me to ask the same questions he does.

"No one. It looks like an automated call from the university." The difference between Oliver and me is that I have no problem telling him it's my mom calling for the fifth time in an hour.

"Don't you think you should answer the call in case it's something important?"

Oliver flaps his hand in the air, shooing off the thought. "Nah, it's probably just a reminder about a fundraiser. It can wait."

I follow him into the spare room next to the main bedroom, finding sunlight splashing against the white walls, forcing us to shade our eyes with our hands as we walk toward the window.

Oliver rests his palms on the windowsill to stare out over the neighborhood but stiffens as if he's spotted something unusual. I scan the outside view to see what's caught his eye. All I see is a middle-aged woman striding alongside her Labrador with a waste bag dangling from her left hand. I loop my arm around his back, resting my head on his shoulder. In response, he flinches as if he didn't know I was standing here.

"Are you okay?"

"Yeah—I just—What now?" He takes his phone out again and silences another call. "Take a hint, will you?"

"Another automated call?"

"Yeah, it's overkill." *I doubt an automated call can take a hint.*

With an attempt to push the phone calls out of my head, I notice a mother and a toddler walking down the sidewalk. The child looks up at our house with eyes of wonder. His glance causes his mother to seemingly panic as she lifts him up and scurries along the sidewalk, continuing down the street.

Oliver leans closer to the window, his nose almost touching the glass as he gazes toward the street. "Did you see that?"

Chills coat the length of my arms as I mentally place the sympathy note with the worried mother. Oliver looks like he might get sick. "Babe, no one even knows who we are yet. All they see is our car and they probably just want to know who their new neighbors are. Plus, the sale was private, so it may surprise people to see anyone here. I'm sure that's all it is." The words roll off my tongue just as easily as they do when I'm deluding the truth in a courtroom to protect an innocent child.

"I'll ask the realtor if she knows anything about the people who lived here."

The sympathy card I found alongside the dead flowers might offer some insight about the previous owners, but I'm not sure the cryptic and accusatory words alluding to the cause of death will offer Oliver any form of comfort... Seeing as I just ensured him all is well with the new house, which might be a blatant lie, it's best to convince myself of the same too.

FOUR

JENNA | NOW

The fan hanging from the ceiling spins like a pinwheel in a passing breeze, just slow enough to watch the five blades whirling around and around. The TV has been on for however long I've been awake, but I'm not interested in watching. The contrast between flashes of bright and dark lights irritates my eyes, making my head ache around my temples.

I want to get up and take care of River, take a shower, and clean up a bit, but each time I move, a tidal wave sucks me in, holds me hostage, and pulls me further out into the sea where I can't decipher the direction that will take me to dry land.

"I'm going to get going. I tidied up the kitchen and placed the food containers in the freezer." A woman's voice grows from somewhere around me.

"You've all been so kind. I can't thank you enough for all the help you've given us over the last week. I'm sure we'll find a way to repay you soon," Oliver says. His fingers are woven between mine. He's on a chair beside me, but I'm not sure how long he's been there.

"No need to worry about repaying me or any of the others. We all just want the best for Jenna."

There's nothing wrong with me. I'm tired. I've just given birth. There must be no grace period for new mothers these days.

"Has the doctor offered any new information?" the woman asks.

I'm not sure which doctor she's speaking about or why she's asking Oliver about my health rather than me.

Oliver lifts my hand. The soft touch of his lips brush against my knuckles. "I haven't gotten any new information. As of this morning, the doctor still thinks she's suffering from a form of postpartum depression but told me to bring her in this afternoon."

Postpartum depression? I'm just tired. The baby-blues is what the childbirth class instructor called it.

"I've never heard of postpartum depression presenting itself in this way," she says. At least she agrees with me. I just wish I recognized her voice.

"The child birthing classes didn't warn us of these symptoms either."

"Well, I'm sure there's a perfectly logical explanation. Maybe it's as simple as her iron levels being too low. I believe it's somewhat common before and after childbirth. Maybe try adding some greens to her diet. Is she still taking the folic acid vitamins?" The woman's words grow closer by the rising volume and form like taffy being pulled into a thin wobbly rope. She's wearing a perfume I've never smelled before. Vanilla and jasmine—the unusual combination sends a wave of nausea through my hollow stomach.

I turn my head to the right and the room follows. My head bounces like a pinball recoiling off a spring. "Hi, Jenna," she says, taking my hand. I blink several times, attempting to focus on her, but her face looks as if it's on the other side of rippled glass.

"Hi..." I use every ounce of strength I have to muster the word.

"We brought you some meals. They're in the freezer so Oliver can heat them up when you're hungry."

My eyes float up behind my eyelids like helium-filled balloons disappearing behind clouds. The room continues spinning around me.

"She needs to keep drinking water," Oliver says. "The doctor said hydration is important right now."

Without warning, a straw rests against my lips. "Babe, you need water." A plastic straw presses between my dry lips and a droplet falls to my tongue, enticing me to pull more liquid from the cup. "That's my girl." I'm not sure how much I've drunk, but my throat isn't as rusty as it was before, and my tongue is no longer as rough as sandpaper.

"When did she actually see the doctor last?" the woman asks.

"Ah, yesterday. The days are all beginning to blend into each other. She said to call back if Jenna spikes a fever or if any new symptoms appear."

From somewhere, an icy palm covers my forehead. "She's not warm. I have a mom-hand-radar for fevers. My Amelia gets them once a month like clockwork. There are just so many viruses running rampant, you know?"

Marybeth. It's Marybeth. I'm not sure I could forget the amount of stories she's told us about her Amelia.

Confusion ripples through me. I think I'd know if I had a fever, and I doubt I have a virus. I haven't left the house.

"No, there's no fever," Oliver confirms, "and she's the same as she was yesterday: lethargic and incoherent."

"Well, I'm not a doctor, but as a mother of three, I think you might need a second opinion from a specialist."

Oliver releases a heavy sigh before he agrees. I'm not sure if he's aggravated, upset, or both. "Yeah."

"This is just an unthinkable situation. I'm sure you're hanging on by a thread too. What can I do to help? I know Peyton would normally be here to lend a hand, but with her current situation, she's obviously tied up."

No one needs to help us. The less help, the better off we'll be. We're managing just fine and Oliver hasn't left my side since River was born other than to take care of him. It's only been a week or so. I'm sure I'll be back on my feet soon. "River?" I utter.

"Oh, gosh. Okay, I'm going to let you be. Call me if you need anything. Hang in there, honey."

"We will. Thanks again for the meals," Oliver says.

The patter of footsteps in the stairwell echoes between the walls, and then a door opens and closes with a thud.

"Where is—River?" I ask again.

"Jenna, babe, we can't do this again..." Oliver combs his fingers through my tangled hair.

"River," I shout, trying to sit up as gravity fights against my weight. "Where the hell is my baby? Why am I in bed, sick like this? I need him." My heart pounds. My pulse thumps within my ears and I try to swing my legs off the bed.

"Jenna," Oliver moans. "Take a deep breath. I'll breathe with you. Come on, we can get through this together."

"No, no we can't. I need my baby."

"Me too, but that isn't an option right now." I shake my head so hard my brain feels like a rubber ball inside of my skull, and I fall backward onto the pillow. "Please," I beg, wishing the fog would clear.

Oliver lies down beside me and wraps his arm around my chest. "Everything will be okay. I won't let anything happen to you."

"It's—it's not...me you need to...care for. Why don't you under—understand?"

FIVE

GINGER | LAST YEAR

I could send Luanne some freezer meals since she won't allow me to help in any other way. I find it hard to go wrong with food, so I'll just bring a basket of goodies and drop it on her doorstep. Of course, I would need to find an address for where she's currently living, which seems to be top secret information. If Peyton has her address, she likely won't give it to me because she'd rather be the best of friends to Luanne right now. If there's anything Peyton does better than everyone else, it's being a devoted friend.

The new neighbors might have a forwarding address for Luanne, but they've hardly been outside long enough for us to casually meet. I stare out the window from my living room, pondering how I can acquire more information about this mysterious death. We all have a right to know what happened on our street and yet, we've been left in the dark with the house that has been swept clean of its former owners.

I pace in front of the bay window overlooking the street and bite down on the tip of my thumbnail, contemplating my options. A whistle sings from between my puckered lips. "Willow, here, willy-girl." I drum my fingers along the curtains in the living room, knowing the space behind the sofa is her favorite place to hide. The swaying drapes release the aroma of lavender fabric spray I used earlier, Willow's favorite scent.

Sure enough, she scampers out whining with a miffed meow. I jog to the front door and open it wide enough for her to escape. After a couple more whistles, Willow spots the fleeting chance of freedom and lunges toward the door. She's a house cat, but I have a terrible time keeping her inside when she thinks I'm leaving. She won't go far.

Willow jolts out and I watch as she sprints down the driveway and across the street to Luanne's old yard. I follow, watching for oncoming traffic or outside lurkers and crouch down when I reach the evergreen bushes in the new neighbors' yard, creeping between the hedges until I reach the gutter along the house siding. Willow is only a footstep away, sitting peacefully in one of her favorite spots. I curl my fingers around the sill of the bay window and pull myself up to peek inside. An unsuspecting pair of eyes meets me at first glance, and I tumble back into the bush. The scent of pine tickles my nose, making my eyes water, but I reach forward and grab ahold of my silver furball. She hisses as I scoop her into my arms. "You little escape artist. I caught you," I say, loud enough for anyone around me to hear.

I press my hand against the thick spring grass and push myself back up to my feet, curling Willow into my folded arms.

The front door of Luanne's old house shoots open just as I step in front of the white Land Rover. The man I saw walking in with his wife just an hour ago is standing in his doorway, searching for the source of commotion. By the sharp angles of his brows, I gather he's flustered. He must also be worn out by the way the sleeves of his white button-down shirt are rolled to his elbows instead of folded neatly.

"Uh, hi. Can I help you with something?" he asks, irritation frowning into his forehead.

I struggle to find my balance while I think of a good response. "Oh, oh, goodness. I'm so sorry. I went to get the mail and my cat snuck out. I apologize in advance, but she's taken a liking to your front—" He seems stunned rather than unsettled, not sure what to make of me I suppose. "She's taken a liking to the evergreen you have below your bay window. I've only had her about a year, but since the day I brought her home, she's had her eye on this one spot."

The man steps out of the house. His dark espresso-colored hair, styled with a side part, is combed into seamless waves flowing away from his prominent facial features. Dark framed glasses highlight a sense of concern within his stormy blue eyes. His casual suit is tailor-made, a silver clip securing his pin-striped tie neatly to his pale-blue dress shirt.

"It seems she's not the only one," he says with an arch in his brow. "I'm Oliver, by the way—the lucky new owners of this beautiful house." He gestures toward the front window as if he's revealing a prize on a game show. "Do you live in one of these neighboring houses?"

"Ah, I see." I try to sound surprised as if I hadn't noticed them earlier today. "How wonderful. It's nice to meet you, Oliver. I'm Ginger, and this troublemaker is Willow," I say, lifting her paw to wave. "I live in the house right across the road, two-forty-five." I point between my house and Peyton's.

Oliver glances past me, toward my house. "Beautiful property," he says.

"Well, thank you. We're all very fortunate on this street, blessed with lovely homes."

"Absolutely," he says. "Speaking of which, what's the word on the street about our house? Anything exciting we should know about?"

I understand most people aren't a fan of neighbors peeping through their windows but if he knew anything about this neighborhood, he might have more appreciation for the watchful eyes around here. "I'm not sure I would be the best person to ask about gossip," I say with a slight shudder. I stop myself from saying something I shouldn't.

"Well, my wife, Jenna and I just closed on the house this morning and we're thrilled to be here. It's been a dream of ours to live in this neighborhood."

I wouldn't be so quick to say that. They'll have this house back on the market in less than a year. "Let me be the first to welcome you to Sapphire Road!"

"Thank you so much..." he pauses and presses his hands into his lower back to stretch. "Ginger, just out of curiosity, were you close with the previous owners?" He cuts right to the chase, and I wonder what he knows or doesn't know about Luanne.

I waggle my head from side to side. "We're all quite close on this street. There's never a shortage of helping hands, which is nice, and we watch out for one another." I may watch more than others, but at least someone has their eyes open.

"How nice to hear. We hope the prior owners left on good terms despite the reason for a quick sale."

"There wasn't a forwarding address left behind for them was there?" I ask.

Oliver juts his chin out and shakes his head. "We don't know a thing about them."

"Nice couple. We'll miss them around here, but it's great to have fresh faces just as well."

The last thing they need to hear about is what Luanne is dealing with. Oliver scratches the side of his neck and squints against the sun. It's my cue to head back home. "I see. In any case, it's so nice to meet you, Ginger." Oliver searches over his shoulder toward the front door as if someone is calling for him, but the street is silent aside from our conversation. "I better get back inside."

"Of course. Don't let me keep you. I hope you have a nice night."

"You as well. Oh, and Willow, too," he says, holding his hand up.

I head back toward my house, realizing how heavy Willow feels after holding her for a couple of minutes.

"The suspense got to you, didn't it?" Peyton chuckles from her sunshine yellow Adirondack chair. I didn't notice her, hidden within the late afternoon shadows on her farmer's porch.

I gasp and almost drop Willow. "Good God, you startled me to death," I sigh, breathlessly.

Peyton leans forward, slicing into the sun's glare, and rests her elbows on her knees, a book dangling from one hand. Her blonde ponytail glistens like threads of gold and her eyes glitter like translucent emeralds. *What is the purpose of posing as a model of perfection all the time?* "I'm so sorry. I thought you were looking right at me while walking up your driveway."

Liar. "You hardly ever sit out here," I point out.

She lifts a hot pink paperback book from her lap and waves it around. "I'm just enjoying the beautiful day with a little romantic comedy. The meatloaf is cooking and I'm waiting on the timer." Her hair sweeps across her face with a passing breeze. I wonder how hard it must be to read when you spend so much time idolizing your reflection in the mirror. We both know she's out here inspecting the new neighbors just like I am.

Except, we are out here for two very different reasons.

SIX

JENNA | LAST YEAR

The moving truck left our apartment early this morning, leaving just a cloud of dust behind. We turned in our keys to the landlord and said goodbye to our first shared space. I didn't have an attachment to the simple one-bedroom apartment, missing a personal touch and a sense of familiarity, that we'd been living in for the last year. It felt temporary from the day we moved in together. I always have my eyes set on what's next. A house to plant our roots, and in this lucky case, one with a grand farmer's porch that wraps around the exterior, a lush lawn with mature trees bordering the property, and a quiet street—it's exactly what I've wanted.

"Incoming call from...Mom," Siri announces as I turn onto the highway.

I press the green phone button on the steering wheel and listen for the call to connect. "Hey," I greet her cheerfully, as I do each morning, but today there's an extra layer of excitement highlighting the one word. Normally, I would be on my way to the office, but the university Oliver teaches at has spring break this week, and I took a few days off so we can settle into the house.

"It's moving day," she announces, as if it might have slipped my mind.

"I'm on my way as we speak." With a glance in my rearview mirror, I spot Oliver on my tail in his polished black Land Rover, the counterpart to my white edition. His mouth is moving and he's laughing, obviously talking to someone over hands-free.

"You must need help with the unpacking, so I'm going to come over and give you a hand in a bit," Mom insists.

"You don't have to do that. We can take care of it, and you shouldn't be lifting anything."

"Jenna, please. I'm just going to take a quick shower and I'll see you in an hour."

"Mom—"

"See you in a bit, honey," she says, hanging up the phone like she does when she requires the last word.

I planned on trying to meet some of the neighbors this morning with hope of figuring out something more about the cryptic sympathy card I found on the chilling dead flowers. If Mom knew I'd found such a thing, she'd understand why I needed some time this morning. She would also ask me if I'd lost my mind for not calling up the realtor and demanding information about the previous owners. It's better off for everyone if I keep the card to myself for the time being.

We did assume she would pop in today. I'm her only daughter, and as a single mom, I don't see her ever giving me a little more slack. She's lonely. I get it, and I try to include her whenever possible.

The twenty-minute drive is behind me as I pull into our driveway, parking in the spot closest to the door. We agreed I should have this spot for when we have kids someday. Oliver has an old-fashioned sense of how our lives are going to pan out after we have children, but I've worked too hard for my career, and I don't plan on giving that up to be a full-time mom, despite how much I eventually want a family of my own.

Oliver pulls up on the left, parking his car beside mine. He's still on a call. When he peers at me through the passenger side window, he smiles, his teeth glistening, pride written across his face, and he ends his call as if nothing else matters right now. The movers already have their truck parked out in front of the lawn. We gave them our set of keys so they could start unloading since we needed a few extra minutes to finish up at the apartment. By the looks of the half empty truck, they moved quicker than I thought they would.

They've propped the front door open, and a path of flattened boxes are in the foyer. The three movers are like a well-oiled machine, never stopping to take a breath, moving from the back of the truck to the inside of the house.

Two of the men are walking our king-size mattress up the stairwell. They're moving with caution, making sure not to snag any corners as they prepare to take a right off the top landing.

"Fellas, I can give you a hand if you'd like?" Oliver shouts up to them.

"We're all set," one replies amidst a grunt.

"I'm just going to check on them," Oliver says, his fists curling. His strong desire to be in control of everything makes him anxious. The trait doesn't bother me since I see it more as passion for what's important to him, but I wish he would let things slide sometimes, at least for his own sanity. He puts every part of him into everything he does, big or small. I can't fault him for that.

"Knock, knock," says a voice from the open doorway, concealed behind a stack of boxes. I step around them to greet whoever is at the door, finding a young, tall blonde, with a smile that looks as if it could reach her ears. She's in black yoga pants, a long white hooded sweatshirt, and running shoes.

"Hi!" That came out awkwardly. I took a second too long to scrutinize her.

"I'm sorry to just barge in on you like this, but I couldn't wait any longer to come introduce myself. My husband, Lincoln, and I live just over there, across the street at two-forty-three. Oh, and I'm Peyton," she says, pointing over her shoulder to the house across the street with cloudy blue shingles and navy trim for the shutters, front door, and garage bays.

"Come on in," I invite her. "The house is sort of a disaster, but it's so kind of you to stop by and introduce yourself. I'm Jenna and my husband, Oliver, is upstairs with the movers."

Peyton scans the foyer as if she hadn't been inside before. The woman across the street told Oliver they were all close, but that could mean anything, I guess. "I can't tell you how excited I am to have new neighbors around our age. Everyone else is somewhat young around here too, but—wait, do you have kids?"

I'm struck by her forward question, but I suppose that would be a typical thing to ask of someone moving into the street. "No, no, not yet. Someday, you know...in the future," I reply.

Peyton laughs. "I hear ya. You must be newlyweds too," she says, her eyes faltering on my ring finger.

"Is it still that shiny?" I ask with a smile, admiring my hand as it catches the light.

She holds her hand up too, and a similar glisten sparkles around us. "It can never be too shiny," she says. "Anyway, everyone else around here already has children, so it's nice that I'm no longer the only one not at that point yet."

I feel the same. My friends have fallen out of the picture over the last few years as their schedules filled with playdates, sports, and school activities for their children. We seem to live very different lives now, but understandably so.

"Oliver, babe," I call for him up the stairs. "Come meet one of our neighbors."

"Oh gosh, I don't want to interrupt the flow. I'm sure we can all meet later when you aren't in the middle of a box catastrophe." She's funny and sweet, and I'm glad there's someone I can see myself becoming friends with already.

Before I can insist on her meeting Oliver, he barrels down the stairs and over to my side, then wipes the sweat off his palms onto his worn painting jeans. "It's so nice to meet you," he says, offering to shake her hand.

"This is Peyton. Peyton, this is Oliver. She and her husband Lincoln live across from us," I tell Oliver, filling him in.

He's out of breath and places his hands down on his knees. "One second. Sorry, I'm out of shape. I forgot how hea-heavy the bureau is."

"That's why we compromised on hiring movers," I remind him with a chuckle as I tap my palm against the chest of his sweat-soaked shirt. Oliver was sure we could handle the move on our own, but I had a feeling it was going to be harder than he made it sound, and I'm not sure how useful I would be, carrying all our furniture up to the second floor. I could hardly get a grip on our mattress; never mind the bigger pieces we'd have to maneuver.

Oliver inhales sharply and straightens his posture. "Sorry—sorry about that." He lifts his head and stares at Peyton. "Peyton, you said?" He presses his hands into the small of his back, stretching backward. "You don't look like a Peyton. Is that a weird thing to say? Do you get that a lot?"

"Oliver," I say, scolding him. I'm not sure if my laughter successfully fills the awkward silence between us. "Sorry, he thinks because he has classes of students, he can match a name to a face," I say, slapping the back of my hand playfully against Oliver.

"It's fine," she says with a laugh. "Anyway, my husband, Lincoln, is at work right now, but I'm sure he'll be so happy to meet you when he gets home later."

"Good, good. I look forward to meeting him too," Oliver replies, still trying to catch his breath. "I need to finish moving the bureau, but uh, Peyton, it was nice of you to stop by and—"

"Yes, thank you for coming by to introduce yourself," I say.

"Of course. It's always overwhelming being the new person on the street. I figured I'd just break that ice for you," she says, shucking an awkward fist into the air.

"Yes, it's nerve-racking, but everyone seems nice as far as we can tell. Oliver met Ginger last night. I guess her cat likes one of our bushes in the front yard."

Peyton holds her manicured nails against her forehead. "Sorry about that. Ginger has a good heart, but she's a little bullish. The other neighbors and I think it's because her youngest son just left for college after the winter break, so she's an empty nester after being a stay-at-home-mom for so long."

"Well, that makes perfect sense. I can't imagine devoting so much time to raising kids and then suddenly they're gone."

"Right?" she agrees.

I glance up the stairwell to make sure Oliver is out of earshot. "Sorry about my husband. This move has been stressing him out. Me too, of course, but I bury my stress in work. He can't do that as a professor, I guess."

"A professor?" she asks. "When you said students, I assumed younger kids."

I tease him about looking the part of a professor, but he doesn't resemble the stereotype aside from his black framed glasses that only seem to enhance his appearance. People often assume he's in sales or finance. It's because he's always so neatly dressed, sticks to a monthly haircut, gets his eyebrows shaped, his nails manicured, and flosses after each meal. He can seem reserved, but doesn't lack confidence since he stands at a podium in a lecture hall in front of college students every day.

"Where does he teach?" Peyton asks.

"Larkspur University, right in town."

"Well, I guess that commute won't be too rough, huh?" Peyton glances down at her smart watch. "Okay, okay, I know I need a thousand more steps before noon and one more glass of water," she says.

"I turned all my notifications off. My mother nags me about everything enough. I don't need a watch to do the same," I joke. I had thrown my watch across the room before I figured out that I could turn the reminders off. The constant buzzing against my wrist made me want to scream.

"Oh my gosh. My mother is on silent mode too. I'm awful, but the '...when are you and Lincoln going to make me a grand-mother...' stresses me out quite a bit," Peyton says with a sigh of exasperation. "She lives out of state, so the phone is easy enough to manage."

I guess I'm not the only horrible daughter in the world—one who deprives her mother of the one thing she wants in life. "Well, our moms can start a grandchild-less club and share in each other's woes because I have the same conversation with mine several times a week, too. She thinks my ovaries are going to dry up since I'm over thirty now. I've tried to explain that our generation is different, but she doesn't want to listen."

Peyton tightens her ponytail, fluffing the top up higher. "Girl, you have just become my new best friend."

"Same," I say without hesitation.

"Anyway, I'll let you get back to unpacking. I'm so glad to have met you," she says, placing her hand on my shoulder. "Oh, one piece of neighborly advice that I had to learn the hard way..." Peyton giggles and leans toward me with her hand cupped to the side of her mouth. "Whatever you do, don't get caught up in the neighborhood rumor-mill. Most of what you'll hear isn't true."

SEVEN

JENNA | NOW

A nudge against my shoulder sends a wave of pins and needles through my arms and legs. "Jenna, babe, can you hear me?"

I hear him and feel the tip of his thumb brushing circular strokes along my cheek. My eyelids might as well be sewn shut with the amount of strength it takes me to pry them open. Oliver's head grows and shrinks like a beating heart. "I'm bringing you to a specialist, per the doctor's suggestion."

"What? Why?" I ask.

"It's been over a week, and you don't seem to be turning a corner toward any hint of improvement. I'm very worried about you."

"I'm okay." I'm not sure that I am though.

"Well, I still need to get you into the car, though." His voice wavers like musical notes on a run, up and down. "Do you think you can walk?"

I summon my legs to swivel off the side of the bed and push my fists into the mattress to sit up, but the moment I make it up to my feet, gravity pulls me back down to the bed.

"Are you dizzy, or just weak?" he asks, sweeping his hand

across my forehead to brush the loose strands of hair out of my face.

I press my hands against my forehead, wishing I could stop everything around me from swaying like a wrecking ball. "Both, I guess."

"Okay, wrap your arm around my back. I'll keep you steady." With sluggish movements, we make our way to the stairs. Each step feels like a jolting elevator stopping at each floor, and waves of nausea course through me. "Where's River?" I ask. "Is he already in—in the car?"

Oliver releases a soft groan. The front door is already open, but he kicks the toe of his shoe against the door to widen the exit. A humid spring breeze sends a chill down my spine as I step out onto the wet pavement. It must have rained last night. It might rain again by the look of the thick clouds covering the sky. It's gloomy, mirroring the murkiness in my head.

He opens the passenger side door and holds on to my arm as I slide into the Land Rover, then tugs the seat belt across my sore waist to secure it in the lock. Oliver's hair smells like pears and coconut, the shampoo he loves. Once he backs out of the car, I grab ahold of the center console and twist myself around to peer into the back seat, reaching for River's hooded car seat. "I'm here, baby. Mama's here. We'll be okay."

As Oliver settles into the driver's seat and backs out of the driveway, he trades his eyeglasses for sunglasses. It isn't until we pull out onto the main town road that I remember River's blanket. "Oh no. Do we have—" I forget what I was going to say.

"Do we have—?" Oliver repeats.

I close my eyes to retrace my thoughts, but I find comfort in the headrest, supporting my neck.

The car halts with a sudden jerk as we pull up to a stoplight. My eyes flash open briefly until a bright red blinds me, forcing me to close my eyes again. The engine growls and we're moving again. Oliver places his hand on my leg. With the light no longer glaring in my face, I blink my eyes open and twist my head to the left, resting my cheek on the seat. I stare at his profile, his pallid complexion and the downcast angle of his eyes and lips. Like a raindrop on a window, a tear skates down the side of his nose, but his dark glasses hide the truth within his eyes. I've never seen him cry. We've stood through funerals together, and at the bedside of his dying grandmother, but he always manages to keep his emotions in check. But not now. I don't understand. "What's wron—?"

"Nothing," he says before I can finish my question. *He's lying.* Something is hurting him, and I can't think what it could be other than me, my current state. Maybe I should be more worried than I am, but *I'm going to be fine.* He said so himself. I think.

"I'm sorry if I'm scaring you," I mumble.

"No, no, you have nothing to be sorry about, Jenna. Don't say that."

"I'm just...so tired."

"Reasonably so," Oliver says.

"It's not," I argue. "He's a newborn. I need to take care of him."

The car stutters over a speed bump, the movement sending a shooting pain up my core and I cradle my stomach like I've done so many times over the last year. Oliver pulls into a spot, facing an old rusty orange sedan that looks to have been parked in the spot for years. "Hang tight. I'm going to come around and grab you."

"I can walk by myself. You need to get River."

Oliver stalls before stepping out of the car, watching as I open my door and test the weight on my foot before sliding the other one out. Once I pull myself up and catch a grip on the car door, the world spins drowsily. I squeeze my eyes closed, trying to find my balance. I've been horizontal for too long. This has to stop. Oliver appears from behind the car, reaching out for my hand. "Wait, stop...Oliver, where is he? Where's River?"

"Jenna, it's okay, babe. I—I'm getting you settled first then I'll get him."

I reach for the back door handle and tug until it gives. "No. Take him out first."

"Okay, okay," Oliver says with a huff, holding up his hands in a defensive motion. Without another argument, he thankfully leans into the back seat to retrieve River. The clips of the car seat base release with a hollow clunk just before he climbs back out with the carrier looped around his arm. "That's the wrong blanket," I say.

Oliver closes the back door and shucks the baby carrier up to his elbow, curling his arm to secure it. "We need to get you help right now. Let's focus on you for the moment, okay?"

He wraps his arm around my waist and takes slow steps alongside me as we make our way through an unfamiliar parking lot. "Where did you find this doctor?"

"She was recommended by your primary."

The pavement feels like soggy grass, each footstep sinking. The air is thick with mist and the scent of incoming rain makes my legs feel twice as heavy as they did before.

The doors ahead swing back and forth rather than sliding doors and I'm unsure how to walk through them, so I stop before coming too close.

"We can't go in this way." I push back against Oliver's arm, trying to make him stop walking. "No. We'll be hit by the swinging doors." He continues forward so I jerk his arm back, forcing him to stop, and he stumbles backward. I almost trip too.

"Whoa, whoa, easy."

"You're going to hurt River," I state.

"Jenna, lower your voice. Don't say that."

Medical aides make their way out of the swinging glass

doors. One has an empty wheelchair. "Do you folks need a hand?"

"That would be great," Oliver replies. "I called just a while ago about some postpartum side effects."

The two medical aides suddenly become four and I don't know where the other two came from. Two have each of my arms in their hold and they help me into the wheelchair that I didn't request. "I can walk."

No one listens. We all keep moving toward the deadly doors and I scream at the top of my lungs, "Stop! They'll hurt my baby. Stop!" The chair continues forward and I twist around to push the set of hands away, but the man's grip is unmovable. "Please stop." My screams turn to crying pleas, but by the time I turn back around in the seat, we're inside the building. A wide lobby sprawls out before me with a reception desk on the left. Plexiglass stretches from one wall to the other, spanning the width of the desk, and reaches as high as the ceiling. There's only a small opening to exchange medical cards, I guess. To the right are empty green upholstered wooden chairs, perfectly aligned down the length of the wall.

Oliver steps in front of me to a window opening. "I'm here to check in Jenna Milligan."

"You can take her right back," the woman behind the plexiglass says, waving to someone behind me. "I'll just need your insurance card and to confirm some of the information you provided over the phone."

"Are you coming in with me?" I ask, waiting for Oliver to turn toward me.

He's searching for an answer above my head. "Jenna, we're going to bring you back first," the aide behind me says.

"Can I say goodbye to River first?"

As if no one heard my request, the chair rolls backward and I'm spun around to face the corridor leading to another door. "Why can't I say goodbye to my son?"

"Everything is going to be okay. We're just going to talk right now."

"Talk? I'm here to meet with a specialist about my fatigue."

I turn back, searching for Oliver and River, but we're moving through the door and turning a corner down another hallway.

Faux wooden floors line the corridor and white hospital grade doors seal each room we move past. Some doors have small windows, some windows have bars—other doors have no windows at all, but regardless, I can't see Oliver and River at all.

EIGHT

GINGER | LAST YEAR

The neighbors have only been here for one day and Peyton is already over there with the wife. The ladies are barefoot, lazily slouched in chairs while sharing a bottle of wine on the front porch, giggling as if they're long-lost pals.

"Of course, I'll join you," I say to my empty living room. I lean toward the coffee table and fill my wine glass with another helping of Merlot. Once I settle back into the couch, I hold the glass up to the television. "Cheers to new neighbors." *Only the new neighbors*, I'd like to add. The live stream would be better if I could hear their conversation, but the microphone on the outside security camera won't pick up much from across the street and someone is mowing their lawn around the corner.

The kitchen timer sounds a long thread of beeps (beep... beep...beep—beep—beep). I stand from my seat, careful not to tip my full glass on the way up and, with my eyes still on the live stream on my television, walk out of the room.

I slip on my daisy yellow hot mitts and pull down the oven door. The radiating heat burns against my face as I reach in for the sheet pan with three perfect rows of chocolate chip cookies.

I kick the oven door shut and slide the pan on the stovetop. The boys would always go crazy when I made their favorite cookies. I wonder if they think about them anymore. I suppose they'd need to think about me occasionally too. Maybe if I sent them all text messages and told them I had freshly baked cookies, they would come visit their mother. It seems they've forgotten about me in the mix of their own busy lives or maybe thinking of me is too painful for them after everything we've all been through. We should see a family counselor but not one of them will agree to do so.

After allowing the cookies to cool for a bit, I place them in a plastic container. With one last long swig of my wine until the wine glass is dry, I head across the street.

Jenna notices me first since Peyton is sitting with her back to me. We haven't met yet, so she's probably wondering who I am. Before I step foot onto the driveway, Peyton twists in her seat and stares in my direction with a flat line across her lips. Something hasn't registered in her head yet that she's forgetting her manners.

"Oh hi, Ginger," she greets me. Her words say she's more pleased to see me than her expression conveys. It's hard to understand the qualms she has with me. Some might say she should be grateful to have me as a neighbor.

"I hope you don't mind my intrusion, ladies. I just wanted to come over and welcome our new neighbor. I thought I'd bring over some freshly baked chocolate chip cookies for you to enjoy with your wine."

Jenna stands up, her hand on her chest and her mouth agape with surprise. "How sweet of you to bring over cookies. I'm Jenna Milligan. My husband, Oliver, should be out any time now. He was just hanging up the last ceiling fan. You are Ginger, right?"

What a doll. "Yes, my name is Ginger. I, embarrassingly, met your husband yesterday when my cat escaped into your hedges." Jenna doesn't seem surprised to hear my story. Oliver must have already told her about our meeting.

"He did mention that. You know, I think your cat was just curious about the new neighbors," she says with a warm laugh. I hand the container of cookies over to her and she takes them, placing them down on the wicker coffee table between her and Peyton. She then promptly reaches her hand out to shake mine. I like her already.

She's adorable in a coming-of-age way, no longer a young adult, and not quite sure of where she belongs in the world yet. If I had to guess, she's probably in her mid-twenties. I assumed they were older yesterday when they stepped out of the Land Rover in business attire.

"Please, have a seat and join us. It's such a beautiful night out here with the breeze after that heat today."

"It's gorgeous out. I'd love to join you," I say, taking in a deep inhale of the thick floral air.

"Could I get you a glass? I've already unpacked those, thankfully."

"How kind. I don't drink anymore—" Not as of five minutes ago. "—plus, I don't want to overstay my welcome. I'm sure you girls have lots to chat about."

Peyton readjusts her position and drops her bare feet down, sliding them into her loose-fitting sandals. For such a pretty girl, she is so uncivil.

"So, what brings you to Lakespur?" I ask.

Jenna lifts her wine glass and takes a sip before replying. "We both work in town and didn't live far from here before, but we were apartment dwellers, waiting to stumble upon our dream house. Everything finally came together for us when we got wind of this house going up for sale."

A dream for Jenna and Oliver, but a nightmare for the prior owner, Luanne. "Yes, it seems everything happened very quickly with the house, didn't it?" I say.

"I guess the last owners were in a rush to move," Jenna says, her statement sounding more like a question. She definitely doesn't know anything about Luanne.

"Yes, I'm afraid so. Life gets tricky when we unexpectedly lose a spouse. She couldn't stay—"

"Ginger," Peyton interrupts. "He didn't pass away in the house or anything." That's about all we are supposed to know about Tommy's death.

"How awful," Jenna says, placing her wine glass down as she returns to her seat.

"Well, in any case...you should raise a toast to new beginnings. I would, but anyway..." I shouldn't have said anything about Luanne. It's too soon.

Jenna readjusts her position in her seat and straightens the straps of her overalls. "Anyway, my husband is a physics professor at Lakespur University and I'm a child-law attorney at Breakers and Cole Law Firm downtown, so everything is very convenient here, which is wonderful." Her voice is forcefully chipper. A child-law attorney must hear a lot of unfortunate stories; she must be well versed in burying emotions.

I don't want to seem surprised to hear she has such a prestigious career, but she strikes me as someone well suited for a classroom full of elementary school children. Looks can be deceiving, which I'm sure bodes well for her in court. "Gosh, I assumed you were much younger. Please take that as a compliment," I say, pressing my hand to my chest.

"I get that a lot," she says, a blush tinting her cheeks. "I'm not typically in overalls with my hair up, but unpacking is the worst task in the world."

Jenna reaches over for the container of cookies and lifts it up, removing the plastic lid. "Would either of you like one?" She glances between Peyton and me.

"Sure, I'll have one," Peyton says.

"Oh, why not?" I follow.

We each take a cookie and I replace the lid to keep out the bugs.

"Oliver loves chocolate chip cookies. I used to bake way more than I do now, and I'm pretty sure that's why he first fell in love with me. Cookies are the way to a man's heart, I guess," Jenna says with a chuckle.

"Yes, I can bribe my four sons and husband with cookies any day of the week."

Peyton clears her throat and adds, "You mean...*could*, as in past tense?" then takes a bite of her cookie.

I try to keep my expression placid, refusing to let her get a reaction.

Jenna takes a deep breath and straightens her shoulders, quickly shifting her focus from Peyton to me. "So, four sons, you said?" Jenna says with a mouthful, cupping her hand in under her lips to catch any crumbs.

"I just sent the last of them off to college."

"You must be so proud," she says.

I'm so proud, it hurts. So very badly.

The front door of the house opens and Oliver steps out. "Pardon me, ladies. So nice to see you both again," he says. Unlike Jenna, he's in slacks and a button-down shirt with a tie. "Babe, can I talk to you for a second?"

Jenna glances at the two of us, seeming embarrassed that her husband is interrupting her afternoon fun. "I'll be back in just a second," she says, scooting into the house beneath Oliver's arm holding open the door.

As soon as the door closes, I lean in toward Peyton and point a finger at her face. "You are something else, you know that?" I shake my head and sigh. "You'll only fool her for so long too. She should know why this house went up for sale."

"What happened a month ago is old news. Let her enjoy the excitement of a new home before dragging her down into the dark hole of despair you seem to enjoy so much." Peyton huffs with frustration and shakes her head. "Did you have another bad day?"

Before I can reply, the door opens. "I'll save you some cookies, babe," Jenna says, joining us back out on the porch.

"Sorry. It looks like Oliver won't be joining us tonight. He was just called into an emergency faculty meeting."

"Lincoln had to work late too." *How convenient. Lincoln works late every night.* "We'll all catch up another night," Peyton says.

Oliver steps out of the house with his briefcase in hand and the couple whisper a quick goodbye to each other. A few silent seconds pass before Oliver is pulling out of the driveway.

"Well, I'm going to leave these cookies here for you ladies and go feed my crazy cat before she gets the idea of running out of the house again."

"Thank you so much for stopping by and for the cookies," Jenna says, standing as I leave.

"Have a good night, Ginger," Peyton follows with less enthusiasm. "We'll see you soon."

Sooner than I wish, I'd like to say out loud.

NINE

JENNA | LAST YEAR

The summer night's sky has embraced the street. The darkness is broken up by a show of interior lights behind curtains and white porch lights.

Peyton tugs at the sleeves of her sweatshirt, concealing more of her hands. Just after Ginger left, the dampening breeze embraced us, so I ran inside to dig out the first sweatshirt I could find.

The few minutes I was inside with Oliver before he left, Peyton's warning about Ginger replayed in my head: *Ginger has a good heart, but she's a little bullish.* The poor woman might be suffering. The dead roses I found yesterday make more sense now, but not the part where the previous owner was seemingly accused of her husband's demise.

"I can see the worry swirling through your eyes," Peyton says, lifting her refilled glass to her lips.

Oliver has always said I wear my heart on my sleeve unless I'm in court with a client. It's rare when I try to hide my honesty from anyone, even clients, but when in court, there's no room for telltale signs of weakness. "Worry?" I laugh as I reach for the second bottle we've uncorked.

"Girl, I'm an esthetician. I can spot worry lines a mile away, and you're too young for those. Although, it's never too soon for Botox, right?" she asks, sucking in her cheeks like a fish. "Seriously though, your house isn't cursed or anything."

I place the wine bottle down beside my glass. "Oh," I scoff, "I don't believe in ghosts or curses." I don't necessarily enjoy the idea of moving into someone's horror story, though. "But that sounds like an exciting career. Do you work in town?"

"I do. I work part-time, waxing, facials, chemical peels, and I assist a doctor with Botox injections. Basically, I get rid of the evidence of age," she says with a laugh. While the thought sounds appealing, the idea of needles stuck into my face makes me cringe.

"I will have to schedule some appointments with you then. It's been ages since I've had a facial," I say. "Okay, I have to know...what happened to him—the guy who lived here before?" I ask, holding the rim of the cool glass up to my lips. With the porch lamps backlighting me, Peyton's face glows just enough that I can make out her expression—her eyelids falling heavy and her lips arcing into a grimace.

"It was tragic," she says, staring into her wine glass. "A car accident. From what I heard. I guess he went through a red light at a busy intersection. Others seem to have varying stories of what happened, but we'll probably never know." I can't help thinking that there's something Peyton isn't saying. "So, you told Ginger you're a child-law attorney. I never would have guessed. You seem..." Peyton lifts her arm to cover her face and laughs. "Sorry, you just seem too sweet to be in such a tough career."

We all have reasons for the things we do, and I take pleasure in knowing how many people take me at face value rather than the knowledge I keep tucked away inside. "Looks aren't everything," I add, trying to respond with the same humor.

"I didn't mean that." Peyton rests her wine glass on her thigh. "I've spent a lot of time with various child-law attorneys, and they were similar in a cold, unemotional, and detached way. I couldn't form a connection with them."

The thoughts stack, one on top of the other, as I imagine why she's needed to speak with child-law attorneys. It could be anything from her parents divorcing to the most unthinkable situations. I know better than to assume. "I'm sorry you've had that experience. We aren't all lacking emotions, but sometimes we have to clear our minds and think without making a case too personal."

"I totally get it," she says, taking a mouthful of wine, followed by another.

"If you ever need someone to talk to—"

She shakes her hand in front of her face. "No, no, I couldn't —we just met, and you do this all day, every day. The last thing you need in your free hours is a whiny neighbor."

With a narrow glint to her eyes, Peyton stares at the wine bottle as if she's staring down the past she'd like to re-cork. I let her have the moment she needs and take another piece of cookie to nibble on.

Peyton breaks her stare and drops her gaze to her wrist. "Lincoln should be home by now. I'm bummed—I wanted you to meet him," she says with a pout. "He's such a workaholic sometimes. But he works so much that I only have to put in part-time hours, which means I can keep up with the house and have dinner ready for him when he gets home."

The way she twists her lips to one side makes me wonder if she's truly happy.

"Does Lincoln work late every night?"

"Most. He won't come home until his last architect leaves." Lincoln sounds like a noble business leader. "Speaking of which —" She reaches into her sweatshirt pocket and pulls out a key. "A couple of the other ladies and I have exchanged keys in case we get locked out during the day. It happens to all of us." Peyton chuckles embarrassedly and sweeps a loose strand of hair behind her ear.

"That's a great idea. I'm planning to make copies of our keys this week. I'll have to bring one to you in case I get locked out too. That's so nice—to have such a tight-knit little community here. It's exactly what I was hoping for when we bought the house."

"Yes, it's the perfect place to live. It never gets old." Peyton glances over her shoulder toward her driveway, disappointment still prominent within her eyes.

"I'm sure I'll get to meet Lincoln soon. The good thing is, we have all the time in the world to meet, right?"

"I would like to hope so," she says, placing her wine glass down on the coffee table. "Time seems to be such a variable in life. You never know what tomorrow might bring, right?" This conversation seems to have taken a turn and I'm unsure if it's the way Peyton truly thinks or if it's the wine shrouding her thoughts. "Want me to clean this out before I go?"

"Don't be silly. You brought the wine. I can handle the glasses. Thank you for being so welcoming today. It's nice to know I'm surrounded by great people here."

"We do all appear pretty great, don't we?" she says, a smile teasing her lips.

Peyton's long pause gives me an uneasy feeling.

"You do," I say. "Thanks again for the wine and conversation."

"Talk soon," she says, slipping her hands into her back pockets before making her way home.

I bring the empty wine glasses and bottles into the house and over to the kitchen sink, feeling a heaviness in my head that didn't set in until I stood up from the porch seat. I must have refilled my glass one too many times.

The house feels larger at night, especially being here alone. I'm debating whether to plant myself on the living room couch until Oliver returns or if I should try to get through a couple more boxes. Mom and I did manage to get through a good chunk of them today, but there are still more than a dozen left.

The couch calls for me as I make my way through to the living room, and I sink into the cushions. The upstairs light from Peyton's house catches my attention as it glows. I wonder if that's her bedroom?

Headlights flash against the bay window and I sit up taller to see if it's Oliver's car, but the vehicle continues past our driveway and pulls into Peyton's. At least her husband is there now.

I can't see well enough to make out a figure, but as the car door clunks shut, the upstairs light absconds into the darkness, making me consider if the light was ever on at all.

TEN

JENNA | NOW

The room I am led to is barren, white walls like a blank sheet of paper and me, a question mark, scribbled in the middle. Ammonia mixed with floor cleaner reeks through the air, highlighting the hospital-grade environment. Then a medical bed surfaces within my focus, as well as covered wall outlets, and a white plastic covered chair. Here, we pause on the taupe linoleum floor as if there is something spectacular to admire within the space. "Mrs. Milligan, I'm just going to help you over to the bed so I can check your vitals," the aide says, looping his arm beneath mine, assisting me as if I have two broken legs. My legs are fine. I'm not sure if he is one of the same men who met us out in the parking lot or someone different. There were four and now there is one.

"Why can't my husband and baby come in here with me?" I ask.

The aide, whose name badge is blurry, takes a seat on the chair, staring at my legs, which dangle off the end of the bed. "You seem very upset, and we want to do everything we can to help you. But first, we need to check your vitals, and then the doctor would like to speak to you briefly before we move any further." The man has a full head of dark curls, tapering down to his ears. His tired eyes make me wonder how long he's been working today. His scrubs are a royal blue, different from the light blue I would normally see in a hospital. "Do you mind if I check your blood pressure?" He's so calm, it would be hard to argue with him.

"Okay."

"I'm Felix," he says, pointing to the name badge made up of fuzzy letters. "You're welcome to ask me any questions you might have or tell me whatever you're thinking."

"What's wrong with me?" I ask, anxiety riddling my sputtering words. A faint smile presses into Felix's lips and his shoulders drop. "I'm not a doctor, just an aide, but I can answer any other question that doesn't have to do with a diagnosis." A diagnosis for what? "Where am I? Could you at least tell me that?"

Felix pulls a key from his pocket and unlocks a drawer built into the wall, its intention: to be hidden. He retrieves a blood pressure cuff and turns back to face me. "Ashlyn Behavioral Health Center," he says while wrapping the cuff around my left bicep.

"Behavioral—" I repeat. "I'm supposed to be meeting with a specialist."

Felix squeezes the gray bulb in his palm, forcing pressure into the cuff with the repeating huff, huff, huff, sound as the arm band engorges around my arm. "Dr. Asmee is a wonderful specialist," he says. "Your blood pressure is low, and your heart rate is too. Have you had your thyroid tested recently?"

I shake my head. My thyroid has never been an issue, and I've had plenty of blood work over the last year. "I was slightly anemic during my pregnancy but took iron supplements."

"Hmm." Felix goes to the open drawer in the wall and returns with a thermometer and an oxygen sensor.

I go through the motions of following his directions, lifting my tongue for the thermometer and sticking my index finger into the oxygen sensor, trying to wrap my head around what's happening to me. "Do you remember what you had for breakfast this morning?" he asks, removing the thermometer.

My gaze falls to my leggings, where I notice a small white feather, a leftover from the throw pillow on our couch. There must be an opening in the seam because every time I look down at my legs there's another feather. I pluck it from the thin fabric and pinch it between my fingers.

"Mrs. Milligan?"

"I'm sorry. What's the question?" I lift my head, trying to focus on the man's face, but the badge hanging around his neck calls my attention as it sways from side to side.

"What did you have for breakfast this morning?"

"Breakfast," I repeat, retracing my steps back to the house. I'm not sure I had breakfast. "What time is it?"

Felix glances down at his wrist. "It's just after two in the afternoon."

"My husband woke me up and brought me here." I've never slept in, not a day in my life until River was born. Now's the time I shouldn't be sleeping much at all, but I can't seem to keep my eyes open.

"Okay, I'm going to help you into the bathroom across the hall. We're going to need a urine sample and for you to change into the gown waiting in there for you. Do you think you'll need assistance? I can bring down a female aide if that would be more comfortable for you."

"No, I can manage." I think.

Felix helps me across the hallway and into the bathroom. "I'll wait right out here. If you need anything, just holler."

I close the door, feeling around for a lock on the handle, but there is no lock. I press my hands against the oak door, my gaze zipping up and down. I've never been in a bathroom without a lock. My breaths become ragged as I turn around, trying to recall what I'm supposed to be doing in here. I find a folded gown resting on a small table next to a plastic cup in between a toilet and sink. *Right, he asked for a urine sample and to change out of my clothes.* A single bar lines the wall like one in a ballet studio, except this one is padded and enclosed by more plastic-like leather. The bar comes in handy with each step I take, feeling off balance and unsteady as I struggle to remove my clothes, dropping everything to the ground. I take the small, flimsy cup, and try to balance myself over the toilet. All I can do is stare at the door handle without a lock. My face burns and my muscles tighten as I try to coerce myself into breathing through this mortifying situation.

Getting into the gown is the easiest of tasks until I reach behind me to secure the ties. My hands fumble against each other, keeping me from securing a loose knot. My clothes are scattered on the floor and as I lean forward to scoop them up, the fabric along my back separates. I pull myself up with the assistance of the padded bar and hold my clothes against my stomach.

I need a third hand to open the door. "I'm all set," I call out, hoping Felix is still waiting and can open the door so I can hold the back of my gown together.

He knocks even though I said I was finished. "May I open the door?"

"Yes."

The door opens and Felix takes my arm to hold me steady as I shuffle across the hallway in my mismatching socks—something I would never do to myself. I'm very particular about matching socks and coordinating colors.

Time hops in flashes as if someone is cutting and pasting me from one scene to the next. I find myself reclined in the hospital bed, with the gown and mismatched socks. The exam room's door is open, and Felix is having a conversation with someone in the hallway.

A new face appears, a woman in a lab coat over white scrubs. Her dark hair is tied back into a long braid halfway down her back. Her eyes are as bright as her smile. She's young, maybe even younger than me. A tablet is pinched between her arm and torso.

"Jenna," she says, a hint of an accent adding a flourishing sound to my name. "I'm Dr. Asmee. I've heard you've been struggling with severe fatigue, confusion, and weakness these last couple of weeks since you've given birth. Is that correct?"

"Yes." There's nothing more to say. She seems to know all my afflictions.

"Your husband, Oliver, said you saw your obstetrician already, and she suggested you follow up with a specialist. Is that correct, as well?"

I don't remember seeing my doctor. I don't remember much at all from the last couple of weeks.

Dr. Asmee pulls the tablet out from beneath her arm and takes a seat on the chair across from me, like Felix did. The tablet rests on her lap, the screen dark from this angle. "I—"

She smiles and peers down at the tablet. "Jenna, how have you been feeling since giving birth?"

"Tired, weak..." She said it all when she walked inside the room.

"Okay. Have you been taking any prescription pain medication?"

"No, none."

"How have you been managing your physical and emotional pain?" I'm not sure what she means. I'm recovering from giving birth.

"I'm not in pain except for a twinge here and there."

"Okay, that's great," she says in an upbeat tone, satisfied with my answer. "Emotional pain is completely normal after a sudden loss. We just want to make sure you have all the resources you need." Dr. Asmee presses her lips together. A firm smile appears as she tilts her head to the side, the disposition of sympathy.

"Loss? I'm not experiencing a loss."

Dr. Asmee pulls the chair closer to the bed, where she can reach for my hand. "Jenna, I'm speaking about the loss of your son."

Like a hammer against a sheet of ice, cracks splinter my perception. "What are you talking about? My son is alive. River. He's out in the lobby with my husband right now. You can go see for yourself."

Dr. Asmee places her free hand on top of the hand she's already holding. "Grief can be a very powerful source of manifestation, but together we can find ways to heal."

I tug my hand away from hers and push myself upright on the bed. "I think you've mistaken me for someone else. My son is in the lobby. I didn't lose him. Please, bring my husband and baby in so you can see for yourself," I plead.

She doesn't move from her seat. Her eyes don't lower from the stare she's boring into me.

The room spins and I close my eyes, hoping to wake up from this nightmare.

ELEVEN

GINGER | LAST YEAR

Baby carrots are caramelizing, the sugary sweet scent warms the entire first floor. The butter is sizzling, potatoes roasting to a perfect shade of amber, and a rump roast is seared and seasoned to excellence, just the way my youngest baby likes it.

I've set the dining room table, and I'm staring at the wall clock hanging above the kitchen's archway. Just a few minutes more.

A notification pings across the screen of my laptop: the camera has picked up motion in the front yard. Carter's truck is loud enough to hear from a couple of blocks away, so I don't think it's him. I lean across the breakfast nook and wiggle the mouse to click on the notification for a live view.

The sun has been setting for the past half hour, but there's still enough light to see Peyton and Oliver outside having what appears to be a tense conversation in the middle of the street. She's trying to hand him an empty casserole dish, but he clasps his hands behind the back of his neck before taking it from her. With a quick shake of his head, he shifts his weight from one foot to the other then peers over his shoulder toward his house. Maybe he's wondering if Jenna is watching their conversation from the window. Peyton looks over her shoulder next. But it's toward my house, probably wondering the same about me—if I'm watching the feed from the cameras. Just before turning back for his house Oliver drops his head and laughs, but it's not the same laugh I see between him and Jenna when they leave for work in the morning.

Peyton pulls her sleeves down over her knuckles and folds her arms into her chest. "Tell Jenna I'll call her later," she says, loud enough for the security camera to pick up.

"Yeah," Oliver replies. "Thanks for the—ah—this dish."

They must have a weekly get together now, just the four of them, so happy and content with their free bird lives. The other neighbors have been wondering about Jenna and Oliver, too but they keep to themselves. Not everyone is as forthcoming as Peyton and I are. It's a shame because they're missing out on getting to know some wonderful people on this street.

Carter's truck rumbles through the speakers. With the volume up high, the frequency causes a squeal and pierces my ears. I fumble to turn the volume down but close the laptop, knowing Carter will walk in at any moment.

I slip my apron off and toss it over the laptop before making my way to the front door. The cha-clink from the deadbolt echoes, and I pull the door open. It's only been a couple of months since he left, but he looks different somehow, older, more mature. He has facial hair. My chest swells with emotion, noticing how much he looks just like his dad now. I see James's face now more than ever before. "Sweetheart," I say, opening my arms wide for a hug.

"Hey, Mom." He slings an arm around me for a blink and drops two bags of clothes by his feet.

"I'm glad you've come home for a few days of your school break." Carter slinks around me, dragging the overfilled bags behind him.

"Yeah, the washing machines in the dorm are always full or

broken, and I need to switch out some of the winter and spring clothes from my closet."

The memory of Peyton giving me a set of vacuum storage bags as a Christmas gift pops into my head. Everyone exchanged nice items with one another at a holiday block party, and I found her gift to be quite unusual. That must be what she thinks of me when shopping. "You know what, I have these vacuum storage bags. I didn't think I'd have any use for them, but I guess we do. You can just put your extra clothes in one of those. They save tons of space."

"Yeah, that's fine. Thanks."

He takes the load of dirty clothes to the laundry room, and I follow, waiting for him to tell me more about school. It seems someone taught him how to do laundry since he left. It's something I should have done, but I enjoyed taking care of my boys, knowing how quick the years were going by. Joel left first just over five years ago and the other three staggered in his footsteps over the following years.

"You separate your darks from lights?" I ask, making conversation with what feels like the wall.

He doesn't respond. He pours the detergent into the plastic cap then dredges the liquid over his clothes, closes the top and sets the dial as if he's done it hundreds of times before. The rumble of the old machine takes the place of our strangled silence.

"I want to know everything about school; your classes, professors, friends...any girlfriends I should know about?" I try to joke.

"I'm going to catch up with Ian and DJ for a bit."

If I look disappointed, he'll feel guilty, and I don't want that for him. "Could we eat dinner first? I made your favorite."

"My favorite?" he asks. His eyes harden and jaw stiffens. "Mom, why are you doing this? Nothing is the same now. Can't you see? Favorites don't matter much anymore. Ever since...Dad

—you should just stop pushing us all so hard. Nothing we do will bring him back."

"I just wanted to make you a home-cooked meal." What reason do I need to make my son dinner?

Carter drops his head full of thick blonde hair and shoves his hands into his pockets. "What do you want me to say?"

I've been a wonderful mother to all four children, and I don't deserve the silence they give me. Being a mother is often a thankless job, but it's like they've forgotten who was here for them every day before and after school, driving them around to sports, clubs, jobs, and dates. I showed their friends love by having an open-door policy. The kids invited friends over for dinner nightly, and I never turned one of them away. The house was always clean, their lunches made, laundry done, pantry full of their favorite foods, and a painfully unbiased shoulder to lean on whenever they had a problem. I wanted to protect them even when I couldn't. I had to let them soar, and I did. Now, though, it's like none of that ever happened.

He won't look up and all I can picture is his big blue eyes staring up at me when he was a little boy, telling me he jumped out of a tree and now his knee was cut and bleeding. As upset as I was that he didn't listen to me, I lifted him up, placed him on the counter, kissed his little freckled nose, and cleaned up his knee. I told him there are lessons in life we sometimes have to learn on our own. He told me he'd never jump out of another tree again.

I reach up to Carter's shoulders and straighten the seams of his thin black fleece. "Have a bite to eat and go out with Ian and DJ. I'll finish your laundry so you have clean clothes to bring back to school with you in a few days."

Carter takes in a lungful of air and lifts his head. "Okay."

"Go sit down. I'll bring the plates out."

I hurry to the kitchen, worried he might disappear if I take too long. "Do we have new neighbors?" Carter asks from the dining room.

His question distracts me as I'm making deep slices into the meat. The butcher knife slips against the edge of my thumb and the numbing tingle zaps through my nerves. I snag a paper towel and wrap my thumb up, resting my elbows on the countertop. "Yes, we do." The blood is seeping through the white quilted paper, so I move to the sink and rinse my thumb before re-wrapping it in a clean paper towel.

"Why did Tommy and Luanne move?"

I didn't tell the boys about Tommy. Their plates are full and they have busy lives. They knew Luanne and Tommy Franklin but were never very close with them. I don't know if it's necessary to drop this news on Carter, especially when he seems out of sorts. "Some things in their lives changed, and they needed to sell the house."

With a paper towel wrapped snugly around my thumb, I finish distributing the food onto two plates and carry them out to the dining room.

"Mom, why do you keep lying to me? I hate having to question everything you tell me lately. It's like one lie blinded you from reality. It's concerning."

I set the plates down on each side of the table. Carter stares down at his steaming food and his shoulders fall forward in defeat of whatever vendetta he has against me today. I'm barely seated by the time he has his first bite. His eyes close as he savors the flavors of the meal, the one he is denying is his favorite.

"What were you asking me?" I fill my mouth with a forkful of baby carrots, relishing the savory, sweet, buttery taste.

"What happened to your thumb?"

"The knife slipped. It's just the top layer of skin. I'll be fine." I'm no stranger to oven burns and skinned fingers from peeling and slicing. It's hard to escape common kitchen injuries as a stay-at-home mom and housewife.

"You're bleeding through the napkin."

I want to tell him I'm not, but I am. "I'll be okay."

"I've counted at least three lies in the ten minutes I've been home. Don't you think this is an issue?" I'm not sure when my youngest son decided he should become my parent, but that's the way it sounds when he talks to me.

"I haven't lied to you about anything. Why say something like that?"

Carter drops his fork against the plate. The clatter rings through my ears. "Jesus, Mom. Just stop already. This is uncomfortable. All you do is lie. The four of us talk, you know, Joel, Michael, Sam, and me. You lie to all of us."

"You all talk to each other but can't seem to find time to call me back once in a while?"

Carter lifts his fork back up and continues to shovel heaps of food into his mouth, likely to end our dinner as quickly as possible. "We think you should talk to a shrink or something. You aren't well and staying cooped up in this house all day doesn't seem to do much good for you."

"You all think this?" Of course they do. Convincing me to find a therapist to speak to would be much easier than one of them making me feel like I still exist in their lives. "If the truth is what you want, son, I'll give you the truth. My thumb needs a couple of stitches. It will still need stitches once you leave to go spend time with your friends and I'll take care of myself then. Luanne sold the house because—"

"Tommy died in a car accident. Mom, why didn't you think to mention this to us? We found out from Stacia Quinn three weeks ago." Stacia, the eldest of the Quinn children who live two houses down. Carter and Stacia dated for a while, but they broke things off this past summer before she left for college.

"Yes, Tommy died from a car accident. The four of you

weren't close with him, and I didn't find it necessary to blanket you with grim news."

"Was there a funeral?"

I'm not sure if there was a funeral. If there was, it must have been for the immediate family only because there was no information in the obituary and Luanne didn't mention it to any of us. Most of us neighbors brought her meals and offered our help in every way possible.

"It was a private gathering for their family."

"It wasn't private. In fact, Joel, Michael, Sam, and I all went and paid our respects, along with the rest of the neighbors on our street. You were the only one who wasn't there."

My appetite has vanished and I'm no longer in the mood to talk, so I take my plate into the kitchen and rinse it in the sink. "Please lock the door before you leave. I'm going to urgent care to have my thumb stitched. Carter, I love you." Before I leave, I take my purse from the coat rack in the foyer and peek back into the dining room. Carter is leaning back in his chair, his head hanging over the back of it as he stares up at the chandelier. "I said I love you."

"Thanks for dinner," he says without moving a muscle.

TWELVE

JENNA | LAST YEAR

My heels click against the marble floors of the Breakers and Cole firm. The echo is only this loud late afternoon when no one is arriving or leaving the building. Plus, the building seems emptier than usual. I know many of the others here take their vacation time during the hottest summer months, and I imagine some associates must have called out sick today to take advantage of the ideal beach weather after the last couple of weeks of scattered showers. The only other person on the first floor is Hazel, the daytime security guard. She steals a quick glance at her watch as I make my way toward her in front of the elevator's golden doors. "You must have been in court all morning," she says.

"Is it the bags under my eyes that gave it away?" I jest.

"Didn't win the case today?" Hazel has been working here for the last five years too. She was hired just a few weeks after me. It's nice to see a familiar face every day, especially one who isn't asking for copies of paperwork and reports on current cases.

"It was a doozy with a whole mess of surprises."

Hazel scrunches her nose and juts out her jaw. "I'm sorry, hun. Life would be boring without surprises though, right?"

"I might be okay with being bored, just once in a while." Hazel presses the elevator button for me, making it so I don't have to wait for the doors to open.

"Well, find that boredom and enjoy it before you and Mr. Milligan pop out any babies," she warns, knowingly. I've heard many stories about her three kids and have seen the dark circles beneath her eyes from sleepless nights. If a court case makes me look and feel run down, I don't know how I'll ever be able to handle a baby.

Find that boredom. Her words ruminate in my head as the elevator soars up to the top floor of the building. Maybe it isn't boredom I'm after, rather just a day without the weight of the world resting on my shoulders. Having to apologize to two kids who wanted to live with one aunt over another aunt after losing both of their parents over a three-year span doesn't make for a great day in court, especially when a will is suddenly discovered, appointing the less favorite aunt as their legal guardian.

The elevator doors open up to the wide cherrywood front desk in front of a wall with the firm's branding in sharp black protruding letters. Reception must be at lunch and the rest of the office space is quiet too. I make my way around the maze of desks and drop the expanding file-folder onto my desk, the smack from the heavy load of papers against the glass tabletop mimicking the way my heart dropped the moment I knew the case was over.

"You can't win them all, Jenna," Leonard Cole, my boss says. He's like a neon light in the dark with his glowing golf tan and snow-white hair. The man knows how to accentuate his tan, judging by the number of pastel colored shirts he owns. He says it's his veneer smile that wins him all his cases, but that isn't the case. I want to be a partner in this firm for a reason. The reputation is untouchable. He walks by my desk and pats me on the shoulder. "Losses happen to us all, kid."

"I know, I know." I do. I knew this career would see more heartache than most others I could have chosen but the benefits outweigh the downfalls. If someone represented Mom after Dad left us, we might have avoided living off food stamps while waiting for our next eviction notice.

"Oh, by the way, I didn't ask. How's the new house?" He stares at me from over his shoulder as he refills his mug of coffee at the small kitchenette in the corner. "You must be settling in by now. What's it been, two weeks?"

"Yes, two weeks and two days. It's definitely our forever home. I just wish the last few boxes with miscellaneous items would unpack themselves." I wonder if the previous owners thought of the house as their forever home too. It's easy to think a thirty-year mortgage is a life insurance policy, but that's not the case.

"Whatever you do, don't save them for later because you know what they say..."

"I'm not sure I do." I can't even force myself to laugh right now. I'm so frustrated about losing the case.

"New house, new..." I close my eyes, knowing what's coming. "Baby!"

He sounds like Oliver. I'm not sure who came up with that ridiculous saying but couples should take their time when settling into a new house. Life is a marathon, not a sprint.

"Not yet," I chirp. "I have a career to focus on." There's my weekly hint that I'm desperate to become a partner here someday.

He takes a slow sip of coffee and walks back by my desk. "To each their own."

Whatever that means.

. . .

My car meanders over the slight incline of our driveway and comes to a stop beside Oliver's car.

"Jenna, I've been calling you for an hour," Oliver says from the front door as I step out of the car. "I was about to come looking for you."

I reach back across the driver's seat to grab my phone from the cup holder and hit the power button. It's impossible to miss a call while I'm connected to Bluetooth. The phone doesn't light up.

"Babe, I'm so sorry. My phone is off. I don't know how I forgot to turn it back on after court."

"You never do that," Oliver asserts.

"I know." I close my car door and the sight of a large red pickup truck in Ginger's driveway catches my eye. She doesn't strike me as the type to spend time with someone who drives a truck.

"Jenna, what's going on?" Oliver is still standing beneath the porch light, his arms crossed.

"I'm sorry, my phone was off. I just had a long day." He holds his arms open wide, waiting for me to make my way to him.

"You lost the custody case?" He holds me tightly against his chest and kisses the top of my head.

"I let them down."

Oliver pulls me into the house, engulfs me within his arms and leans his forehead against mine. "I love you for how passionate you are about your career, but sometimes things aren't always going to go as you want." He brushes his nose to the side of mine and kisses me sweetly while squeezing his arms around me a bit tighter. "Come on, take a load off." Oliver leads me to the couch where I plop down. He takes a seat on the coffee table; his legs frame mine. "Babe, I know you don't like when I say this to you, but I think you're draining yourself with these cases. Remember when we talked about leaving work at work?" We had that conversation because there were a few weeks when Oliver was so stressed out that he was in an awful mood every night and went to sleep just after dinner. It was concerning. But I don't get like this all the time. I don't have a reputation of losing many cases though, so when I do, it hurts.

"I know, but it's just this one time, and I feel crappy."

"We need something more in our lives than just work. It's why I want to start a family with you so badly." I don't know why he would pick this moment to start a conversation that always gets the two of us worked up.

"Oliver, I—you know how I feel."

"Why can't I have a say in this? How come it's just your decision?"

"It's my body," I reply without having to think longer than a second.

"We're married. We said we want kids, and now I feel like this is only up to you," he says, his eyes filled with endearment and sorrow. I'm doing this to him, letting him down, but I'll be letting myself down too if I don't stick to my plan.

"It's not just up to me, but it's half up to me, and I'm not ready." I press my head back into the couch cushions and close my eyes, wishing I didn't have to feel any more guilt than I already do right now. I don't want to have an argument with him, especially about children after I just let two down.

"Great," he says, standing up from the coffee table. "I'll just reheat the lasagna from last night."

I pull myself up off the couch, kick my shoes off and follow him into the kitchen. "I can reheat the dinner. I'm sure you had a long day too."

"It's fine," he says, already pulling the plastic food containers out of the fridge.

A casserole dish on the island catches my attention. "What's this?" I don't recognize it. All our baking dishes are royal blue. We got them in a set for my bridal shower. This one is white.

"Peyton gave it to me and told me to thank you for letting her borrow it."

I lift it up, perplexed because I can't recall loaning anything to Peyton. Not that I wouldn't if she had asked, but she hasn't. Maybe she confused me with Ginger. She said they borrow kitchen items from each other on occasion. "This isn't ours."

"Hmm." Oliver scoops out the lasagna into a round blue dish to reheat in the oven. "She called me halfway across the street to grab it when I got home from work. I can run it back over there after we eat."

"I'll just go do that now since you're reheating dinner." Oliver doesn't respond right away. He sets the oven to preheat and rummages through the drawers until he finds the roll of foil to cover the lasagna. "I'll be right back."

"Okay," he responds. "Oh, wait, no, Jenna? I think she's busy tonight."

Just as I reach for the door, the bell rings. *What now?*

I open the door, finding a tall woman in a pencil skirt and matching black jacket, perfectly made up, in front of me with a microphone in her hand. "Are you the new residents of this beautiful home?" she asks.

I look behind me, wondering if I'm part of a practical joke. "I'm sorry, who are you?"

"I'm Kandice Burke with Channel 3 News and I was hoping to ask you a couple of questions regarding the ongoing investigation with the previous owners of your residence?"

Just before she finishes her long-winded question, I spot a cameraman behind her, dressed in all black, camouflaged with the night aside from his pasty complexion and the small green dot lit up on the camera.

"Please turn the camera off. I haven't given you or anyone permission to record me."

The woman, Kandice, spins around and waves her hand at the man with the camera. "Shut it off."

As his light goes dark, I notice a glowing window upstairs in Peyton's house flickers off too.

"I'm not aware of any ongoing investigation regarding the previous owners. We were not given any information about what happened to the residents prior to us purchasing the property."

Oliver steps up behind me with a dish rag in his hand. "Can we help you?"

"Yes, we're here to—"

"There is nothing to investigate. Please see yourselves off our property and do not return," I say firmly.

"What's going on?" Oliver takes my arm and pulls me behind him, a protective gesture. "It's late and you're at my door with a camera. Do you have any common decency?" He takes a step forward, causing Kandice Burke to take a heavy step backward.

"Sir, are you aware that there has been speculation of foul play from the prior resident—"

Oliver sighs with frustration and throws his head back. "With all due respect, I'm not taking my news from a person who is trying to garner information from a couple who wasn't living here when this supposed incident occurred. Good night," he says, closing the door in the woman's face—something I've never seen him do to anyone.

"Why would they come here looking for answers?" I ask, knowing Oliver doesn't know any more than I do.

"Foul play?" Oliver repeats. "They must be looking to fill airtime."

"What a nerve," I say.

Oliver takes my hand and pulls me around to face him. "Babe, I don't want to argue with you. I just want to enjoy every single minute of being a newlywed with you. You know, I think about you all day, even when I'm teaching, which is wildly inappropriate...but I can't help it. Then you go and do things like demand that a camera crew leave our property at once, it drives me wild." The last part, he whispers into my ear.

"What about dinner?" I whisper.

"You'll be hungrier when I'm done with you."

We hardly make it into the bedroom when Oliver's phone vibrates in his back pocket. He ignores it at first. "What if it's work?"

He groans and slips out the phone, scanning the display for a quick second. "They can wait," he says, tossing the phone to the floor.

In our dark bedroom, with my clothes slithering down my body and my husband's lips brushing over my collarbone, I should be lost in the moment of desire, but instead I'm left trying to figure out why Andrea Lester is calling him again out of the blue.

THIRTEEN

JENNA | NOW

People have been pacing in and out of this same exam room for what feels like hours since I arrived here. Each person asks me the same set of questions with minimal variation. I'm not sure if they're waiting for my answers to change or if they need multiple rounds of confirmation, but one thing I know for sure is that they will not allow Oliver and River to visit me in this suffocating room.

"You seem more alert now," a woman says, a doctor, maybe. She hits the hand sanitizer dispenser on the wall and rubs the liquid into her hands and between her fingers. I'm not sure if I've already met with her. There have been at least three doctors or maybe nurses, or—I'm not sure who they are but they all stare at me as if I'm a reptile inside of a terrarium. "On a scale from one to ten, how angry are you feeling?"

Her question catches me by surprise because I'm not sure why they think I'm angry. "I'm not mad, just upset. I truthfully don't know why I'm here at this facility. I just want to be with my family."

The woman has dark hair pulled back into a low ponytail. Her mint-green scrubs and white Crocs give her skin tone a tan glow. I like to wear colors that complement my complexion too, but right now I'm wearing neutral shades that make me look pasty and sick.

She nods her head with what seems to be a gesture of understanding, but I think she's trying to keep me calm, or maybe from asking any more questions. I still don't know who she is, and without an introduction of any sort, I could assume we've already met but there have been too many faces to keep track of today. "I understand why you're upset, especially if your mind is in a fog," she says. "Jenna, have you experienced any suicidal thoughts or thoughts of harming others?"

I find myself watching her lips move, wondering why the words don't seem to be matching up with the sound of her voice. "Suicide? No, I'm not sure—"

"Okay, and harming others? Even family members?"

My jaw drops as I question why she would be asking me this. "No, I couldn't hurt anyone."

Her brows furrow and her lips grimace as she subtly nods her head. "Okay." She takes a moment to come up with her next thought. "Are you able to list the current medications you're taking?"

"Why? Is something wrong with me? Should I be on medication?" I chew on the inside of my cheek, thinking about the question I'm asking. Shouldn't I know?

Her eyes narrow as if she's trying to summon a different selection of words out of me. "I believe you are dealing with a lot of grief, postpartum hormonal changes, and exhaustion, but I also think there's more to this that we need to get to the bottom of."

I cross my ankles and pinch my knees together as my mind recoils like a boomerang slinging through the air. "Grief? I'm not grieving."

"Of course," she says. "We all have different ways of expressing pain following a sudden loss."

Sudden loss. Dr. Asmee referred to my situation with the same words.

My chest feels like it's caving in and my body is stiffer than a block of ice. "What loss are you referring to?"

The woman interlaces her fingers together and rests them on top of her crossed legs. Her gaze drops, as she takes a moment to pause then peers back up and straightens her shoulders. "Jenna, your baby was stillborn. It appears you are in a state of psychological shock due to the trauma you have experienced."

Stillborn. The word falls apart as it ruminates. Stillborn. I release a heavy breath and force a smile across my lips. "My son is in the lobby with my husband. I think there has been some confusion."

"Your husband has been very concerned about you and has tried to be understanding of your denial, but it's been nearly two weeks since you gave birth, and you aren't able to come to terms with the fact that your son didn't make it. A loss like this is understandably unfathomable to any parent." It's hard not to wonder if I'm imagining this conversation as I lean back against the propped-up bed. My eyelids flutter and close as I think back to the moments just after River was born. I distinctly remember holding him against my bare chest as tears of joy flooded down my hot cheeks. His body was warm, and his cry was the most beautiful sound I had ever heard. I felt a form of love I never knew possible, and it filled my heart to the brim. All I could think at that moment was how I had ever convinced myself I wasn't ready to be a mother when I couldn't imagine my life without this sweet little boy.

"If my husband has been concerned, why was he holding on to a car seat with our son secured inside?"

The woman stalls before responding. She leans in and rests her forearms on her legs. "The car seat was empty."

I can't stop myself from shooting her a glare. "That's impossible," I argue.

With a heavy nod, she responds, "Jenna, when is the last time you recall holding your son?"

I close my eyes again, pleading for more memories to fill my foggy head. "I'm sure it was just a few hours ago."

The woman pulls a small tablet out of her coat pocket, taps the screen with a stylus pen then jots down a note. "Do you know the last time you fed him? Was it by bottle or breast-feeding?"

My plan was to breastfeed or pump so I'm sure that's what I've been doing. "Breastfeeding."

"You've been here for several hours at this point. Do you need to express the milk?"

I press a palm against my chest, noticing only a dull ache. "I'd like to go home." I'm doing my best to remain calm so we can come to an agreement that there has been a misunderstanding.

She taps her pen against the tablet a couple of times and glances down at her notes. "Understandably so. However, after evaluating your current mental health status, we have decided to admit you as an inpatient for the next seventy-two hours to see if we can help you through some of this grief. Within the next few days, you will be evaluated again, and we can determine then what is best for your well-being."

I'm already shaking my head no before she finishes her sentence. I haven't agreed to this, nor did I voluntarily bring myself to this hospital, whatever this place is. I'm not sure if we're even in Lakespur anymore. "I have a right to reject treatment. I do not want to be admitted."

"Yes. Your husband, Oliver, said the two of you spoke about this already today and you agreed so you could get better. Jenna, have you been experiencing any suicidal thoughts or urges to hurt yourself or others?"

"No, no. I haven't had any of those thoughts. I haven't had many thoughts at all, to be truthful, which is why I know we didn't speak about this at all. I was probably asleep. Maybe he thought I was awake and responding, but I wasn't. He's—he's wrong. I don't want to be here. I want to go home. I've just been tired and stressed out from birthing a child. This is normal." I want to prove to this woman that she has confused me with someone else and that River is sleeping in the car seat carrier next to Oliver in the lobby.

She gives me one slow nod. "As I mentioned earlier, I'm Dr. Kasper and I've been evaluating you to decide whether I think you may be a danger to yourself or others. While I don't find you to be a danger to anyone, you aren't cognizant of the reality we're in, and it would be dangerous for me to release you. Your husband is also very concerned for your well-being and doesn't think he's capable of giving you the care you need at this moment. That's why you're here."

She never mentioned her name before now. I didn't meet her earlier. "He never said this to me. I would remember if he had. Please, I'd like to talk to Oliver."

Dr. Kasper swivels around on her stool and presses a button in a column of five on the wall behind her head. "We sent him home. I'm sure if we let him stay, he would have, but we find therapy to work better when a patient is isolated from their usual environment."

"Where are my belongings? My purse? I need to call him."

"He has them. They're safe with him. He's going to bring back some clothes for you to be comfortable in during your stay here."

"When? I want to see him when he returns."

"Jenna, we're going to move you to a different area of the facility where you will be around others who are going through similar challenges. All the rules will be explained to you shortly."

Rules? I'm here against my will and I haven't hurt anyone or done anything to deserve this type of treatment.

"No," I snap, sliding my legs off the side of the bed. An unexpected breeze sweeps against my back, reminding me that I'm in a hospital gown. I clutch the fabric over my backside while trying to devise a plan to get out of here somehow. "Please let me show you why this is a mix-up."

Dr. Kasper stares at me for a long moment until her gaze falters. I wonder if she's debating whether to let me show her proof that I'm not mentally ill, but the moment my sock covered toes touch the cold ground, the door opens and another aide rolls in a sheet covered gurney, blocking my only possible exit. White straps dangle from each corner. There is no way out of here.

FOURTEEN

GINGER | LAST YEAR

I thought this absurd investigation with Luanne was over but now the news crew is back for more, and so late at night. What a nerve. They're not going to gather any new information from Jenna and Oliver. They've been living in the house for less than a few weeks. I'm surprised the news crew didn't come to my door too.

I shouldn't be watching doorbell footage before bed. I promised myself I would stop the compulsive behavior but it's like an addiction. I just wish knowing what's happening outside of my house every minute of the day would give me peace of mind, but it doesn't.

Carter said he wouldn't be coming home tonight since he's staying at a friend's house so I've closed all the blinds and the deadbolts on the front door and back patio sliders are secure. I jerk the doorknob of the interior garage entrance to check that it's still locked as I walk by.

Everything is fine.
I'm alone.
No one will bother me tonight.
Everything is fine.

I'm alone.

No one will bother me tonight.

"Willow," I call and whistle for her, "time for bed."

She scampers out from the living room and leaps up the stairs toward the bedroom. I follow, flipping off all the light switches except for the one in the stairwell. I don't know what it is about an empty house that feels so loud, but everything creaks even though the place is barely twenty years old.

The TV in the bedroom is already on as it's automated to do every night at nine. I have such trouble falling asleep to the noise and the flickering lights but James can't fall asleep without the TV on, so we always turned the volume down to compromise.

Having finished my nightly routine of washing up and chasing down my pills with a cup of tap water, I turn down the bed and slip in on my side, closest to the bathroom. James has always insisted on sleeping closer to the window in case of an intruder. I never understood why since it would be more likely that someone would break in downstairs rather than the upstairs window, but he would tell me, "You never know." Always so overprotective.

I scoop my arm beneath his pillow and pull it in against my chest. "Goodnight, sweetheart. I still love you."

FIFTEEN

JENNA | LAST YEAR

"You're up and dressed early for a Saturday morning," Oliver says, stretching his arms over his head, the tangled sheets pulling away from his body. "After last night I could use a day of doing nothing but lying in bed with you." The corners of his lips curl and he pins me with his devilish stare. It was the same look he gave me last night, that kept us up much later than usual.

The guilt drives through me. We're still newlyweds, only six months into our marriage. I shouldn't be leaving my charming, adorable husband in bed all alone like this on what should be a lazy weekend morning.

"I made plans with Peyton last night before bed. I had texted her about the reporters and she told me we should grab breakfast. I told you, remember?"

Oliver sighs and shifts onto his side to face me. "Yes, I remember. I was just hoping you would change your mind and stay with me instead."

"Why don't you call your ex-girlfriend, Andrea, back?" The words slip out like an avalanche neither of us saw coming. I even cover my mouth, wishing I could shove the words back where they came from.

"What? Where did that come from?"

"Well, she called you last night."

"No..." he says, sounding perplexed. "No, she definitely didn't." He laughs and I can't help but feel like I'm losing my mind, but I know what I saw.

"Yes, she did. Look at your missed calls. It was when your phone rang and you tossed it to the ground."

Oliver leans over to the nightstand to grab his phone, scanning through something then throws the phone across the bed to me. "Nope. Andrew called. I'll see him at work on Monday. If it was something important, he would have left a message."

I look over his missed calls and only find Andrew Lahey as he said. "Oh. I don't know why I thought—"

He raises a brow at me. "I have nothing to do with Andrea." Oliver tilts his head to the side and pouts his lips. "Babe, exes will be a part of our lives no matter how hard we try to get rid of them, but what matters is that I'm married to you. I love you. Nothing will ever change that, no matter how nutty you act." Oliver circles his hand around my side of the bed. It would be a good time to tell him he acts just as nutty, but it's not worth arguing over. "So, with that said...what's a few more hours here with me? Tell Peyton you'll meet her for lunch instead."

I lean back against the wall, torn. Oliver sits up and turns his head toward the window. "Did you hear that?"

I remain still, hearing a faint murmuring of shouts growing louder in the distance. I race to the window and peek out between the blinds. "It's Peyton and who I guess is Lincoln. They're arguing just outside their front door."

I step away from the window, not wanting to be nosy. I wouldn't want anyone watching us if we were having an argument.

"Well, maybe now it's best if you don't go to breakfast. They probably have something to work out."

I spin around and cross my arms over my chest. "She probably needs a friend right now, or whenever they stop yelling at each other."

"You don't have to solve the world's problems, and maybe he's the one who needs a shoulder to lean on. It's not like you know Peyton all that well yet."

A car door slams. A front door follows with gusto. The rubber from a car's tires squeal and the engine burns into a rumble before everything becomes silent again.

"Damn. That didn't sound good." Oliver drops his head back into his pillow. "I'll just have to wait until later I guess." He pulls the covers up to his neck and the jealousy of him still being in bed almost makes me cave.

I climb up on the bed and tease him with a kiss, payback for making it hard for me to leave. He groans and I call it a win. "I'll be back soon. I promise."

"Love you, babe. Don't get in the middle of an argument that isn't yours." His favorite saying always leaves a pause before the punchline. "Unless you're in court."

I shake my head at the lame joke. "Love you too, you nut."

The sun blinds me as I step out the front door with my key fob in hand. I pull my sunglasses down just as a warm wind, deceivingly refreshing, blows my loose strands of hair away from my face. It's going to be another hot one today. The heat always makes people act grouchier than usual, which could explain the argument between Peyton and Lincoln.

Before slipping into my car, I peer across the street, noticing Peyton's car is missing. She must have been the one who took off like a lion after its prey earlier.

The drive is just long enough to get through one song from my curated "Sing at the Top of Your Lungs" playlist I listen to when I'm alone. I question if I'll have time for another song while debating if Peyton will be waiting at Starbucks or if she went somewhere else. I was thinking we'd drive here together.

As I pull into the parking lot of the strip mall with a variety of mismatched shops, ranging from a florist to a boutique clothing store for children, I spot her car in front of the chalk painted cold-brew advertisement on Starbucks' windows. Maybe she needed a few minutes to cool down from the argument. My curiosity piques, wondering what I'm about to hear regarding the news crew and now her public argument. I won't bring that part up unless she does though.

As I walk in through the glass door, I spot her off to the right, waving at me with a smile anchored to her lips. She holds up two grande-sized cups of iced-coffee and I make my way over to her, trying to hide the confusion I feel inside. I'm not sure I told her how I like my coffee, but it's the thought that counts.

"Hey, girly!" she says, standing from her seat to give me a hug. The urge to ask her if everything's okay feels like holding a fly in my mouth.

"You didn't have to buy the coffee. I'm the one who probably woke you up last night."

"Girl, you have nothing to worry about." She pushes the cup across the table, and I take a seat.

"Well, thank you," I say, holding it up in cheers to her.

"So," she begins. "I didn't want to put this in a text message because—well, it's a lot, but I can't believe that news crew showed back up at your house last night. I thought they were done with that when Luanne moved out."

I take a sip of the icy drink, recognizing the flavors of mocha and caramel. That was a lucky guess at my favorite Starbucks drink. I usually hold the whipped cream, but it hits the spot today as I anxiously wait for Peyton to fill me in.

"Her husband died in a car accident though, right?" I confirm.

She nods before answering. "Oh, yeah. But one of the more private rumors is that Luanne was trying to take out a life insurance plan in Tommy's name the day before the accident so one string of gossip led to another and, before you knew it, the news was on the case. The police too, obviously. It's all a big mess but I honestly think it was just a crazy coincidence. Luanne would trap a bee in her house and take it outside to set it free. She's not the murderous type, you know?"

It sounds like I'm missing a big piece of this story. "That's— wow, that's kind of crazy."

"I know," she says, taking a sip of her coffee.

So, why were you and Lincoln yelling at each other outside twenty minutes ago? She's staring through me, almost as if she can hear my thoughts. "You heard us, didn't you?"

"Heard what?" I play dumb.

Peyton tips her head to the side, her blonde ponytail brushing against her shoulder. "We both have big mouths and loud voices, but we love each other to death."

I hold my hands up, my palms facing her. "No judgment. Every couple has their moments. It's unhealthy if you don't."

She bobs her head from side to side. "Well, we have ours more often than most maybe."

I'm about to ask her why and bite the bait, but she continues talking before I can.

"It's the post-traumatic stress for me. I'm sensitive and overly emotional at times."

I'm not sure whether to pry or wait for her to continue talking. When I offered her an ear the other night, she wasn't ready to talk about whatever happened in her past. She takes a napkin from the holder in the center of the table and begins to tear off little pieces, dropping them one by one into a pile.

"So. I can't have kids."

I wasn't expecting this statement. I had a thousand other assumptions. "Oh, I—"

She shakes her head. "Don't—there's nothing good to say, trust me." Another pause stolen by another sip from her cup. "I had this boyfriend of sorts. Not really a boyfriend, I guess. It was a fling. He was older. I was seventeen. I got pregnant. He forcefully convinced me to abort and took me to this back-alley place where I didn't have to give my name or age. I ended up with a serious infection, but thought the pain was a side effect so I didn't seek medical attention right away. In any case, I'm basically sterile now, or so three different obstetricians have told me."

My stomach plummets for her. "I'm so sorry. You were seventeen?" The question flies out of my mouth.

"Yup," she says, taking another swig of coffee. "Stupid me."

"How old was he?"

"Thirty-one."

It would have been considered statutory rape in the state of Delaware. It still could be if she has enough evidence. "Did you press charges against him since you were a minor?"

She rolls her eyes. "I couldn't afford a good attorney and I didn't have enough evidence for a crappy one."

"I can help. It's not too late, you know? There is no statute of limitations when it comes to statutory rape." I try to keep my voice as low as possible.

"No, but thank you. It won't fix anything. I have my own ways of coping. *Alternative therapy*, as I refer to it. Everyone heals differently, right?"

"Therapy?" I ask.

She grins and bites down on her lip. "I know not everything can be solved by sitting in a chair and blurting out details to a stranger."

"Do you still have contact with this man?"

She huffs a groan and a laugh at the same time, leaving me to wonder which she intended it to sound like. "It doesn't matter. Anyway, Lincoln and I were arguing because he decided after we got married that he does in fact want kids when I told him I didn't want them before we got married."

"I'm sure he understands, knowing you can't have them, right?" I would hope so. It's clearly out of her hands. She's had nothing but wonderful things to say about Lincoln, and aside from their argument this morning, I never would have assumed there was any trouble between them.

"I'm sorry for dumping that on you. I was trying to keep myself from blurting this all out. We just met and I could just use a friend."

I reach across the table for her fidgeting hands. "I'm sorry for what you've been through. You can always talk to me. I'm very good at being non-judgmental, ironically."

She sweeps her hair behind her ear. "That's good because I haven't told anyone this before. Even Lincoln, ashamedly." I don't tell her that I think Lincoln should know her reason for saying she doesn't want to have kids. "You must be a real good attorney if I managed to blab that all out to you after only meeting you a few times. I'm sure this goes without saying, but please don't tell anyone. I don't want anyone to know my business or the real reason we aren't having kids. It makes me look—"

"You were a seventeen-year-old kid. We all did things we regret at that age."

"True, but I guess some things just don't wind up hiding out in the back of our minds, right?"

SIXTEEN

JENNA | NOW

I've been listening to a nurse, or maybe she's a counselor, spout off a long list of rules, most of which don't apply to me since I don't have any clothes from home, a purse, or any means of communication. "No shoes with laces, sweatshirts with ties, belts, or jewelry either," she continues.

"I don't have anything," I remind her, but I don't think she's listening. No one seems to be listening to me.

"You'll meet with two different counselors, one psychiatrist, and attend two group sessions each day. A personal care assistant will be around to help you with your needs throughout all hours of the day. It's common to feel overwhelmed at first, but I assure you, you're in excellent hands," she says, attaching a plastic bracelet to my wrist. Her statements might as well be automated. I'm just another face passing through these halls. Except they've mistaken me for someone else who needs to be here.

I'm still on the gurney and I'm not sure why, but they have brought me into another room, one that looks like the last but with an additional empty bed and a window covered with bars. The sight makes my pulse thud within my ears as I clench my hands so tightly my fingernails burrow into the flesh of my palms. Bars are for felons, and I've never even received a speeding ticket. Is this how they treat all their patients...with fear?

"Breakfast is at eight, lunch at noon, and dinner at five," she continues, rattling off too many facts at once, sounding as if she's in a rush and needs to check a box next to my name. "A nurse will be with you shortly to help you shower and check you over for any baseline bruises or wounds." She smiles forcefully, then lowers her clipboard and pivots, walking out and leaving me here alone.

I lean my back into the pillow and stare up at the stucco ceiling lined with fluorescent lights.

Oliver brought me here. He knows I'm not mentally ill. I wonder if he knew what they would do to me after the exam. He couldn't have. He wouldn't have. More importantly, I can't understand why they think River isn't alive. The thought of losing my baby is like the tip of a knife puncturing holes into my heart, as I bleed out. I know it's not true. It's not possible.

I squeeze my eyes shut, searching for my last memory of cradling River in my arms.

"Jenna," a warm, calm voice wakes me. I must have dozed off. Another new person here to greet me in this hell. "I'm going to help you get cleaned up." I blink a few times before my focus clears, finding a young woman in a black fleece and blue scrubs, with her hair tied back into a low blonde ponytail like the last nurse I met.

"I want to go home. This is a mistake." How do they all act as if they can't hear me? "I'm an attorney and I'm aware of my rights. Holding me here against my will is illegal." This isn't true. Per Section 5150 of the Welfare Institution Code, a doctor can deem me unstable or at risk of harming myself or others for a seventy-two-hour holding period. I haven't posed a threat to anyone, though.

"You will be re-evaluated within seventy-two hours by a doctor," she says, proving she knows the legalities behind my accusation.

"I don't understand any of this. I need to be examined by a doctor for a physical condition, not psychiatric symptoms."

The woman takes a hold of my arm and helps me off the bed. "Do you feel stable when you walk?"

The floor isn't swaying like it was the last time I moved about. My head still feels heavy, but I can move on my own, which was more difficult a couple hours ago. "Yes."

"That's an improvement. We'll take it," she says with an unnatural tone of cheer in her voice.

While taking small steps down the hallway, I spot a phone mounted on the wall. "Could I call my husband, please?"

"Not just yet. Let's get you cleaned up right now."

I'm not dirty because I showered this morning. I think. The first thing I do when I wake up in the morning is shower. "I would like to speak to a doctor."

The woman inhales slowly, in through her nose and out through her mouth. "I understand."

"Do you? Because I've been suffering from exhaustion, confusion, and dizziness. My memory is in a fog. What psychological condition does this fall under? How does everyone here know what kind of treatment I need?"

"A therapist will answer all of your questions once we're through with a shower."

I had nightmares about giving birth to an audience watching. I'm a private person; discreet, and reserved. None of that matters when a woman is in labor. But I'm not in labor now and a woman is watching as I shower, reminding me to use shampoo. I've never taken a quicker shower than this one. She helps me into hospital-grade cotton underwear and a clean gown with matching socks that have rubber grips along the soles. I'm given a toothbrush, toothpaste and odorless deodorant, and I can't help but compare this mortification to what felons must experience upon their admission to prison. What crime have I committed?

"I'm going to bring you to meet with Laura, one of our therapists. She's the one who will answer your questions. Once your session is over, I'll take you back to your room." I know I've mastered the art of hiding my emotions while on the job, but this woman still has a stick-figure smile drawn across her mouth.

More hallways, all identical to the ones I've seen today. I wouldn't be able to find my way back to the room they assigned me to, but I know it doesn't smell of canned corn and pork like this one does. We stop in front of an open door and find the woman whose name I still don't care to learn, since she'll disappear like the last five or six people I've met. "Laura, I have Jenna here to see you."

Laura spins her chair around at her desk like a school principal waiting to lecture a naughty child. "Have a seat," she says, waving her palm out toward the one green faux leather chair sitting across from her desk. Like all the other women I've seen today, she has her hair pulled back, a clean face without a hint of makeup, and scrubs. She appears older than the others, older than me. Maybe she's fifty.

The aide, whatever her name is, closes us into Laura's office. I slide back in the chair to lower my elbows on the wooden armrests as I feel the rush of questions threatening to escape me all at once.

She lifts a single piece of paper from a stack of others on her desk and places a thin pair of glasses on the bridge of her nose while reviewing whatever is on the paper. She removes her glasses just as quickly and places them down on top of the paper before clasping her fingers together.

"This is a mistake," I say, "and I've said so to every person I've spoken to since arriving here today. No one seems to listen to me, and I'm very frustrated." I do my best to use careful words that will label me as innocent instead of whatever everyone here thinks I am.

Laura nods her head as if she understands, but I'm already sure she doesn't. "Your symptoms are quite serious. Are you aware of this?" she asks.

My eyes widen in response before I answer. "Yes, which is why I'd like to see a doctor for a physical evaluation."

"There is a reason for your symptoms, one we have definitively proven. If we thought your physical health was in danger, we would treat your case differently."

I open my hands, holding them up in front of me. "What have you proven?"

"Substance abuse is a common way to ease grief, but it can lead to dangerous, even deadly, outcomes."

Just another reason to prove they have confused me with someone else. "I don't have a substance abuse issue. Again, I think there is some confusion with whatever initial reports they filed about me when I arrived."

Laura unclasps her fingers and places her palms down on her desk. "Diagnostic testing is quite accurate." I know this but I haven't abused substances.

"I've taken common over-the-counter pain pills as prescribed following the birth of my son. I haven't misused them or taken more than what I was supposed to take. I haven't had alcohol in over nine months."

Laura pulls out a notepad and a pen from her desk drawer and jots down a few words. "We found more than over-the-counter pain medication in your lab work."

"That's impossible," I lash out. "Just as impossible as

everyone here wanting to convince me that my baby was stillborn."

Laura stands from her chair, pulling it around the side of her desk and in front of me, so close our knees are nearly touching. "Jenna, your son, River, did not make it. He was born without a pulse. Losing a baby is excruciating and unfathomable. Nobody blames you for your coping mechanism. You can't remember anything about your son because he isn't alive. Oliver has tried very hard to explain the reality of your situation to you, but he said that you would fall unconscious just after he would remind you. Then you would sleep for hours before waking up again in denial."

I don't recall Oliver telling me River didn't make it. He's been sitting by my side when I'm awake. He's spoken of River and carted around his car seat or baby seat in the house. If this is true, why would he have—

"It's easier to let someone come to terms with traumatic information on their own time, and Oliver was trying to allow that after trying to help you understand, but your decline in awareness was concerning to him, and us, and that's why you're here now."

She's lying. I don't know her. I've never seen her before. How does she even know Oliver? I've never taken a drug in my life. None of this makes any sense.

Laura reaches behind her and retrieves a mustard yellow envelope from her desk. She pinches the silver fastener and releases the tab, then pulls out a bottle of pain relievers. "Do these look familiar?"

"Yes." I've always taken the same brand of pain reliever.

"We asked Oliver to bring whatever medications you take regularly, pain relievers included. This was the only bottle he brought." I watch as she untwists the cap and pours a few pills into the cup of her hand.

"Do these look familiar?"

I shrug. "Yes."

"Okay," she says. "These pills look very similar to your average pain reliever, but unfortunately, they aren't. They're opioids, a very potent drug. Your medical records state you picked up a prescription for opioids two years ago following knee surgery."

I try to picture myself walking into our en suite bathroom, retrieving the one bottle of pills from the medicine cabinet—the one I refused to touch even after painful surgery—and pouring them into an empty bottle of pain relievers. I couldn't have done something like that. How would I forget doing that?

I wouldn't.

How would I forget that my sweet baby was supposedly born without a pulse?

I couldn't. It's a lie. These are all lies.

"No. Those aren't mine."

Maybe they are mine, but I didn't take them. At least, I don't remember taking them.

SEVENTEEN

GINGER | LAST YEAR

Another argument between the supposed lovebirds next door. It's what I wake up to on most Saturday mornings lately. For someone who seems so happy most of the time, Peyton doesn't seem to worry about airing out their dirty laundry. The wall in my bedroom is all that separates me from their driveway. I would think she would do a better job of hiding her secrets from me at least. Many of us keep our windows open at night when the temperatures are mild like they have been the last couple of days and, if she took a quick look, she would see I'm one of them.

Peyton isn't the type to want anyone to know they are constantly disagreeing over which doctor she should see or the fact that she isn't seeing any doctor for an apparent health issue. It's always the same back and forth. It's obvious to me that he's fighting her on the subject because he loves her, but I could easily assume Peyton would prefer to live in her ideal world of cupcakes and rainbows rather than face a less than ideal truth.

Lincoln is a good man, a hard worker, and a devoted husband, but I feel there are secrets contained within the walls of his house. He is too good for her, that much I know.

The telephone rings and startles me half to death. It's too early for anyone to be calling right now. I twist my bedside alarm clock to get a better look at the large digits. It's not even nine.

I lift the cordless phone and connect the call. "Fowler residence," I answer.

The pause before someone speaks irritates me. I can already tell I'm on some calling list. "Hi there. This is Ronald from Landmore Bank," the man begins in a drawl. I imagine he must be sitting in a cubicle with a headpiece, dressed in professional attire even though customers will never see him in person. "I must let you know that this call may include an attempt to collect debt and will be recorded for training purposes. May I speak to James Fowler please?"

"He's not in," I respond, reaching for the pen and notepad next to the phone cradle. I write down his name and the bank he's calling from to check on it later.

"We have been trying to reach him for quite some time. Is there a better number to try or do you know when a good time might be to try back?" Probably never, is the only real answer.

"I'm aware you've been trying to get a hold of him. He's a busy man, and I'm afraid I don't have a helpful answer. His schedule is unpredictable at best, but please feel free to try back again later."

The number from the caller ID is the next piece of information I jot down so I know not to answer any more of his phone calls.

"Thank you. Have a good day, ma'am."

Everyone wants whatever James owes them. I'm living off our retirement fund, hoping since it's just one of us now, it'll be enough to sustain me for however long I have left. Never, in my wildest dreams could I imagine ever feeling so frustrated and disconnected from my husband that I could commiserate and relate better to a debt collector on the other side of a phone call.

EIGHTEEN

JENNA | LAST YEAR

A perfect house can only be perfect when no one is living inside. It's the tenants and owners who leave dents, scratches, and create shadows in corners where secrets can hide like dust bunnies.

We've been living in the house for a month, and I believe we've met each person on our short street at least once. I now know there are twelve children between the ages of two and eighteen, and seven unique sets of families. We all wave when passing one another on the street, sometimes we stop to discuss the weather or a strange sound from the night before, but none of the conversations are deep and meaningful, not like the ones I've had with Peyton. Her story, her past, it breaks my heart.

"Did you get the red onion?" Oliver asks as the sizzle of butter pops and snaps in the frying pan.

"It's in the vegetable drawer."

We've met Lincoln twice, but they were passing meet and greets, either on his way home from work or on his way there. He seems like a nice man with a busy schedule. I'm hoping to learn more about him tonight when he and Peyton come over for dinner.

As Oliver locates the onion and splits it in half, my eyes burn. "Babe, cut the root off last. Remember?" I remind him with a chuckle. Tears are running down both of our cheeks as I brush the onion peels away from the cutting board where Oliver is slicing to toss them away.

"That's a myth," he argues with a smile.

I take a step closer to his side, taking a whiff. "I think that onion might be bad. Maybe we should skip it and just use the garlic."

Oliver leans down to smell the onion even though I can tell something isn't right from a couple feet away. "It's fine. It's just onion-y," he says, planting a wet kiss on my cheek.

I scoff and laugh before returning to the bowl of salad I'm putting together. "Oh, don't mention anything about what I told you about Peyton. Lincoln doesn't know about her past." I shouldn't have told Oliver what Peyton confided in me, but her story was eating away at me and I was researching similar cases, wishing I could help her in some way. Oliver happened to see what I was reading on my laptop. He isn't one to typically comment on what he might see on my screen, but this time he seemed taken aback along with his comment of, "Yikes, what's all that for?" Then he insisted on knowing more about the assumable case. He knows I keep my clients' cases confidential and will tell him if I can't discuss something, but because this wasn't about a client, I didn't want to lie. Husbands and wives share everything, or at least that's what I thought life would be like once we were married.

The doorbell rings just as we finish setting the new dining room table that we're about to use for the first time. Since it's just the two of us, we've been eating dinner at the kitchen island most nights. I've always seen the function of a dining room to be the place to entertain guests.

Upon opening the door, I see Peyton and Lincoln are both dressed up as if they're going to a fine dining restaurant. I'm not quite as glamorous but I've changed out of my uptight work clothes into a sundress. Oliver rarely finds time to dress casually so he fits in with them more than me. His work clothes are suitable for most occasions.

"Something smells incredible," Peyton says, pulling me in for a hug. "Thank you for having us over tonight. It's been a while since anyone has had us over for a homemade meal."

Lincoln steps in after Peyton passes by. It's the closest I've ever been to him, and I didn't realize how tall he is. I have to press up on my toes to give him a hug, but he seems used to dramatic height differences as he leans down to meet me halfway. I assume he's come right from work based on the fitted gray suit with a black button-down. The dark accents of his clothes match his slicked back hair, thick brows and lashes that frame his golden-brown eyes.

"I'm so glad to finally spend some time with you two tonight," he says. "Peyton hasn't stopped gushing about you in weeks." A kind, relaxed smile follows.

"I've heard nothing but the same about Peyton," Oliver says, making an appearance from the kitchen. He clears his throat and juts out his hand to shake Lincoln's. "I'm glad you could make it tonight."

"Thank you for having us over. It's nice to officially meet you, man."

"Same, same," Oliver says, waving him over to the dining room where Peyton is already admiring the spread that we might have gone overboard with. We started with a charcuterie board of meats, cheeses, jams, and an assortment of toasted breads and crackers. Oliver insisted on making a four-course meal with the starter spread, salad, chicken Florentine over mushroom risotto, and then an apple cake for dessert. I'm not sure how he got so much done before I got home from work, but he pulled it off.

"You didn't have to do all this," she says.

"We like to cook and it's nice to have friends to join us for dinner," I say. "Oh, speaking of which," I say, standing up from the table and rushing into the kitchen to grab the casserole dish we've been holding on to. "I've been meaning to give this back to you. Oliver said you returned it, but this isn't ours. Maybe it's Ginger's?"

"Isn't that ours?" Lincoln asks Peyton with a confused arch to his brow and a quiet chuckle.

"No, it isn't ours. Maybe it is Ginger's. Sorry about that. I don't know why I thought it was yours," Peyton says.

"I'll just put it on the side table next to the front door so you can take it home with you. They all look the same, don't they?"

"I can't even figure out which pan to use for a casserole or just a pie sometimes," she says, tapping the heel of her palm against her forehead.

"Can I get you a beer or wine, something stronger?" Oliver asks Lincoln. We have two bottles of wine out on the table already and I see Lincoln eye the bottle of red.

"Red would be great. I can get it though. You don't have to run circles around us. We're easygoing." Lincoln places a hand on his button-down shirt as he leans across the table for the bottle. "Do either of you want red too?"

"No, thank you," Oliver replies.

"I'm all set too, but thank you," I say.

"Honey?" Lincoln turns to Peyton. "Red for you?"

"Oh yes, please," she answers.

Oliver fills his and my glass with white then hands the bamboo salad bowl and tongs over to Peyton.

The conversation has been flowing smoothly and it's nice, comfortable, being myself with others. I'm hoping Lincoln and

Oliver will enjoy each other's company as much as Peyton and I do.

I lift my wine glass to initiate a toast. "To new friends."

"Cheers!"

"Hear, hear."

"To friendship," Peyton ends the round of responses.

After just one sip of the wine, my stomach turns, and my throat tightens. I place the glass back down and wait a moment for the wave of discomfort to pass. "Girl, you are paler than hotel bed sheets. Are you okay?" Peyton asks.

"Yeah," I say, waving her off. "I skipped lunch today so my blood sugar must be low. I'll be fine."

I've convinced myself I'll be fine until I hold a fork full of lettuce up to my mouth. My stomach churns again and I place my fork down. "Will you excuse me for a moment?"

Oliver stands up just as I do, but thankfully doesn't follow me as I don't want to be any ruder than I'm already being. I must sound like an elephant stampeding up the stairs, feeling a wave of nausea rise through the core of my body.

My head dangles over the porcelain bowl in our bathroom and I'm waiting for something to happen or the queasiness to subside, but I can't figure out what I ate earlier that would make me feel this way. I had a bagel with cream cheese for breakfast and I skipped lunch.

In no other time in life would I be caught with my bare arms on the edge of a toilet bowl, and at this very moment there's a knock on the door.

"It's me. No judgment. We've all been there. Can I come in?" Peyton mumbles through the crack in the door.

"One second." I wouldn't want her to see me like this, never mind anyone else, but she's going out of her way to check on me. I flush the toilet for no other reason than to create a barrier of noise so I can prop myself up before opening the door to let her inside.

"Are you okay?" she asks, holding a glass of water. "Oliver was on his way up, but I told him I'd check on you."

"I don't know what just came over me. That never happens."

"I've seen this before," Peyton says with a sigh. "You either have food poisoning from your invisible lunch or you're pregnant."

"Oh my gosh, no, no," I say, trying to laugh off the assumption. "Neither. There must be a third possibility." The thought of pregnancy didn't enter my mind because we've taken precautions, and the odds of being part of the one percent unaffected by birth control is hard to believe. There must be another explanation.

"I'm sure it's some little bug."

Peyton presses the back of her hand up to my forehead. "No fever, so that's good."

"I think I'm okay now. I don't want to ruin our dinner. I'll be fine. I promise," I say, resting my hand on her shoulder. I'm not sure I have the desire to eat but I can at least sit at the table and be cordial.

"We can go. If you don't feel well, the last thing you want to do is feel like you have to entertain us."

"Please stay. I don't want you to leave. Plus, Oliver would be so disappointed. He's been looking forward to spending time with Lincoln just as much as I have."

"Okay, but one more flash of white on your face and we're leaving you be."

I follow her down the stairs and back into the dining room. Oliver has his hands on the table, staring at me with a look of worry. "Are you okay?"

"I'm totally fine. I bet my breakfast was bad. I got a bagel from the corner store near work and—those late expiration dates can go unnoticed sometimes," I say, trying to make a joke of the situation.

As Peyton and I take our seats, I notice Lincoln staring at Peyton, watching her every move, waiting to catch her eye as if he wants to silently give her a message, but she remains focused on the table, and her salad.

Oliver places his hand on my knee beneath the table. He knows I wouldn't call off dinner no matter what the situation.

The nausea subsides but I feel more and more run-down as the night progresses. I've taken the time to listen to the conversation between Lincoln and Oliver, finding all the tidbits about his architecture firm to be interesting, which explains his long hours. Peyton has been unusually quiet, not taking part in the conversation between the two men. She's scrolling through her phone, and I notice her jaw grinding from side to side.

"You know, Jenna, what if you are pregnant?" she says, taking the glass of wine from in front of me. I haven't touched it or the food.

"Pregnant?" Lincoln asks with delight. The thought seems to surprise him, likely just as much as it shocks me that Peyton just asked this question out loud.

Oliver's hand squeezes around my knee. "What?" he utters. "Why is she asking—"

It's becoming harder to fake my response to Peyton's suggestion, but I force another smile. "Trust me, I'm not pregnant." With a quiet huff of laughter, I loop my hair behind my ears, a telltale sign to Oliver that I'm uncomfortable.

"You kind of have a glow," Peyton says. "Maybe you should take a test just to see."

"It's the chandelier," I say with a chipper inflection.

"Babe, is it possible?" Oliver asks, trying not to be overheard, which is impossible when there are only four of us at the table.

"No," I say. I mean, yes, there's a one percent chance my birth control didn't work, but no...

Peyton sniffles and she pulls her fist up to her mouth.

Suddenly she pushes her chair out from the table, the loud scrape from the wooden legs against the floors reminding me to get felt for the feet. "I'm sorry," she mutters, running to the front door.

"Peyton," I call after her. "What's—" The door opens and closes between blinks and the three of us are left awkwardly sitting at the table, staring at one another.

"Let her go," Oliver whispers to me. "My God. That was uncalled for."

Lincoln pushes his chair out from the table. "I am so so sorry. I better go check on her. She's weird around the topic of babies. She doesn't want them, but she acts like she does, and we think there might be a medical issue. You know…I'm talking too much and have already said more than I should. I should go," he says pointing at the door. "Oh, I'll bring this home too. Thanks again." He grabs the casserole dish from the side table before opening the front door.

"No worries. We understand," Oliver says.

When Lincoln leaves, Oliver leans back in his chair and runs his fingers through his hair. "What just happened?"

"She can't have kids. She thinks I'm pregnant because of a wave of nausea."

Oliver twists in his chair to face me and takes my hands in his. "Babe, forget about Peyton for a minute. Are you okay now?"

"I'm fine," I say, lying because I still feel nauseous.

"I'm sorry dinner was ruined. I was hoping the night would go well. There will be other opportunities, though. Don't worry," he says, leaning toward me to give me a kiss on the nose.

"I feel so awful that I upset her."

Oliver closes his eyes and shakes his head then pushes his chair away from the table. "Babe, I don't think Peyton is of a sound mind. You may want to keep her at an arm's length for a bit. Neither of us need that kind of drama in our life right now."

"Someone's trauma isn't drama, Oliver," I remind him. "Peyton is my friend."

"Jenna, that's only true if the trauma is real. If it happened. If she isn't just looking for attention from a child-law attorney. You trust so easily and I just don't want to see you get hurt."

NINETEEN

JENNA | NOW

My arrival here yesterday has bled into today, a new day, the second day. I hardly remember falling asleep last night or moving about to eat breakfast this morning. I was in a room alone except for an aide sitting beside me like a guard, but they said I would be placed into a different room today. I'm not sure why. It's like I'm circling around in a thick fog with no path to clarity. My head is so heavy.

"Just this way," an aide says, leading me to the next scheduled activity. "Group therapy is a great way of handling domestic issues, mental health stress, or drug and alcohol abuse. Hopefully you'll find this to be a positive experience for you."

I'm being shuttled around from room to room, corridor to common space, and I just follow like an obedient pet. There are so many people here that they all seem to be circling around me, staring as if I'm an exhibit. Maybe I'm having a nervous breakdown.

Not once had I imagined myself in one of these chairs, a circle of others staring at each other with tired eyes. The aid pulls one of the chairs out for me and gestures for me to have a seat. Again, all eyes are on me.

"We have a new friend joining us today. Jenna, would you be interested in saying a few words?" I didn't catch the group leader's name when I sat down. I've barely scanned the circle we're sitting in. I've been staring out the window to our left, wondering how I've become a prisoner in this building. Upon taking a closer look at everyone around me, I notice a common gray glow throughout the various tones of complexions. The variance of clothing options are mostly different color sweatpants or flannel pajama bottoms and solid color T-shirts or loose-fitting sweatshirts without hoods. The ages range from an older teenage girl to a man who appears to be in his late fifties. There are more women than men, and the majority seem to be in their twenties or thirties. Each person seems to portray a unique flavor of sadness, making me wonder what brought them here—how long they've been here.

The teenage girl won't look up from her lap. Her scraggly dark blonde hair dangles over her eyes as she plucks at a hangnail on her thumb. She reminds me of many of the clients I've worked with—abused, neglected children, left to rot. I should be helping someone like her, not being treated as if I have similar troubles. The facility is wasting time and money on me when there are people here who clearly need more than group therapy. I continue studying the others, finding one woman to be convulsing while tears stream down her cheeks as she mutters a prayer over and over. The man beside her is sweating, holding the back of his head while subtly rocking back and forth in his seat. I hear his erratic breaths from across the circle.

"I don't think I belong here," I say. I'm sure the others all feel the same about themselves—that they don't belong here either. I stand up from my yellow plastic bucket seat, lift the chair and move it back a few steps so I can exit the circle.

"Jenna, we'd all really like it if you stayed here with us for this group session," the woman says. It's like a cult here. That's what this is.

"No, thank you," I reply, quickly leaving the open communal area. Footsteps sound behind me and I'm sure it's the personal attendant chasing after me, but as she can see, I'm not as unsteady or dizzy as I was when I arrived here. My head isn't as foggy either. I make it to the hallway where I saw the telephone and stop right in front of it. I grab the handle and rest it between my ear and shoulder. A dial tone hums into my ear and I tap out Oliver's phone number.

I turn to look down the hallway, finding a hand reaching for me. "You can't do that right now." She tries to take the handle out of my grip. I refuse to release my hold.

"No, no. I need to speak to my husband right now." I'm so busy fighting to hold on to the phone that I didn't notice another hand pulling down the hook switch, ending the call. "Shit!" I yell in her face. "I have human rights, and a baby at home who needs his mother. This treatment is asinine, and I demand to speak to an attorney right now."

"Jenna, I'm going to need you to take a deep breath with me."

I stare at the woman for a long second, vaguely recognizing her from the swarm of faces I've seen today. She's the one who followed me down to group therapy. I think her name was Mel. She's a head taller than I am and she has a lot of muscle, even compared to most physically fit women I know. "I don't need to take a breath," I say, annunciating all my words like a sharp pencil against coarse paper. "You are going to let me make a phone call. One measly little phone call."

"It's in your best interest that you don't," she says. Her eyelids look heavy as if this conversation is keeping her awake.

"My best interest? Do you care about my son's best interest, or the fact that he doesn't have a mother right this minute? Do you care that someone set me up to look like I'm mentally ill and then..." I laugh sardonically, "and then, you people have the audacity to try and convince me that my son—the child I gave birth to not even a month ago, is—"

"Jenna," Mel says, holding her hands up as if I might swing at her. I've never hit anyone, not once in my life. Just another assumption made here. It's shocking, really. "Your son has passed away. He's in a bet—"

Another laugh storms up through my lungs and I palm my chest. "I'm sorry, I'm sorry," I squeal, "were you just about to tell me my son is in a better place?"

"Okay, I'm only going to ask you once—"

"You're right. You are right, Mel! My son is in a better place, because any place that isn't here fits that description, doesn't it?"

"I know this is difficult," she says.

"Screw you," I shout, turning on my heels to make a run for it. But I hit what feels like a brick wall. "Let me go!" My scream bellows and bounces off the walls around me like a haunting echo.

There's a jab against my arm and by instinct, I try to touch the area of my skin, but my arms are being pulled behind my back. My knees sink into the floor as if the tiles are made of marshmallow, and a warm embrace clings to my skin.

A hazy vision of Oliver pacing back and forth in our living room with River wrapped in a bloody blanket floats above my head.

"What do I do? Where do I take him?" I can hear Oliver's voice so clearly.

"Why is he bleeding?" I try to ask but the words don't come out. "Oliver?" I can't hear myself speaking. He's so worried, but River is fine, can't he see? His eyes are open, he's staring right up at his father, wondering why he's panicking. "You're scaring him," I say, panic in my voice. "You're scaring him."

TWENTY

GINGER | LAST YEAR

A notification pops up on the screen of my phone as the device buzzes against the side of my leg. I place my bowl of popcorn down on James's side of the bed and mute the television.

Motion has been detected at the front door.

As it always does, my curiosity gets the best of me. I do try to ignore the motion detector at night so I can settle down before I go to sleep but I'm interested to see if there's activity at Oliver and Jenna's house so soon after the start of their dinner date with Lincoln and Peyton.

With one glance at the live footage, I see she's at it again. I expected Perfect Peyton to contain her demons for longer than a month, but maybe she's becoming weak with her game. It's rude to run out of someone's house when they invite you over for dinner. I would never run out on Jenna and Oliver like that, but apparently, they don't want to give me the same opportunity to prove my hospitality. Maybe my invitation got lost in the mail.

Peyton has her hands pressing into the front of her face as

she runs from Oliver and Jenna's. With Lincoln only seconds behind her, I would think the house is about to erupt into flames. Although Lincoln doesn't have the same urgency in his pace as Peyton. He even takes a moment to peer up to the sky and shake his head. Poor guy.

An argument ensues the moment their front door closes, but I can't make out much of what they're saying, only the rise and fall of their volume. If they were in their bedroom, I could hear more.

Minutes pass but then the background static of their tempered exchanges becomes quiet. The kind of quiet I walked into on that snowy day two winters ago. It was the unknown calm before a storm—a small window of opportunity to tidy things and secure all loose ends.

I lift James's framed photo off my nightstand and rest it on my chest, then trace the tip of my fingernail around his smile. "Do you blame me for being angry, James?" We had everything we could have asked for in life. I thought we were perfect. But we weren't, were we?

TWENTY-ONE

JENNA | LAST YEAR

In the bathroom, the scene around me plays out as if it's a silent film. It's been five days since our dinner disaster, five days that I've felt queasy, tired, and moody. Oliver never asked if my period was late. I would have told him but it didn't really cross my mind until now. It hasn't been something I've been worried about.

Denial is easier than facing a fact, for me at least.

I appreciate the way Oliver is remaining calm, knowing this isn't what I want right now even though it is the very thing he desires the most.

One hundred twenty seconds. I've been counting for eighty when a thread of letters pops up within the test window. I close my eyes and reach for the plastic stick. My heart pelts like hail against glass. I might shatter.

Oliver doesn't say a word. I'm not sure if he's even taken a peek yet, but I squint through my lashes, finding the depiction of the rest of my life transcribed in only eight letters.

"Deep breath, deep breath," Oliver says, placing his hands on top of my shoulders. I place the test back down on the edge of the sink and lift my gaze to witness the expression on Oliver's face, one I should have dreamt about like so many people do after they get married. The moment their spouse finds out they're going to be a parent is supposed to be life changing. It should bring tears to my eyes and make me feel a new level of love for him.

His slate blue eyes are watery, his cheeks are red, and his jaw muscles are tense. "I know you're not ready," he whispers.

I turn around and wrap my arms around his waist, leaning my head against his chest. His heart is racing just as fast as mine. I stare at the bathtub, the pale green shower curtain scrunched up against the tiled wall. I imagine bubbles overflowing, water splashing everywhere, giggles erupting like the crescendo of an uplifting melody, and both Oliver and I soaked from trying to give our perfect baby a bath.

"I wasn't ready until right this very moment," I reply.

Oliver's arms tighten around me, and he buries his face in my shoulder, releasing the tears he was holding in for my sake. "I love you."

"I love you, and our baby—our family of three."

TWENTY-TWO

JENNA | NOW

A foghorn of voices stab through my ears and I blink over and over, waiting for the blurry film to clear. A woman is standing at the foot of the bed. I've never seen her before but she's in a simple gray sweatshirt and black baggy cotton pants. Her light brown hair falls into curls and her pale complexion contrasts against the dark circles beneath her eyes.

"Who—are you?" I force my head from side to side, deciphering where I am, but while doing so, I find my body feels like it's being weighed down.

"I can be your new best friend, or a nightmare. Your call," she says with a shrug as she coils a strand of her hair around her finger. "I'm also your roommate. Kinley."

I try to sit up, but I don't have the energy. "Why—"

"Don't fight it. Trust me. I'm on week three with another week to go. I could have been out of here last week though."

Kinley walks around to the side of my bed and pushes her sleeves up to her elbows. Puffy pale scars line both of her arms, giving me an easy conclusion as to why she's here but I'll try not to assume. "I shouldn't be here, and no one will listen to me."

"No offense," she says with a sigh, "we've all said that upon arrival. It's like human instinct or something."

My wrist itches from the clammy sweat on my skin beneath the plastic patient bracelet. "My husband brought me here because I was suffering from fatigue and confusion after having a baby. He must have thought this was a regular hospital." Would he think that? We always go to the same hospital—Lakespur Union. He would never do this to me. They may be keeping him from me just as they are keeping me from him.

"We're in a mental health facility, not a hospital," she says as if it's common knowledge. "Well, seeing as you were put into a room with me, it's safe to assume you have a drug issue too. Am I right?"

I choke out a silent laugh. "No. They think that's what they found in my blood or urine—opiates or something, but I've never taken drugs. I'm an attorney."

"Yeah, and I'm a first-grade teacher..." she says with laughter.

My chest rises and falls hard and fast as I try to place all my thoughts together. "No, I haven't taken drugs."

"Then why else would you be here, involuntarily, I assume?" She flops down onto her bed as if she's a teenager in the comfort of her bedroom.

"I thought I was suffering from postpartum depression but maybe something else was happening to me. The doctors or counselors, therapists, whoever here...they're all telling me my baby is dead when he's not. He was here with my husband when they brought me in."

"So, why do they think he's dead then?" Kinley asks. Her matter-of-fact question steals the air from my lungs, and I clutch the fabric over my chest, digging my fingernails into my flesh. Why does a simple question feel like a physical attack from someone I've just met?

"No, no, no, he's not." He wasn't stillborn. I remember his face. I remember holding him. Oliver was holding him.

"You seem unsure," she says, as if she's known me for longer than five minutes.

"I'm not unsure. My child is alive."

"Then why were you taking drugs? That's not a good way to start your new life as a mother." I close my eyes, wishing I could fall back into whatever trance I was in. I feel like I'm trying to speak through static. "Anyway, for what it's worth, you don't look like you just gave birth. So, good on you."

The urge to wrap my hands around my swollen belly calls an ache into my heart. I can smell his head, the sweet powdery baby scent, and feel the soft feathery hair from his head tickling my chin. I wouldn't remember these things if he wasn't alive.

I wonder if Peyton knows where I am right now. I'm not sure Oliver would tell her, but she would be wondering where I am. She would be checking on me as she had been. We've spent so much time together over the last nine months, but maybe this is too much for her to handle.

A figure at the door catches my attention and I recognize her as the woman who has been following me everywhere and likely the reason my body feels like it's four hundred pounds. "You have a visitor. I'll take you to the visiting room."

"Who? Who's here?"

Mel, the member of staff, peers over at Kinley then back at me. She helps me up to my feet and my muscles ache as if I just worked out too hard, lifting weights I shouldn't be lifting without warming up and running miles when I can barely run one.

"Maybe it's your dead baby's daddy coming to explain," Kinley says. I recoil as if her statement was a swinging fist and though I wasn't struck, I feel as if I just took a blow to the chest, leaving me winded and dizzy as I try to convince myself she must be talking about someone else's life rather than mine.

"Enough," Mel says, "mind your own business."

"How else would I know so much if Jenna didn't share the so-called business?"

Mel rolls her eyes and waits for me to pull myself together up on my feet. "Follow me."

I do. My feet are heavy, barely lifting off the floor with each step. I might as well be shuffling down the hall. "Who's here?" I ask again.

She doesn't answer. Instead, she stops in front of a closed door, opens it and gestures for me to walk inside. Another empty room, no windows, just chairs, and...

"Mom," I utter, trying to make my way over to her as fast as my legs will carry me.

She wraps her arms around me and rests her head on my shoulder. Her embrace is as good as it was after my first day of kindergarten when a fourth grader stole my lunch box. I held my tears all day until I got off the school bus and the moment my arms were around her, every emotion I felt came rushing out. She let me cry until I felt better and like magic, I was okay again. I wonder if she could somehow make me feel better now —maybe step in and fix everything just once more.

"I'll give you two a few minutes. It's nice to meet you, Deborah," Mel says, offering Mom a different type of smile than the one she's offered me. "There are cameras watching for your safety." Whose safety? Neither of us would hurt each other.

Mom combs her fingers through my hair, curling strands behind my ears. "Sweetheart—"

I shake my head furiously. "Don't say it," I warn her.

"I'm your mother and you need to listen to me," she says, holding my face between her cool hands. The fragrance of the freesia perfume she's always worn makes me wish she won't ever release me. The scent is a reminder of the times when Mom has been waiting with open arms. "River did not make it. Oliver said the umbilical cord was around his neck for too long.

There's nothing you could have done differently, right?" I'm not sure what kind of question she's asking or why she's taking Oliver's word over mine. None of this is right. My favorite fragrance is now tainted by the ammonia filled air in this room and worse, Mom's jarring words.

"I remember him, Mom," I cry out.

"You held your baby. Oliver said you held him, and you soaked him up and gave him all the love you could give. But he didn't have a pulse. You couldn't have heard him cry, Jenna. Oliver's been coming to terms with this on his own while trying to support you in every way possible. He didn't know they were going to admit you. He was trying to get you the care you need. We've been by your side for the last two weeks but you're not okay, sweetie."

"I would have seen the umbilical cord wrapped around his neck if I remember holding him. Can you understand this?" I cry out. Tears are running down her cheeks. I notice now she's not wearing makeup like she always does. Her eyes are red-rimmed, and her cheeks are raw with rosy patches. Even her hair is a mess and up in a ponytail—a style she hates for herself. "If he's...he's—" I try to catch my breath and find my words, "de-dead, why was he with us when Oliver brought me here?" The last words hardly form with sound, but I think she understands.

"You gave Oliver no other choice. He didn't want to hurt you any more than you were already hurting."

"Mom," I cough out, "Mom, no, they said they found drugs in my system. I would never—"

"Jenna," she says, taking in a stiff breath through her ruddy nose. "When people are in a fight or flight mode, we do things we wouldn't normally do. We survive by whatever means, and Oliver found the bottle of pills in your nightstand, but not until two days ago. He had no choice but to bring you here." Mom's chin trembles and I know she's trying to remain strong for me, but she's not seeing the bigger picture.

"I don't remember any of this," I say, staring directly into her eyes. She must believe me: her daughter, the one person who has always been there with her. We've never doubted each other, not once, and I've done nothing but stand by her side since I was old enough to do so.

My hair slips out from between her fingers, and she takes a step backward. A shuddered breath quakes through her chest as she presses her hand over her heart. "I believe you, sweetie, but the lab tests don't lie. They showed me the reports."

"You saw reports stating the umbilical cord strangled my baby? Why weren't you there? You told me you'd be there."

"No one told me, Jenna. I had no idea you were in labor. And no, I didn't see any report. Oliver said he died from strangulation from the umbilical cord."

I shake my head and swallow against the dryness in my throat. "No, no. Oliver called you. I know he did."

"Sweetie," she says, shaking her head, her forehead lined with deep wrinkles. "Maybe he thought he did but he was wrapped up in the moment with you."

"What? No. Mom, it's the house. I'm telling you...we never should have bought the house. It was all a big mistake. I didn't think—" My statements aren't helping because I never told her about the people who lived in the house before us or about the news crew that showed up, the rumors...but that's all I can think about now.

"I don't understand what you're talking about. What does River have to do with the house?"

"Someone did this to us. Someone didn't want us living in the house. Someone killed River—it wasn't the umbilical cord." My face sears with the heat of a roaring fire. "You need to listen to me, Mom. Please. I'm not mentally ill. You know me better than anyone else in the entire world. Please."

Mom lifts her hand from her chest and presses it against her mouth. She clenches her eyes until tears spill out from between her lashes, then sucks in a lungful of air and holds it for a long second before exhaling.

"Jenna." My name is stern on her tongue. "I need you to tell me the truth right now. Was it you who killed him?"

TWENTY-THREE

GINGER | LAST YEAR

It's been days since the dinner party crisis, and I still haven't seen the two women conversing. I'm dying to know if they had an argument. Maybe Jenna saw past the pretty face Peyton wears so well. As an attorney, I would expect she has a sixth sense about people, but then again, even the smartest people can be fooled.

As a mother of four, I have a different extra sense, so I've made Jenna some soup. Her car hasn't moved in two days. Though it's been muggy and damp this week, the weather hasn't seemed to hold her back before which can only mean one thing.

I make my way across the street and ring the doorbell, glancing around in every direction as I have a habit of doing. A scuffling sound comes and goes from the inside, but the front door opens, revealing Jenna in a dark blue bathrobe that makes her look quite pale. "I had a suspicion you might be sick," I say, handing her the plastic sealed bowl of chicken soup. Hopefully the savory scent of the chicken broth doesn't upset her stomach.

"Ginger, you're too sweet. Really, you didn't have to go out of your way for me." She pulls the bowl in against her chest and glances over my shoulder toward Peyton's house. The look in her eyes sparks my curiosity. "How did you know I was sick?"

I twist my lips to the side. "I noticed your car in the driveway for the last couple of days when you're normally at work."

"You're very perceptive," she says. "I'd invite you in, but—"

"Germs don't bother me. Four boys, remember? Come on, I'll heat you up some soup. Even hardworking women like yourself need some care sometimes."

"Oh," she says, taking a step back away from the door as I forwardly walk inside. People like Jenna need to be pushed to take help or they will never accept any.

"Get comfortable on your sofa. Daytime TV isn't so bad." I take the bowl of soup back from her hands and continue past the fact that she hasn't blinked in what feels like an entire minute. I'm already in the kitchen by the time she closes the front door.

Rather than relax on the couch, she follows me into the kitchen. "I'm not sick with a cold, virus, or bug," she says.

I stop moving just after peeling the lid off the plastic bowl. Dear God. I hope it's nothing serious.

"What is it, dear?"

Her tired eyes form into crescents as she presses a firm smile onto her lips. "I'm pregnant. I haven't told anyone. My doctor's appointment is tomorrow so I'm not sure how far along I am, but it might be seven or eight weeks."

I place the lid down and press my hands together over my chest. "Good gracious." It's hard to forget each of the four times I found out I was pregnant with the boys. The excitement was overwhelming and then bam, it was like I got hit by a sack of bricks as the morning sickness set in—exhaustion, nausea, and a sudden aversion for most foods. "Morning sickness generally starts around seven weeks, sometimes sooner, sometimes later, but the good news is, most of the time it subsides by the second trimester."

"I'm hoping for sooner rather than later. I don't want to lose my job."

The thought of that makes my shoulders tense. I said the very same thing. I was in my last year of earning my Master's degree for clinical psychology when I found out I was pregnant with Joel. It shouldn't have been a surprise and James and I should have been more careful, but we got married the summer before. Life happens. I thought I would be able to continue on too, but the morning sickness got in the way and the fatigue left me in a brain fog. I promised myself I would get back to the classes after he was born, but I will most likely forever remain eight credits short of my degree. "I'm sure whatever happens is the way it's meant to be."

She doesn't look pleased with my response. "Unrealistic expectations. That's what I have, right?"

I rummage through her cabinets until I find the soup bowls and take one down. I spot a ladle in a glass jar of cooking utensils, then fill the bowl.

"Everyone is different. It's up to you what you do with your family and career, and no one should have any influence over that. My best advice is to listen to what your body tells you to do."

"My mom says the same whenever I'm sick," Jenna says, pulling her robe tighter over her chest.

I hold a finger up in the air and smile. "Smart woman."

The soup is heating in the microwave, and I usher Jenna back into the living room so she can put her feet up. "The more rest you get now, the better off you'll be."

"You're really kind to do this for me. I'm sorry I haven't gotten to know you better yet. I guess I was so wrapped up in—"

Perfect Peyton. "You don't need to explain. At your age, I would have been just as thrilled to have neighbors the same age across the street. It's a nice situation for you all." *Is it? Because I'm not sure the two of you have spoken in almost a week.*

"Absolutely. I'm just not ready to tell Peyton I'm pregnant yet so I've been a bit quiet and fibbed a little, telling her I have a bad cold. I haven't even told my mom yet because I'm waiting until after my appointment tomorrow. I don't want to get her excited until I know everything is all right."

The microwave timer beeps, and I scurry back into the kitchen and circle around before finding a potholder. The spoon is last on my scavenger hunt. I open both of the wide drawers and find the silverware on the right. I take out a spoon and reach to close the other drawer, but my belt loop catches on the knob of the drawer and rattles everything around inside.

"Are you okay?" Jenna shouts in.

"Yes," I laugh. "I got caught on the knob of the drawer."

"That happens to me daily," she says.

I unhook myself and reach in to straighten out the silverware organizer, finding the corner of a card poking out from the exposed side of the drawer. I lift the organizer to place the card back where it was but not before glancing at what appears to be a sympathy card.

The words written in familiar handwriting send a shiver up my spine. This note must have been left for Luanne, and only one of us on this street thinks she could have done something so malicious to her poor husband.

We send our deepest condolences
The darkest of nights might seem blue
But the sun will again rise
Unless it's you...
The cause of his demise.

I just can't understand why she would have left this behind. I wonder if it was Jenna or Oliver who found the card, and why

they chose to keep it, then hide it beneath the silverware organizer—the one place most people don't look.

I shove the card back where it was and close the drawer.
Jenna is flipping through the channels on the large flat-screen
television, so I set the bowl down on a table coaster. "Here we
are. Soup fixes everything," I say.

"Thank you again, Ginger. I truly appreciate all of this."

"If you need anything, I'm going to leave you my phone
number so you can call me." I pull out a sticky note from home
that I've already written my name and number on for her. "I'll
leave it right here for you." I place it down next to the bowl of
soup.

"I appreciate it," she says.

"Oh, and don't worry. Your secret is safe with me. My lips
are sealed until you're ready for others to know." Peyton is going
to despise this news. I can't wait until she finds out.

TWENTY-FOUR

JENNA | LAST YEAR

"We should wait a little longer," Oliver suggests. "It will be like adding salt to the wound."

The secrets are making me feel crazy. I told Ginger and I never would have if I wasn't cornered by her. But the fact that she knows, and Peyton doesn't, is keeping me up at night. It's obvious there is some sort of disdain between the two of them and with how easily Ginger spoke about the folks who lived here before us, I'm not sure how likely she is to keep a secret from Peyton. Ginger seems envious of Peyton, but there's something more I can't seem to put my finger on. Peyton doesn't talk about her much, but the couple of times she did, the expression on her face changed and she looked like she had a spider crawling up her neck that she needed to shake off.

"I can't. It's been two weeks," I reply. "She still thinks I'm mad at her for the outburst at the table then running out of the house. I've told her I'm not, but there's an awkwardness between us, a shift in the way we chat over texts." We live across the street from each other, and I don't want any unnecessary discomfort, especially since I've enjoyed getting to know her. If anything, I understand why she was initially upset.

When someone wants something they can't have, it can seem like the entire world has that one thing. In this case, she was correct about her accusation, and it doesn't help that she keeps asking me how I'm feeling.

"Are you just going to go knock on her door and say: guess what?" Oliver asks, seeming a bit fearful of my response. I'm not sure why he's so against this decision since we've already told our families.

"I suppose. There's no other way to do it, is there?"

Oliver shrugs. "I guess not, but maybe we could just wait another week or so?"

"Babe, it's stressing me out. You don't have to come with me. I'll handle it on my own. Isn't there a game on or something?" I ask, reaching for the remote on the coffee table.

"You always know just the right thing to say to win your argument," he says, looping his arm around my waist and gently pulling me in for a kiss. "Fine, fine, fine, if you insist, I'll watch the game."

"I do. Relax. Put your feet up and don't think about anything else."

"I wish you would do the same," he says, his voice lifting an octave.

"I will as soon as I get back. I promise." Oliver drops down onto the couch and slouches into the cushions. I hand him the remote and give him a peck on the cheek. "I'll be right back."

I rush out the door and head across the street, finding Ginger outside watering her perennials along the side of her driveway. She waves with a smile and I'm thankful she leaves the passing interaction at that so I can get this confession over with.

My heart tremors in my chest as I ring Peyton's doorbell. "Just a minute," she shouts.

She opens the door and she's out of breath. Sweat is beading along her forehead and her hair is wet and pulled back into a ponytail. "Sorry, I was on the treadmill," she says through heavy breaths.

"Oh," I say, peering past her and then back toward my house, unsure if I should tell her I'll come back later. "I didn't mean to interrupt your workout."

"Oh my God. Stop it," she says, pulling me into the house. "I'm glad you're here. I've missed you."

"Work has been—" It's a lie and I don't want to lie. "I'm pregnant," I blurt out as she reaches for her water bottle on the living room coffee table.

"Yeah, I know," she says with a dry laugh, lunging forward to give me a hug—a stiff hug, but a hug, nonetheless.

"What do you mean? How did you know?" As she steps back, I glance down at my stomach, knowing I haven't begun to show much other than some mild bloat, and I have one of Oliver's Lakespur University T-shirts on—not exactly form fitting. I've been looking for a hint of a belly and there is nothing about my stomach that says pregnant.

"I'm twenty-seven. Do you know how many of my friends have gotten pregnant in the last year? Everyone starts with a response of denial. The nausea, the glow, the silent treatment: check, check, and check," she says, a light-spirited laugh follows. "But didn't you say you weren't ready for kids yet and were making sure it wouldn't happen anytime soon?"

"I did, but I feel differently now."

"Were you on the pill or something?" she continues.

"Yeah, why?"

She chuckles. "You should play the lottery, being that one percent no one ever hears about."

"Maybe I will. It's true. It's hard to wrap my head around. I never thought birth control could let me down, but I'm just glad it did now instead of—" I realize what I'm saying and wish I could take it all back, knowing what happened to her in the past.

She waves her hand at me, shooing off my blundering words then pulls me over to her couch. "Sorry if I smell, by the way. Breathe through your mouth."

"You—you don't." I try to laugh but I end up coughing through the dryness in my throat.

"So, crazier things have happened, but the dinner at your house—it was life altering for me."

Peyton seems genuinely happy, and I can't imagine that night did much of anything except bring up some painful emotions for her—kind of like today, again. "How so?"

"Well, I'm late..." She lowers her hands to bouncing knees.

"Oh." I'm sure she knows that doesn't always mean what I think she's hoping it means.

"No, you're supposed to say, 'Peyton, you need more proof than that, silly.'" That would be completely inappropriate, and hurtful. I would never say that.

"But—"

"I took a test, Jenna. I took one yesterday because I was three days late, so I got one of those early pregnancy detection tests and a minute hardly passed by when it popped up with the word pregnant," she says, delight oozing off each word. Her excitement is palpable, so much so that she's out of breath just talking. "Don't worry. I went to the doctor this morning. They took blood and confirmed that everything looked the way it should look for being just over four weeks along. When I asked for an explanation after being told it was impossible for me to get pregnant, the doctor shrugged and asked me if I'd been around anyone else who is pregnant. I laughed, obviously, because that's the most ridiculous question I've ever been asked. I'm pretty sure everyone knows you can't 'catch' a baby, right? Wrong. Pregnancy *can* be contagious. That's what he said. It's some psychological thing, I guess. Of course, that confirmed my thoughts on you being pregnant, and me becoming pregnant later that night thanks to the make-up session Lincoln and I had."

This entire visit feels surreal. This seems more like a miracle than a psychological coincidence. She's staring at me, waiting for me to show her the same joy she showed me when I walked into her house. "I'm stunned and—"

"I know, I still feel blindsided too. I keep thinking I'm going to just wake up from this dream and I don't want to, Jenna."

Tears surface in the corners of her eyes and her chin dimples. I reach for her and pull her into my arms. "I'm so incredibly happy for you. This is just the best news." I hope her doctor warned her about complications and the fragility of the first trimester. She would be devastated if something happened.

"I know nothing is for certain and I'm going to take it easy until my ultrasound at the eight-week mark. My doctor said the risk of a miscarriage will lessen each week so I'm going to keep praying and doing everything I can to be healthy."

"I'm truly, truly happy for you. Good things come to those who are patient, and you've been through a lot, so maybe this is just the universe's way of making reparation to you." I take her hands in mine, feeling the same clamminess in her palms as mine. It must be a pregnancy thing.

"If all goes well, we get to do this together—two unsuspecting expecting moms-to-be," she says, her smile slinging between her ears. "How many weeks along are you?"

"I'm eight weeks along as of yesterday. So, you're—"

"I'll be five weeks along on Tuesday. So, we're only three and a half weeks apart of each other," she croons. "Oh, and I'm not telling anyone else until I'm thirteen weeks just to be safe. Ahh! We get to go shopping together for maternity clothes and little, tiny baby clothes. Maybe one of us will have a boy and the other will have a girl—oh God, I'm getting way ahead of myself."

I'm pretty sure we're all programmed to think the same way.

Peyton just has a habit of saying what she thinks out loud. "This is all amazing news. I'm so happy to have someone to go through this with, especially since I've been sicker than a new sailor on choppy waves for the last week."

"I read that morning sickness starts at around six to seven weeks along. It all makes sense. I have a week before I'll probably be in the same boat."

"Not everyone turns green every time food appears within a ten-foot radius. Don't worry. I'm just special in that way," I joke, trying not to laugh too hard, which would stir up my stomach again. It seems I have an initial wave of sickness right when I wake up, then another just before lunch, and the afternoon is mostly just nausea. Just thinking about it makes me feel like I'm rocking on a boat. I stand up because I know the feeling won't subside, not unless I at least get some ginger ale into my stomach.

"Speaking of morning sickness," I say, holding my finger up. "I hate to cut this celebration short, but this munchkin has other plans for me."

"Oliver must be so happy," she says, staring at me with a glow in her eyes.

"He's over the moon. That's for sure. Lincoln must be the same."

Peyton drops her gaze and picks at a hangnail over her lap. "I didn't tell him yet. I'm worried about getting his hopes up and something happening. Soon, though."

I can't stop the concern from etching two lines between my eyes. "He's your support system. You're in this together."

"I know," she says with a nasally huff and a small smile. "We should be."

I'm in a daze as I make my way back home. I'm not sure I even checked for oncoming cars before crossing the road. I step into the living room, finding Oliver in the same spot I left him, but with a glass of water in his hand. He was mid-sip when the door closed behind me.

"Peyton is pregnant too," I tell him.

Oliver's stare doesn't sway from the television as he spews the water out of his mouth. "What?" he says, running his knuckles beneath his bottom lip.

"Yup."

"I thought she couldn't—"

"It turns out, she can. So now our baby will have a friend right across the street. It's perfect, right?"

TWENTY-FIVE

JENNA | NOW

"Mom, come back!" I scream as someone grapples my arms, pulling them behind my back so I can't move. All I can do is scream—scream until my voice gives out and all that's echoing around me is the last bit of air from my angry lungs.

She's just walking away from me like I'm a beggar on the street asking for drug money. She asked if I hurt River. My mother. My flesh and blood. How could that thought even linger in her head long enough to ask?

"You can release her."

I turn to find the person giving the instruction. Her name is flying around in my head like a butterfly, and I don't have a net to catch it. "We can stay in this room if you'd like?" She seems prepared to go anywhere, with a leather tote bag slinging from her shoulder.

I met with her yesterday, soon after I arrived or was imprisoned. She's the one who had a bottle of pills with my name on the label. She's the one who quietly diagnosed me as a drug addict who gave birth to a stillborn baby. She's the one causing my family to question me, to wonder if I'm a murderer of all things.

Since I don't respond to her question, she takes a seat in one of the chairs, places her bag down beside her and crosses her legs, before cupping her hands around her knee. Her body language says: we're all waiting on you now. I can hear a teacher's voice, staring down at the students whispering to another without a clue that they're being watched.

I drag my tired, grimy sock covered feet over to the chair, the rubber nubs on my soles squeaking like a new driver behind the brakes of an old car. Once I'm settled, I take a moment to focus on the badge adhered to this woman's chest. Laura. That's right.

"Jenna, we need to try and recall some of your memories from the last couple of weeks. Are you willing to participate?"

She must know if I could remember one thing significant enough to get me out of this place, I would have spoken up by now, but there are barricades in my head, keeping me from connecting pieces of a life I should know better than anyone else.

"If you know a way to help me remember facts, I will share them with you," I say, flatly, twisting a chair around to sit down and face her.

"Great," she says, leaning down into her shoulder bag and pulling out notepad and pen, placing them on her lap. "Do you know what date River was born?"

I stare off to the side, recalling the date. "I was due on March twenty-second, but I was almost two weeks late when my water broke." I remember thinking I would be a full two weeks late in two more days, which meant I would need intervention that I didn't want. "The third of April—that's when River was born."

"I have in my notes that you and Oliver decided on a home birth with the help of a midwife. Is that correct?"

"Yes." I don't feel like indulging Laura on my reasons for deciding to go with the plan of a home birth.

"Can you recall the midwife's name?" Laura isn't finished writing her last note when she asks this question.

"Yes, her name is Celeste Brown. She came highly recommended with dozens of raving referrals." She didn't ask about Celeste, just for her name. But I feel the need to defend her as I get closer to the incriminating questions I expect to face soon.

I watch as she scribbles down Celeste's name in larger letters than the rest of her notes, then wraps it in a thick circle.

"Home births are typically non-medicated, is that right?" I thought Laura was a therapist of some sort, but now I'm almost positive she's a social worker. Her questions are not showing concern for me as the patient, but for River.

"That's correct."

"Were you aware of the pros and cons of a home birth?"

"Yes, but during my prior appointments with Celeste, she called me an ideal candidate for a home birth. I also live less than a few miles away from a hospital in the chance something were to go wrong."

Laura rests her pen on the pad of paper and clasps her fingers together. "Something did go wrong, but you didn't end up at the hospital, nor did River."

"Celeste stayed with us to tend to my care and River's after his birth."

Laura places her burgundy polished finger down on the top of her notepad. "You were stable when she left? What about River?"

"I held him. Oliver held him too. He was alive."

"The cause of death was an umbilical cord accident, and he was born without a heartbeat. These uncommon and unfortunate situations are usually a cause for both the mother and baby to seek additional help at the hospital, but according to the midwife's report, you were deemed to be stable postpartum and therefore denied hospitalization care for yourself."

"No," I shout at her. "None of this is true. If something had been wrong with my baby, I would never deny him medical care. As for me, I was told I wouldn't need to be admitted to a hospital after a home birth so long as I was stable during and after birth."

Laura taps her fingers on her notepad. "Unfortunately, it's too late to conduct an autopsy to prove any other theory."

"What? Why is it too late? If my child is what you say...it isn't too late for an autopsy," I say through gritted teeth.

"I'm afraid that's not possible, Jenna. River wasn't buried, he was cremated."

"No, no, I would never agree to a cremation. My family and I feel that cremation isn't an end-of-life option for us. This proves something is wrong with the notes that you have or the story you've been given. How can I accept that my son is dead when I have no recollection of almost everything you are telling me?" Both of my knees are bouncing furiously and I'm light-headed from breathing too heavily. All I can do is press my fingernails into the tips of my knees to stop myself from screaming out at the top of my lungs.

"Are you saying you recall moments with River being alive at times throughout the last two weeks at home?" Laura asks, her nerves at ease unlike mine.

I move my hands from my knees to my forehead, pressing at the skin that's begun to loosen over the last few years. "I can't remember anything, but I know he's not dead."

"Okay, we're going to stop here for today," she says.

"No, please. I need your help. I need someone to believe me. That's why I want to talk to Oliver. He could clear everything up. This is all a big misunderstanding."

Why did Mom tell me it was all true? Why did she ask if I was the one who ended River's life?

"I'll see what I can do about bringing Oliver here, but for the time being, I want you to take this notebook—" Laura pulls a red composition book out of her bag and a thin plastic-coated tube of ink with a short dull, metal tip.

"What is this?" I ask, inspecting the instrument.

"A safe pen. It's flexible and will allow you to write as much as you want before I meet with you next. I would like you to jot down anything you remember about the last two weeks so we can keep a record of even short memories." They don't even trust me with a pen. I wouldn't even know how to hurt myself or someone with a writing instrument.

"I want to be released from this place," I tell her, trying to stare into her eyes. But she won't look up from her notepad.

"We just need to work together and get you to a point where we can all agree you aren't a danger to yourself. We're here to protect you, Jenna." If that was the truth, she would look at me and say so.

Mel must have been listening to the conversation since she walks in almost on cue. "You have some time before dinner. Do you want to go to your room or the common area?"

"My room," I mumble.

My room. My room is in a two-story colonial with a master suite that I share with my husband. I live on a wonderful street, in a beautiful community surrounded by wonderful people who act like an extended family in a time of need.

Yet all those wonderful people must think I'm delusional enough to be admitted to a psychiatric facility. Everyone's been convinced of this story, but I have no idea who wrote the narrative.

TWENTY-SIX

GINGER | LAST YEAR

When it rains, the dirt washes away.

I don't remember when I replaced Dateline with live stream doorbell footage. I blame reality TV for making me want more, more of what I shouldn't have—more of what I shouldn't always know. If people are willing to give up their discretion for the sake of being on television, it's easy to see what some would do when they don't know they're being filmed.

The police officer standing in my driveway peers in every direction before leaning down to check his teeth in his side mirror. It's just after lunch. We've all been there. This particular officer has shown up at my door more times than I can count over the last couple of years. I'm not expecting him today though.

I wait for the doorbell to ding and dong before casually standing up from my sofa with the remote to power off the television. I scoot into the dark kitchen before approaching the door and snag a yellow rubber glove, slipping it over my left hand.

"Good afternoon, Officer Drell," I say, greeting him upon opening the door. "Is everything all right?" I look past his shoulders, trying to seem as though I'm unaware of what's happening outside in the heavy rain. "Come in, come in." I take just a few steps backward to let him inside, but I don't plan to make this meeting any more formal.

"Mrs. Fowler, it's always lovely to see your bright cheery smile, especially on a crummy day like today. I do apologize for interrupting your day," he says, glancing down at my one yellow glove, "but I was wondering if you might be able to help me with a name."

"A name?" I ask, resting my gloved hand over my other arm.

"Yes, we received an anonymous tip to investigate a person of interest regarding an ongoing local case. The tip suggested you might have information regarding this person."

"I'm sure I don't know what you're talking about, or whomever left an anonymous tip like that, but try me."

"Are you familiar with the name—" he pulls a small pale-yellow notepad out of his back pocket and unfolds it, "Andrea Lester?"

I should have known it's been too long, not hearing of her or from her. I press my fingers to my mouth as I give the appearance of jogging my memory. "I'm sorry to disappoint you, but I don't think I've ever known an Andrea."

"No need for apologies. I couldn't ignore the tip, but I'm glad we don't have to involve you in anything. You've certainly been through enough these last few years with James."

"Bless your kind heart, Officer Drell. But of course, it is my civil duty to help whenever possible, so if I do come across anything, I'll be sure to let you know."

"Take care, Mrs. Fowler. Tell Joel I say hi and to stop being a stranger when he's in town." *As soon as Joel gives his mother the time of day.*

"I certainly will. Stay dry," I say, waving him off before I close the door.

Andrea Lester.

I wait for Officer Drell to back out of my driveway and leave the street before reopening my door. Once he's gone, I grab this morning's newspaper and flap it out wide to hold over my head as I run to Lincoln and Peyton's house. I knock harshly against their off-white door, thankful to be covered under their front porch from the downpour.

The door opens and Peyton pushes me back by stepping outside of the door to greet me. "Ginger, what are you doing out here? It's raining buckets."

"Do you know of someone by the name of Andrea Lester?" Her eyes squint and her forehead contorts with thin lines. "Is she around here somewhere?"

"Who are you talking about?"

"You've never heard the name? Not once?" I scrutinize the look on her face, waiting for an indication of a lie.

"No, Ginger, I don't know who this person is..."

"There was an anonymous tip left with the police department and my name was attached to someone called Andrea Lester who could be a lead for an ongoing investigation in town. Who else besides you would use my name in a tip like that?"

Peyton takes another step forward, bullying me into taking another step backward on her porch. "I don't know, Ginger, who *else* would feel the need to use your name in a tip to the police?"

"My blood will be on your hands. You should know that," I threaten her.

"I'm not even sure what that means," she says with a giggle before a frown tugs at her lips—a frown of sympathy. "Look," Peyton says, placing her hand on my shoulder. "I wish you would go talk to someone—a professional. Ever since James— you just haven't been yourself. Isn't it true that neurosis can grow out of control if it's not acknowledged? Aren't you the one who told me that?"

"Don't insult me," I hiss at her.

"This is exactly what I mean. I'm not trying to insult you.

I'm trying to help, Ginger. I feel bad that you're suffering so much. I can't imagine what this feels like, especially for someone with the knowledge of a psychiatric degree. I'm sure you're aware that this isn't healthy, and I can't be a part of these illusions with you anymore. I have a lot going on in my life right now and these accusations need to stop, for your sake more than mine."

TWENTY-SEVEN

JENNA | FOUR MONTHS AGO

After the longest morning of my life, sitting at my desk at work, tapping my pen against a legal notepad, it's finally time for my much-awaited gender scan appointment. Oliver and I are meeting here at the ultrasound clinic since he had to work this morning too. It isn't a surprise to spot each other in the parking lot twenty minutes before the appointment, both beyond eager to hopefully learn the answer to our undying question.

Oliver meets me at my car door, opening it to help me out. Snow begins to salt down over us in big flakes, making this moment feel more like a dream than reality.

"Just so you know...despite my guesses of whether we're having a girl or a boy, I'm just hoping for a healthy baby and wife," Oliver says, wrapping his arm around me as we walk inside.

"I love sharing this moment with you," I murmur, my cheek pressing against the side of his arm. "I know we'll always remember today."

Oliver's cheeks are rosy, and his dimples are undeniably deep, trying to maintain his excitement as we make our way from the parking lot and in through the main entrance to check in at the front desk. I love watching him fawn over what will be the most important part of our lives. A nurse greets us almost immediately and takes us back into a room, helping me get comfortable on the exam table as Oliver takes a seat beside me. "The ultrasound technician will be right in," she says.

I appreciate the speed in which they move here as the wait feels like an eternity. The technician comes in, greets us, and sits down on her rolling stool before tapping in some information on her computer. The corner screen lights up with a neon green frame centering a black box. I feel like there is a boulder resting on my chest and the gel squirting out onto my belly is colder than ice, but all I can think about is the flicker on the screen across the room. The skeletal outline of a baby comes into vision and my heart pounds as I fall more in love with this little person growing inside of me. "Look at the little nose," I coo.

"The teeny hands and feet," Oliver continues, walking closer to the screen.

"Everything looks good from what I can see, but your doctor will follow up with you for a full report," the ultrasound technician says, handing us an envelope with the gender written down on a piece of paper inside, just as we requested.

"Thank you, ma'am," Oliver says, helping me up from the table. "Where might we find the restroom?"

"It's right next door. You wouldn't believe how many pregnant women make a run for the bathroom after this appointment," she says with laughter, knowing she's the one who insisted I have a full bladder upon arriving for my appointment.

Oliver has been standing outside of the restroom, waiting for me and as I step back out into the corridor, I find him holding the envelope between his hands, looking like he just won the lottery and doesn't know what to do with all the money. "I'm praying to the traffic gods that we don't hit any stoplights on the way back to the house. This wait might kill me," he says.

"Me too, but it will be even more special to open it together at home." I don't know when I became so patient in life because the immature person inside of me wants to rip that envelope out of his hands and pull out the paper, throwing away the idea of sacred memories for this moment. I just want to know. But, I am mature and can wait through the ride home.

We leave the building, both staring at the envelope as if it might reveal itself. "You can take it," Oliver says, handing it to me. "It'll be safer with you." He laughs, hinting that he might lose his restraint on the way home.

"Okay," I sigh heavily. "Just a few more minutes. I'll see you at home." We kiss goodbye and I take the envelope, feeling it burn a hole through my hand. I rest it down on the passenger seat in the car, wanting to secure it with a seat belt so it doesn't fly away. Maybe it would have been better if Oliver took it with him.

I was studying each movement on the screen as the technician took down measurements so I have a slight suspicion about the gender. Oliver was sure he knew before the appointment, but because of old-wives-tales.

The surprise is on me as I turn the corner onto our street, finding Mom's car parked behind Oliver's. He must not have gotten stuck at the same four red lights I did on the way home, and Mom is here a half hour earlier than she was supposed to be but I should have guessed that would happen when I gave her a spare key. I guess it's good he didn't have the envelope.

Jitters and little baby kicks flutter around my stomach as I make my way inside, the envelope tucked deeply into my puffy maternity coat pocket.

Out of habit, I watch my step along the driveway and foot-path toward the front porch, making sure there aren't any small icy patches. I've had my eyes glued to the ground for the last two months, worried I'll slip on any remnants of snow or a puddle that has frozen over. The larger my belly grows, the less

I can see directly in front of me and it's been flurrying for the last couple of hours. Thankfully, the winter has been mild so far.

I walk in, finding not only Mom and Oliver but Peyton and Ginger too, all sitting around the living room, as a round of introductions seem to be wrapping up. "Deborah, it's so nice to finally meet you," Ginger says to Mom, holding her hand in hers.

No one heard me walk inside so I let the front door close with a bit of oomph. That does the trick. Everyone quiets down as if the chatter was shut off by a switch, and all pairs of eyes are staring at me, waiting for an answer.

"Is the surprise for me or for all of you?" I ask with laughter.

"It better be for all of us," Oliver says, standing up to greet me.

"I'm innocent. I know nothing," I say, my voice higher pitched than usual. "Are your parents going to make it?" I mutter the last part under my breath. Oliver's parents haven't been involved in our lives too much this past year. Oliver says they've always been this way, but they were around more often when we were only dating. There was an evident shift in their behavior toward us over the last year and a half, but I can't seem to figure out what changed. I think we all get along well, but I have gotten the sense there is history between the three of them that Oliver hasn't shared with me. He says his parents are closer with his brother because he has three kids, I could guess that's why Oliver wanted to have children so badly.

"No. They can't make it today but they said to video call them tonight so we can share the news." They live less than twenty minutes from here but make it seem like we're in another state.

"It's a good thing the baby cooperated," I tell everyone.

"Jenna," Mom says. "I have been sitting in this chair for

forty-five minutes with palpitations. I need to know, sweetie." She presses her palms together and rests them over her chest.

I pull the envelope out of my pocket and Oliver helps remove my coat. "It doesn't matter either way. I love our baby and you," he says in a whisper that everyone could hear as they follow with a round of awws.

My hands tremble as I fuss with the envelope flap and pull out the folded paper. Oliver snags the paper, holding it in front of us both as we reveal the technician's writing.

I knew it. Something in my gut just told me. It's like the sky is clearing and the sun is embracing me in its warm glow—a slice of heaven for me. Oliver presses the back of his fist up to his lips and a silent sob chokes out as he pulls me into his chest. "It's a boy!" he shouts through a broken rasp. "It's a boy—our boy."

Everyone around us is cheering, hooting, and hollering, and I'm soaking in the tender moment of Oliver's emotions. He must be picturing days of T-ball, soccer, or riding bikes. I'm picturing a little hand curling around my finger, a sweet face with big eyes like his daddy. He will always look at me with wonder as I try to make his world perfect every day for the rest of my life. Mom's arms fold around us as her big elephant tears plop one by one onto my shoulder. "He is going to be one spoiled little boy and oh-so loved," she says.

"I might be biased by saying boys are a treasure," Ginger says from the other side of the room.

The only quiet voice is Peyton's. I know she's eagerly awaiting to find out the sex of her baby, but her gender-scan ultrasound isn't for another couple of weeks. "Peyton's next! We should all make our guesses now to see who's right after she finds out," I say.

Peyton's eyes widen and her face becomes pale. My heart jolts as I question what I've said to startle her. She said she was going to announce her pregnancy when she hit thirteen weeks.

Ginger lets out a loud horse-like laugh. "I'm sorry, did I miss another announcement?"

I mouth the words: "I'm so sorry," to Peyton. I didn't realize she hadn't told Ginger.

"Today isn't about me, Ginger," Peyton says, sitting back against the plush couch cushion.

"I'm just asking if I missed something. That's all."

"No, you didn't miss anything," Peyton replies, a cold snap to her response.

"You're pregnant though?" Ginger continues.

"Yes," Peyton says with a groan, staring off into the opposite direction.

"Well, I'll be...I thought you said you and Lincoln couldn't have children," Ginger continues.

Peyton's jaw drops. Her cheeks redden and she stares right at me, her brows arching as her eyes fill with tears. I shake my head before I can verbally deny what she must be thinking. I would never tell Ginger something so private.

"Jenna didn't tell me anything," Ginger interrupts, her eyes bulging. "Clearly if I didn't know you were pregnant until now, why would you think she would run to me with other details about you?"

"I never told you that Lincoln and I couldn't have kids," Peyton insists.

"Yes, you most certainly did. I suppose when the booze dries up, it's hard to remember."

With the paper and envelope pinned against my chest, my eyes bulge in response to Ginger's comment. I catch myself holding my breath, feeling the evident tension thicken between Peyton and Ginger. I can't understand why Ginger would say something so bold and crass.

"You know what...I brought over some tea cakes. Is anyone interested?" Mom asks, standing up from her chair as if cake is going to stop what's happening between Ginger and Peyton.

"In any case, it's water under the bridge because miracles happen every day and you are living proof, aren't you?" Ginger says. "How far along are you? I must say I hadn't noticed and well—I notice more than people realize." Her laughter must be like lighting a match against a short fuse for Peyton.

"About seventeen weeks," Peyton mutters.

"Oh, how lovely. Your babies will have a built-in best friend right across the street from one another. Congratulations. I am truly happy for you," Ginger says.

Mom slithers off into the kitchen almost unnoticed. I can't say I blame her. I'd like to do the same, but we're in my house.

"I haven't officially congratulated you yet either," Oliver says. "I'm thrilled our two children will have each other, like Ginger said, just across the street from one another."

"Is the father excited?" Ginger asks. "Well, he must be. What dad-to-be isn't, right?"

"You mean to say Lincoln," I suggest, trying to correct Ginger's oddly worded question.

"It's never appropriate to assume these days," Ginger says with an exaggerated sigh. "In any case, congratulations again. This is just marvelous." She stands up from her seat next to Peyton and circles around. "I'm going to go see if your mother needs a hand in the kitchen. Us old hens can catch up while you dote on your exciting futures."

By the time Ginger is out of sight, Peyton's cheeks are the color of summer strawberries and she's lost in a stare, her eyes fixated on the coffee table in front of her.

I take the empty seat beside her and reach for her hand. "I promise you I didn't—"

"This is supposed to be about you, and I just keep stealing your thunder," she says, a tear falling down the side of her nose. "You must think I'm a terrible person."

"What? No, no...I could never think that. We're in this together, bestie and bestie with buns in the oven." I try to make her laugh but all I end up with is Oliver clearing his throat behind me. "And Oliver too."

"Ah, that doesn't sound very good," Peyton says with a small chuckle.

"I got you to laugh though," I say, pointing at her.

"Funny," Oliver adds. "I'm going to find those tea cakes."

I swat my hand at him and take Peyton's hand back into mine. "Everything is fine. Ginger is Ginger. She doesn't know what she's talking about half the time, and we all know she eavesdrops. It's all she has to live for. Even you said that yourself."

"I didn't tell her that though. You're the only one I've ever confessed to."

I hate that she's questioning me. If there's one thing I know how to do well, it's keeping a secret safe. My job depends on it most days. "Maybe she assumed."

"Maybe," Peyton agrees.

"Don't let her get to you." I sweep Peyton's blonde strands behind her ear. "No one can stop us from being the best moms in the world."

Peyton smiles, a forceful tug of her lips, but it counts. "Do you mind if I take off while everyone is occupied? I do want today to be just about you and I think that might only happen if I'm not here."

"Whatever makes you comfortable," I say.

Peyton leans forward and gives me a weak hug. "I'm so, so, so, very excited for you and this little man."

She leaves quicker than I can think of an excuse to keep her here longer. I didn't invite Ginger or Peyton over, but they knew when we were finding out and with Mom's car here, I can assume one saw the other strolling over.

I wish I understood the animosity between the two. It's like there's a past neither of them wants to let me in on.

"That's it," Oliver says, returning to the living room. "I don't want her in our house anymore."

I'm blindsided by Oliver's blunt remark, especially with Ginger and Mom in the kitchen.

"Honey, I feel like I must agree with Oliver on this," Mom says, stepping into the living room with a tray of tea cakes, Ginger following close behind. "Something is very strange with that girl. You don't need any added stress or anxiety in your life right now."

While Mom and Oliver are giving me a firm look, Ginger is nonchalantly nibbling on a slice of cake over a cocktail napkin cupped within her palm. Mom has only met Peyton one other time and thought she was wonderful. Oliver doesn't like when anyone steals my time from him, and Ginger is a bored trouble-maker. I can't be the only one who sees this all so clearly. Then again, they don't understand what Peyton has lived through or how important this pregnancy is to her.

"Personally, I think you both need to learn to look a little deeper into someone's soul before judging them," I say. "Peyton needs a friend just as much as I do. And Ginger, if you know something about her that she hasn't made public knowledge of, it's polite to keep those thoughts to yourself."

Ginger clears her throat and places her hand over her neck. "Oh my gosh, Jenna, I am so sorry if I made you uncomfortable today. I didn't like that she was stealing your thunder and she can be quite dramatic and unaware of other people's feelings."

"She wasn't stealing my thunder if I'm the one who mistakenly announced her unannounced pregnancy."

Ginger scoffs. "I'm just looking out for you, just as I'm sure your mom would if she was living next door." Ginger gives me a quick, charming smile and Mom eats up the sentiment. "Peyton has another side to her—one you don't want to see. Just keep that in the back of your head, okay?"

TWENTY-EIGHT

JENNA | NOW

There are certain things one can expect to learn about their spouse in the first year together. Oliver and I have been together for just over three years. One year as boyfriend and girlfriend, the second year as fiancées, and the third as newlyweds, soon-to-be-parents, and now...this. I should know an awful lot about him for the time we've been together and what we've been through as a couple. Yet, here we are, Oliver and me, face to face in the same dingy room my mother and I sat in yesterday when she asked me if I was the cause of my son's death. I'm not sure how it's possible, but I almost don't recognize the man sitting across from me and it's hardly been three days since I've seen him last.

I'm supposed to have my psychiatric evaluation today to determine whether I can be released from this facility. Everything I say and do is noted, and if I accuse my husband of lying, setting me up, or fooling me into believing our child is alive or dead, I will be the convict and he will be the victim.

How could this handsome man with his endearing façade, bright eyes, and full lips—always perky with a smile—be capable of deceit?

He can't be. I've spent my entire adult life in a career that requires me to decipher degrees of honesty. There's no way I could have been living with and loving a liar.

It hurts to look into his eyes because I love him. I love him so much I would do anything for him.

He has his hands folded, resting on a cafeteria style table between us. He's toying with his titanium wedding band, the one I struggled to press over his rigid knuckle on our wedding day. We joked that he was stuck with me forever since the ring would never come off. In truth, it would have to be cut off if anything happened to our marriage. But that thought wasn't a concern. It isn't a concern.

I'm not allowed to wear my engagement ring or wedding band here because it could be used as a vice to hurt myself or someone else. *The irony.*

"All I want is the truth," I say, painfully holding my stare against his face. I've never had such a difficult time staring pointedly into someone's eyes, no matter the situation.

"I've given you the truth, but you wouldn't accept it —understandably."

"Look me in the eyes, Oliver. Tell me what happened to River—our son."

I'm doing everything humanly possible to convince myself that he is alive, because the moment I'm convinced of anything else, I am going to break. I will fall to this floor, curl into a ball, and cry until I pass out. I will pray I never wake up again. Denial is much easier to handle, and I've been able to hold on to that feeling until now.

He shakes his head and I'm not sure if he's telling me he can't look at me or can't tell me what happened to River. "He's gone, Jenna." No eye contact. No attempt to lift his head.

"I remember him crying," I seethe through the boiling anger raging through my blood. "I saw his eyes open and felt his warmth."

Again, he shakes his head. "That didn't happen." He pulls his hands in toward his body and lowers them to his lap beneath the table. "Celeste took him upon your final push. She unwound the cord from around his neck, his face was—" He chokes on his words and his breath. "His face was blue, Jenna, his lips too. She checked him for a pulse, then attempted resuscitation, but he was lifeless. She wrapped him in a blanket and handed him to you. It was like you hadn't heard a word she said. You took him and held him against your body and cooed at him as if he was—"

I press my hand to my mouth, feeling every muscle in my face tighten into steel. My chest swells with pain and my stomach retches, searching for the small serving of oatmeal I had this morning. "His eyes—"

"They were open. She thought you'd want to see his eyes before she closed them. You handed him to me proudly, excited to watch me hold him for the first time. I wanted to keel over from the pain I was in, but I did it for you, with hope that it would help you through that horrible moment. Then, you fell asleep. Celeste said your brain was trying to protect your heart from the internal pain you were fighting."

Oliver's figure blurs in front of me as I take in this information as if it's the first time I'm hearing each fact. It is the first time. I would remember if it wasn't. I push my fists against my cheeks and up to my hair, grabbing chunks and pulling to relieve myself from the torment searing through every cell in my body. A guttural scream spews from my lungs and I can't hold my body upright. I fall off the chair, onto the ground, and pull my knees into my chest, squeezing them as hard as I can. I can't slow my breaths.

I ignore the barrage of hands grasping me.

I want them to drug me.

To numb the pain.

To kill me.

After all, that *is* why I'm here.

TWENTY-NINE

GINGER | FOUR MONTHS AGO

"Kids never listen to their parents. It doesn't matter how old they are. It's like whatever advice we give counts for nothing." Deborah is both flustered and confused by her daughter's behavior, but in Jenna's defense, she has been blindsided by the effects of a pretty smile and a sad past—Peyton.

"They don't, do they?" Deborah asks. "Why is that? Surely, they know we only want what's best for them."

"My four boys think I'm the world's worst mother, and I choose to believe it's because it's easiest to blame the person they're closest to...for everything," I say.

"I'm so sorry to hear that, Ginger. All we can hope is that when they have children of their own, God willing, they will understand what it's like to have uncontainable love."

As Deborah and I stand by her car on the driveway, shivering with each passing gust of wind, I spot Oliver and Jenna staring at us from inside the bay window. I'm sure they're wondering what Deborah and I are talking about. The poor couple should be focused on the good news they received today. I take Deborah's hands in mine and smile—mother to mother.

"Jenna will find her way. We all know how friends come and go in our twenties and thirties."

"You're right," Deborah says with a sigh. "All I can do is hope I've done right by her. I can't fault her for having a big heart—it's obvious by the attention she's giving that girl across the street. Jenna wants to fix the world, one person at a time. She's determined."

"I think that's an admirable trait. You and your husband should be proud of the job you've done raising her." I hate being so assumptive about someone's personal life, especially when she was here without a husband or spouse. But without a little bait, no one would ever come any closer. Jenna has never mentioned a word about her father, and I find that peculiar. Girls always love their dads, or so I've been told. I was always told boys will always love their mommas best. Someone clearly had that one wrong.

"Oh, him," she says, rolling her eyes. Deborah combs her fingers through her dark blown out bangs then shakes them away from her eyes. "That lousy son-of-a-bitch left when Jenna was about five. A tail chaser with a wad of cash spilling out of his pockets. Jenna doesn't have anything to do with him. They speak occasionally, but he's remarried to some yuppie just a few years older than Jenna. The misery he caused her—I could kill him for what he did."

"You know, the outside world always looks better from the inside of a window, almost like a mirage, but once outside, the view never looks the same." Deborah studies me for a moment, analyzing my riddling words. If we don't share our stories, we'll never know what we might have in common with someone else. "My husband is no longer in the picture either. Though, I can't say he's managed to find what led him astray."

"I'm so sorry," she says.

"Oh please, don't be."

"You know, we should have lunch sometime. I enjoy talking to you," she says.

Her suggestion almost brings a tear to my eye. I don't remember the last time someone has invited me to do something. "I would love that. Name the time and place and I will be there."

"How about Paloma on Saturday at noon?" She pulls a scrap piece of paper out of her purse with a pen and scribbles down her number.

"I'll be there," I say, taking the note from her hand, "and I'll send you a message with my phone number so you have it too. Until then, I'll have my mom-eyes on Jenna for you. I can't do much, but I can be convincing if need be."

"I like this," Deborah says, pointing back and forth between the two of us.

"Me too," I say, placing my hand on her arm. All I've ever wanted is to be needed.

THIRTY

It looks like Peyton and I picked the right time to go shopping and registry scanning. The department store is empty this morning, appearing larger than I remember. The scents of baby powder and lavender fill the air, closely resembling the way the nursery already smells, somehow. I wonder if it's a consumer trick to entice moms-to-be to spend longer shopping, purchasing more items. I can't even recall the last time I'd been shopping on a weekday morning, never mind a cold, rainy morning where most want to stay snuggly in their bed.

"I think I've gone overboard with my registry," I say, scanning the barcode of a package of organic burp cloths to go with the four packages of non-organic ones I added.

"No such thing," Peyton says, running her hand around her belly. "Our boys will be spoiled. No questions asked." I love that she finally knows she's having a boy too. The peanut wasn't cooperating during the first ultrasound, but the second time, she was able to get an answer. Whenever she says *our boys*, it's so easy to imagine two little boys playing out front until the sun goes down. How perfect a life.

Peyton seems distracted as she one handedly aims her cart

toward an aisle away from where we've been awwing over cute items.

I'm still dawdling around the feeding aisle when I come across a display of bibs with cheesy sayings embroidered across the fabric. I grab two of the bibs that catch my attention then hunt down Peyton, finding her down the bedding aisle inspecting crib sheets. "I think we need to get these on behalf of our husbands. They'll love them."

Peyton smiles and takes one from my hand. "Moms rule and Dads drool. Yes. Going in the cart."

"Have you talked to Lincoln about cutting back on his hours yet? I know you were worried about having that conversation with him."

"Yup. He can't. I should have figured. He hasn't done a thing to prepare for the baby. I painted the nursery myself last weekend while he sat on the phone crunching numbers with his accountant."

"Have you told him how you feel?" It's such a silly question but I see so many couples break up because they forgot how to utilize the one tool that could save a marriage.

Peyton scans the barcode on a sheet set into her cart then peers up at me with a lost look in her eyes. "He thinks I cheated on him."

That came out of nowhere. "Why in the world would he think that? Obviously, it's not true. You said...the night of the dinner party—"

She shrugs her shoulders, holding her palms up. "I don't know. I wasn't home when he's gotten home a few times in the last month. I was running errands, but he began questioning my 'excessive trips' to the grocery store because...pregnancy brain... I keep forgetting everything, and then he decided the grocery store must be a coverup for wherever 'I'm really going.'" Peyton sighs. "Honestly, if I was going to lie about where I'm going, I would come up with something more exciting than a grocery store. Whatever the case is, he's obviously got it all wrong. I think work has been more stressful than usual for him, which has been causing him sleepless nights. I think that's why he's been jumping to the wrong conclusion. We don't talk about the baby much, but it feels like there's a barrier between us now and I can't seem to find a way to fix it. I mean, we haven't been intimate the entire time I've been pregnant, and now...I can't even fathom the idea with how monstrous I feel." *Monstrous*. She looks far better than I do and seems to be carrying most of the weight all in her belly. Still, I understand the feeling.

"I'm sure he has pre-baby jitters along with the stress of work. Life's changing for all of us now, but I don't think that's a reason for him to think you cheated on him. But you know... Oliver and I get like this all the time too. It's childish, but love can make a person act in strange ways sometimes. I always think some girl, or an ex-girlfriend, is calling his phone when it rings and he silences the call. Then he's always asking me who I'm on the phone with."

"But he didn't actually accuse you of cheating, and I'm sure you don't think he's being unfaithful to you," she says, grabbing a package of pillowcases and scanning the code. "In any case, we concluded that I might need a new doctor or at least a second opinion. After interviewing several other doctors in the area, I decided to go with a midwife and opt for a home birth."

It's only been a few days since Peyton and I have spoken, but I had no idea she was going through all of this.

"A home birth? Are those safe?" I've only seen the documentaries on TV, but I haven't done much research on the option.

"They are perfectly safe, and the baby is welcomed into a much calmer environment. This midwife has loads of reviews and several referrals. Everyone raved about her and most of the referrals were moms who had a hospital birth with their first child and chose a home birth for their second or third." Peyton pulls her phone up and taps on this woman's website. "It's the first thing Lincoln and I have talked about that has made him lighten up a bit. So, it's a no brainer for me."

"I'm so glad you found something to patch up the trouble and it sounds like a great solution." Although I'm not sure I understand what a midwife has to do with Peyton cheating.

"I can send you the link if you're interested?"

"Sure, that would be great." I don't think I'm interested, but I don't want to insult her.

Peyton scans the surrounding shelves, preparing to switch from one topic to another abruptly like she often does. "What do you think about baby monitors? Are you thinking of one with video capabilities or just sound? I don't know if I want to be that person who watches my baby breathe all night. I feel like it would cause so much stress, but on the other hand...it would be peace of mind if I wake up worrying in the middle of the night too."

"I'm definitely going with the video monitor, but he'll be sleeping in our room for a while anyway."

"Really? I heard that wasn't healthy for the baby. They should know their boundaries from the start—I must be reading different articles than you," she says with a chuckle while pushing her cart toward the next aisle.

"Different articles?" I question. "What articles are you reading?" I'm waiting for her to laugh, tell me she's joking, or something, but she doesn't. "I'm not sure babies can understand boundaries, but I understand that sharing a room with a newborn isn't for every new parent."

"Well, this baby," she says placing her hand on her belly, "will learn to live with boundaries, trust me." She replaces her hand back on the handle of the cart and pushes it ahead at a quicker pace than mine. It's clear she would like to end our odd conversation.

THIRTY-ONE
JENNA | NOW

The one time I wish they would have knocked me out or drugged me, they let me cry and wail until dry heaves took over. I feel like the roadkill everyone drives by and tells themselves it's just another animal.

"Coming to terms with your problems is seen as a good sign here." I wasn't aware my roommate, Kinley, was even in the room because I've been facing the opposite wall, staring at the imperfections of the paintbrush strokes. I've seen five or six cases while working for Breakers and Cole involving divorcing couples who suffered the loss of a child, but still shared another child. Grief and loss can kill a marriage and anything in between. I couldn't understand the blame between the spouses, particularly with my cases because the deaths were by no fault of either party. Still, neither could bear the thought of looking at one another or remembering why they were together in the first place.

Tears streak down my hot cheeks, as I consider the anger I feel toward Oliver—a feeling I'm not sure I'm entitled to have. I could drop fault on Celeste for not foreseeing an issue soon enough, but it was my—our—decision to use a midwife and to have a home birth. I was aware of the risks involved and the benefits, to me, outweighed them. The statistics were in my favor, or so I read online.

I glance up at the clock on the wall, silently noting that it's eleven-seventeen, the very moment I forfeit the internal battle and face the reality. My son is gone.

River might have survived if I was at a hospital and his heart was being monitored. An emergency C-section would have been the solution. As his mother, this is my fault. I'm to blame and I feel that through every fiber of my being—the vicious ache in the pit of my stomach, the heaviness in my heart, and the pull of loose skin around my midsection that will not allow me to forget the life that was meant to be.

"The feeling of denial has been easier to endure," I reply, sweeping my knuckles beneath my bottom lashes to hide the flow of tears.

"What about the drugs? Do you have to go through the detox program before you can go home?"

Drugs. "I don't use drugs."

"That's what they all say...Although, you don't seem to be dealing with the same withdrawal symptoms as I was a couple of weeks back. Consider yourself lucky."

I never got to the bottom of why there were traces of opioids found in my blood. I can't imagine fishing around for that bottle or reasoning with myself to take them. If I was in denial about River, why would I drug myself?

"How are you doing, Jenna?" Mel asks, walking in with a folder full of papers. What am I supposed to answer? "Dr. Kasper is here for evaluations, and I need to escort you down to her office."

I've met so many patients, therapists, doctors, psychiatrists, psychologists, social workers, and aides in just three days, I can't remember what Dr. Kasper even looks like. I know she's the one who admitted me for the seventy-two-hour psychiatric hold though.

"Did Oliver leave?" I'm not sure he had a reason to stay. I'm sure they escorted him out when they saw how upset I became after listening to what he had to say.

"He's waiting in the general lobby to find out what Dr. Kasper's plan will be." If I didn't ask them to bring Oliver in, I might have had an easier time being released today, but after that scene, she'll probably decide to keep me here for another three days, or worse. Then again, had I not come to terms with Oliver's truth, it would have been enough of a reason to keep me here longer.

"I can move on my own." I squirm off the bed and follow Mel into the hallway. With each step, I feel a hollow swish move around my stomach, reminding me of the extra skin I still have, and the baby I lost. I didn't know how much a heart could hurt. It's heavy in my chest like my body is dragging it around as excess baggage. A year ago, I wasn't ready to have a baby. Now, I would give up my life so River could experience his. This isn't a heartbreak that time will heal. I'm forever changed, never to be whole again.

Mel knocks on a door we approach. "I have Jenna Milligan here," she says.

Mel waves me into the office and closes the door as I sit down on the coarse upholstered seat across from a high back leather smoking chair. I remember Dr. Kasper now as she sits with her legs crossed, her focus on a sheet of notes rather than me. I imagine her job must be hard, telling people they aren't well enough or trusted to be set free outside of these walls.

"I'm sure you're planning to renew my seventy-two hours after being restrained and having a breakdown today."

Dr. Kasper places one hand on top of the other, resting them on her desk. Her cheeks pucker as if she has something sour in her mouth and she narrows her stare at me like she can read something written on my face. "Since arriving, you haven't shown signs of withdrawal from the opioids in your system, which leads me to believe you were experiencing a severe form of shock along with the use of inhibitors, but not enough to cause dependency. It's clear to us that you are coming to terms with what has unfortunately happened to you. Under typical circumstances, we don't tolerate patients breaking rules or fighting with the attending staff. However, in your case, I think it's best for you to be in the comfort of your home while you grieve and mourn your loss. I don't see you as a threat to yourself or anyone else currently. Of course, you are welcome to voluntarily admit yourself if you would like to seek further treatment here with us."

She makes it sound so simple. After three days of begging for someone to listen to me, it's like there was no reason for me to be here at all. All I had to do was tear open my heart, retrace memories that hardly exist, lie to myself about what I must have imagined, and finally, say the words that would unlock the gates to this place: My son is dead. This pain will never cease.

"I'd like to go home," I say. I'm doing everything I can to keep the rest of my thoughts to myself because there is still much more to what led me here than denial. I want an investigation of what was happening to me prior to being admitted because I'm certain I was being drugged, or somehow, unknowingly drugging myself. But so long as I verbally accept the stories being fed to me, I am no longer considered a threat to society. The rage fires through me and I hope she signs whatever papers are necessary to let me the hell out of here.

I clench my jaw so tightly my face and neck ache but she's filling out papers. "We are always here if you ever feel unsafe or need help." I bite back my response. She's the one who should feel unsafe right now.

. . .

With a clear bag containing the couple of non-dangerous outfits approved for me to wear here, I follow Mel out of the alarm sealed double doors and past the initial exam room where I was tricked into being admitted. Finally, I'm back in the lobby, spotting Oliver sitting in a lonesome chair, leaning on his elbow with the side of his face propped up on his cheek. He must be so tired from everything he's been through, but could he possibly be more tired than me? The woman I was two weeks ago wants to run into his arms and make him promise never to leave me again, but the woman I am today knows he brought me here.

I don't know if I'm supposed to go back in time and act as if this is a hiccup in our marriage. A knot forms in my throat and I can't think of one word to say to him.

The door closes behind me and Oliver snaps his head upright. "Jenna," he says, pushing himself out of the chair and holding his arms in front of himself like I'm a rabid animal about to attack.

I stop moving forward to allow him to put his arms around me. I wish he didn't feel like a stranger. I don't want to be angry with him but there's some sort of negative magnetic field between us. "Let's go home, babe."

Outside, the air feels different. It's warmer, more humid than it was a few days ago. While we're walking, I wonder what he's done with all the baby furniture, the car seat base, the stroller we had stored in the trunk. I have no idea what he's been doing these last three days. He could have been sitting at home, agonizing, grieving, or maybe he was back at work for the sake of a distraction.

He opens the passenger door of the car for me, and I slip inside and reach for the seat belt. He closes the door and I take the moment he's making his way around to the driver's side to peer into the back seat. There's no car seat base, no car seat, no spare blanket, no sign that there was ever a baby. I clutch the fabric over my aching chest, needing to feel my knuckles pinch against my sternum as I acknowledge Oliver's solution to grief is to remove reminders of our son. Putting River's belongings away is final, it's a goodbye and I'm not ready for that when I've hardly been able to come to terms with the thought of him being gone. I refuse to act like he didn't exist. I won't do it. His belongings make him real.

It's easier to stare out the window while we leave the parking lot, than try to find the right words to say.

"I didn't know they would admit you," he says. "I was hoping to reach a solution on how to help you."

I twist my head to stare directly at his profile. "You took me to a behavioral health facility, not a doctor's office. What did you think was going to happen?"

"I don't know, Jenna. In case you aren't aware, you were scaring the hell out of me. I couldn't wake you up or get you to talk. You were confused and in denial. It's not like I've had to navigate this situation before."

I can't argue with his point. "They found opioids in my system. Do you know anything about that?"

The car vibrates over the warning strip on the side of the road and Oliver jerks the wheel to the left to straighten out our direction. "Opioids? What? Why—how is that even possible? We don't have that in the house."

"We do, from when I had my knee surgery. I never took them."

"I see, so you decided to take them now?"

"Jesus, Oliver, no, I didn't decide to take them, but somehow they were found in my system and I'm trying to figure out how."

He glances over at me for a brief second before returning his focus on the road. "Are you insinuating I had something to do with that?" he asks, clearly appalled by the thought. "You know how I feel about drug use. I don't understand—"

"Was anyone else in the house between the time—" I catch

my words in my throat, trying not to let my emotions spill out again. "Up until you brought me to Ashlyn Behavioral Health Center?"

"Yeah, most of the neighbors stopped by at one point or another. Your mom came back a few times. Peyton was over every day until..."

"She had her baby?"

Oliver clears his throat and nestles uncomfortably against his seat. "Yeah, I guess she had him a week early. At least that's what Ginger told me. Lincoln wasn't even home, apparently. He had a last-minute business meeting in Texas, so she ended up alone at the hospital. She's home now, and so is he. So, from what I've heard, everything is okay there."

"Well, thank God for that," I say, shifting my view back out the window. That was cold, even for me, and I feel the prick of guilt. But I can't believe that Peyton, who convinced me how much better a home birth would be, ended up giving birth in a hospital. Now, I get to watch her son grow up, all while knowing he was supposed to have a friend. He was supposed to have River, but that's not going to happen. I was supposed to have River.

"No one wished this on us."

"I did, didn't I?" I didn't want to get pregnant. I wasn't ready for a baby. I regret every one of those thoughts. I would do anything to take them all back.

THIRTY-TWO

GINGER | TWO MONTHS AGO

There is nothing worse than a baby shower, never mind two in one month. We haven't had a block party or any neighborly get-together in the time Jenna and Oliver have been living here so this will be the first occasion. Jenna wasn't interested in an over-the-top pastel themed party. Her only request was for a casual low-key affair. Oliver made it clear she doesn't like surprises, so here we are, all snug in their freshly decorated backyard. The air is dry and the sun warm. The seasons are just beginning to change, but the grass is already much greener this year than it was last spring just before Jenna and Oliver moved in.

I place the last tray of finger foods on the round patio table, hoping the assortment of tea sandwiches and mini quiches will hold everyone over until the pizza arrives.

"You must be so excited," Marybeth from next door to Jenna at two-forty-four Sapphire, shouts over everyone talking. She has a volume control issue. It's always a surprise how loud or quiet she'll be.

Jenna looks beyond the point of uncomfortable, sitting in a canary yellow sundress with a white cardigan. Her ankles are crossed, and a plate barely balances on her knees. She's out of room, the poor thing. "We are. We can't wait to meet this little guy who has been playing some serious rounds of soccer in my belly." Her laugh is for show. I can see the look on her face. She wants to be laid up on the sofa with her feet up and a bowl of chips resting on her belly.

"Well, gosh, when Amelia was born, we didn't have half of the gadgets available in the stores now. It was like raising a child in the stone age just seven years ago. But when Drew and then Noah were born, there was more to choose from thankfully. Each baby got easier and easier thanks to all the grand commodities available now."

No one knows what Marybeth is blabbing about. Her oldest is seven. It hasn't even been a decade. Not that much has changed.

"I just realized that this is the first time we've all been together at this house since Luanne left. Did anyone send an invitation to her mother's, where she's staying?" Tanya asks. The third grade, always inclusive, teacher has to make an awkward moment for Oliver who did most of the planning for this shower. He's never even met Luanne.

"I doubt she would want to come. She doesn't know Jenna and Oliver, and I'm not sure being here would be a wonderful reminder for her," I say.

Tanya straightens her shoulders. "It's unfortunate, isn't it, Ginger?"

"It is." I think we all can agree on this.

"The pizza is here!" Peyton staggers in through the back gate as Oliver follows with a stack of pizza boxes clutched between his hands. The aroma of pepperoni and onions is potent enough to whisk through the humid air. Hopefully they remembered to get plain cheese for Jenna as Oliver requested.

Peyton is still as fit as ever, even at thirty-two weeks pregnant. She's one of those optical illusions—no baby from the front, and all baby belly from the side. She knows to wear black to enhance that appearance. Who wears black to a baby shower?

Jenna pushes herself up from her seat, taking her plate along with her, and greets Peyton with a bump-to-bump hug. "I may not have the same kind of buoyancy at your shower in a couple of weeks," Jenna tells her with a quiet laugh.

"Oh, stop it. All I did was carry over a gift. Oliver is doing the heavy lifting with the pizza," Peyton says as he places the stack of boxes down behind her on the covered table.

"Which hospital are you delivering at?" Marybeth shouts again. "Here in Lakespur? They have a great maternity ward."

"Actually—" Jenna says, glancing over at Oliver who's separating the varieties of pizza. "After much debate and research, Oliver and I have decided to give the whole modern, slash, regency era home birth, a try. It's just a beautiful, natural, medicine-free experience, which is so much better for the baby."

Dear God. The girl must be insane.

"Jenna, what on earth are you talking about?" Deborah asks, carrying a tray out from sliding doors. "You haven't mentioned a word of this to me."

Jenna knows what her mother's opinion will be, and rightfully so.

"It's a personal decision we've made together. We have a great midwife and feel confident that the experience will be exactly what we're hoping for."

"Peyton, didn't you say you were doing the same?" Cora, who lives on the other side of me, asks. I'm surprised she took a break from running her multi-million-dollar influencer business to be here.

"Yes. In fact, we're using the same midwife," Peyton says, taking a couple of boxes of pizzas into the house.

"It's a new world. That's what I'm always saying. To each their own," Cora says.

Deborah seems less than pleased, if not angry with Jenna

for springing this news on her. She takes her by the arm and pulls her to the side of the yard. I can't hear their conversation, but Jenna has a way of smoothing things over with everyone. She's always calm and has a list of reasons for every decision she makes.

"We'll talk about this more later. This is so unlike you." Deborah's voice carries, louder than it was.

I make my way inside to see if anyone needs help in the kitchen and I only find Peyton. Perfect Peyton in the most compromising position.

THIRTY-THREE

JENNA | TWO MONTHS AGO

I love my mother dearly but trying to enjoy a baby shower while knowing she plans to give me an earful when everyone leaves, isn't adding much sparkle to my day. I already know what she's going to say about the home birth—it's why I hadn't brought it up with her sooner. I knew she would want to influence my decision and I didn't want that. She was a nurse for almost forty years. She knows more pros and cons about everything in the medical field than I could ever find online. But my gut tells me this is the right decision especially after the number of times I've been scoffed at following my statement of wanting a natural birth without pain medication. Every woman with childbirth experience that I've innocently shared this desire with has told me we all have this ideal, but it never pans out. Apparently, I'll be screaming for pain medication within hours. I don't want that type of pressure, so this idea feels more than right to me, and she can't fight with that. I'm a grown woman and this wasn't just my choice, but a plan Oliver and I came up with together.

As if she's revving her engine, I see Mom's hands gripping the lawn chair she's sitting in, waiting not so patiently for Tanya to give us each her third goodbye. I'm sure the sudden draft of chilly air that's eating up the perfect amount of warmth we've had this afternoon will send her on her way. Even Ginger has gone home. In fact, she left before everyone else which is unlike her.

The very moment Tanya sees herself out through the back gate, Mom scurries over and grabs my hand. "What in God's name are you thinking, Jenna?"

"Mom, this is what I want. We want..." Oliver bravely joins our conversation after stacking up all the gifts that need to go inside. He wraps his arm around my back, resting his palm on the side of my belly, then gives me a gentle kiss on the cheek. A smile stretches across his lips as he sets his gaze on Mom, likely trying to win her over with charm.

"We don't want you to be upset with our decision," Oliver says, digging his free hand deep into his pocket, probably so he can clench his fists like he does when he's anxious. "We have an enormous amount of respect for you and your years of knowledge as a nurse, but the two of us have fallen in love with this plan, and we're excited—over the moon, really—and know this is what will make us the happiest. I assure you, after meeting with the midwife, I'm confident—"

"We're both confident," I add.

"That this is what feels right."

"What if something, God forbid, goes wrong while you're in labor? Jenna, you could hemorrhage. Your placenta could detach. The baby could struggle, and you wouldn't know without the proper fetal monitors. A midwife can't perform an emergency C-section. Surely, the childbirth class explained that surgeons are prepared to have the baby safely surgically delivered within two minutes. These are medical benefits you won't have at home, and they're serious."

I swallow against the knot in my throat, knowing that what she's saying is accurate. However, I've studied statistics on these instances and how frequently they happen. I realize there's a chance, but we're an emergency call away from the hospital if anything was to go wrong. There would be time to act accordingly since we live just two miles away from the hospital. We could get there in just a few minutes.

"I understand everything you're saying, but I've also done research on the advantages of delivering a baby at home and there's a less likely chance of something happening to me with a natural birth in a comfortable environment. Besides, over fifty-thousand women have home births every year and from that only one out of a thousand women need to be transferred to a hospital for something that's gone wrong. I'm pretty sure I have the same odds of getting hit by a bus today, and that's not going to happen."

"How is it safer for the baby, though?"

"I will be checking in with the doctor every couple of days leading up to going into labor, and we'll know if there are complications to be concerned about." I hope she can see that we've grown in love with the idea of a private, personalized, labor experience without the pressure of taking pain medication or possibly inducing labor to speed up the process. Every reason I have has an outcome of a happy, healthy baby, born free of the ordinary stresses that a hospital includes.

"This is ludicrous. It's dangerous. There's no reason to take on these risks."

I know she will continue badgering me until I look like I might cave. Not this time. I want this. *We* want this. I've been thinking it over day and night for weeks and I've made up my mind without a question or a doubt. "I understand your feelings," I say, rubbing my hands in a circular motion around my swollen belly.

Mom's gaze drops to the grass by her feet, and she intertwines her fingers. "Can I still be here when you go into labor? You said you wanted me by your side. Do you still?"

Relief fills my chest, knowing she's about to end this argument. "Of course, Mom. I couldn't imagine going through this without you."

"Me neither. I might pass out, so—" Oliver says, smiling coyly at Mom.

Mom nudges him with her elbow and tries to hide her smile. "I don't like this, but I will support your decision and be here by your side."

I give Mom a hug. "Thank you for everything you did to help Oliver today. It was a perfect shower."

"Peyton too," Mom says.

"What did I do?" Peyton asks, stepping out from the sliding doors. "Kitchen is clean!"

"You helped out so much with this beautiful shower," I tell her.

"Well, this amazing momma needs to go put her feet up now, but I hope you had a nice day, girly. You deserve it."

"It was wonderful," I tell her. "Thank you, and I owe you... in like three weeks," I say with laughter.

"If you don't burst by then," she says, poking my belly.

"Okay, okay, enough out of you. Go home. Tell Lincoln I say hi and thank him for letting me borrow you for a few hours."

"I sure will." Peyton takes a few steps toward the side gate but stops and turns back to face us. "Oh, if you see Ginger before I do, ask if she's all right. It was the oddest thing earlier. I didn't even know she was in the house, but as soon as I stepped out of the kitchen, I caught her flying out the front door, booking it back to her place. Maybe the margarita upset her stomach? In any case, I'm surprised she never came back—*not exactly heartbroken, though*." Peyton mumbles the last bit.

Margarita? "Were people sneaking drinks in the kitchen or something?" I ask, laughing at the thought of hiding it from me. I wouldn't care if others were drinking just because I can't.

"Not that I'm aware of," Mom says, confusion pressing into

the corners of her brows. "Although I did see a bottle of tequila in the kitchen. I guess I just didn't think much of it."

I suppose she's right, but I'm not sure tequila is the most common item found at a baby shower, or maybe it is for the guests who are trying their best to act like this event is as exciting for them as the mother-to-be. I'll have to remember that trick in the future.

THIRTY-FOUR

JENNA | NOW

We turn the corner onto our street, and I pray no one is outside, waiting to pounce. I want to get into the house, draw the curtains, and hide. Everyone knows where I've been. Oliver said they were all visiting beforehand. I don't want to see the pity in anyone's eyes or feel the warmth of an embrace. I need to feel the cold.

The house is clean and the last nine months seemed as though they never happened. The living room looks just as it did a couple weeks after we moved in.

"I'm going to go take a shower," I tell Oliver. I doubt soap and water will do much but a shower without someone standing a few feet away, water warmer than body temperature, and soap with fragrance will remind me I'm home. I'm here, not there.

"Do you need anything?" he asks, placing my plastic bag of clothes down by the couch.

"No. Nothing, in fact."

Oliver's shoulders slump forward, and he presses his lips together. If I was standing outside of this bubble we seem to be in, I'd feel sorry for the way I'm making him feel. But I can't seem to see past the crushing grief swallowing me whole.

I reach the top of the stairwell, unsure of what to expect. River's bedroom door is closed. In our bedroom, there is no bedside cradle, a white noise machine on our dresser, or burp rags folded in a pile at the edge of our bed. Those are all things I must have imagined—that's what I'm supposed to keep reminding myself. I wish it would become easier to believe, but I'm fighting my subconscious and it's unnatural. Over everything else, I should be able to trust my thoughts.

Once in the bathroom, I lock the door, needing the extra privacy, even from my husband. I step out of the sweatpants and pull off the T-shirt, dropping them into a pile on the ground. My stomach looks like a deflated balloon, one that was once overfilled. I rest my hands on the granite countertop and stare into the mirror, forcing myself to come to terms with what I truly look like now. Pale, saggy, despondent eyes, dark inflammation beneath my eyes, and my hair looks like I've been wrestling beneath a wool blanket.

"You can take these pain relievers every six hours if needed." Celeste's freckled face appears in the mirror—she's standing beside me. *"Hydration is important, and so is sleep."* She places the over-the-counter bottle of pills down on the counter.

"Thank you," I say, my voice hoarse from groaning and pushing.

"You'll be sore for a day or two, but you did great."

I study her reflection, the strands of strawberry blonde tendrils dangling over her forehead, her eyelids heavy from coaching me through the midnight hours.

A faint, high-pitched cry travels up the stairwell and swirls around the bathroom.

"He must be hungry."

"I—I don't think so," she says.

I shake my head to sweep away the images fooling with my mind and pull open the mirror to expose the shallow shelves of the medicine cabinet. I scan each row, knowing Oliver had organized each bottle alphabetically because things must be in order or it stresses him out. There's a space between the Omega-3 vitamins and a narrow tube container of Dramamine. The over-the-counter pain relievers are on the top shelf, the bottle Celeste gave me is third in from the left. I take down the bottle and twist the cap off, finding the red and white gel coated pills. It's all I recall taking. Of course, I only remember snippets of time between the day I went into labor and the day I was admitted to the behavioral facility. What if I did take something else?

The shower feels as restricting as the house. Despite having hot water and my favorite soap and shampoo, nothing works to ease the heavy burden from my chest. I don't want to see my naked body and I don't want to feel the emptiness in my stomach. I can't run away from myself.

I wrap myself in a towel, telling myself to appreciate the plush material in comparison to the over-bleached thin terrycloth towels I was given in the facility. I wrap my hair up with a second towel and open the door to release the excess steam.

Outside, car doors close, one after another, and I wonder if Oliver is taking things out of the cars.

I pad across the bedroom carpet to the window and pry my fingers between the blinds to peek outside. There are a few cars parked in Peyton and Lincoln's driveway. An older couple is walking toward their front door with two baby-blue gift bags and a large stuffed giraffe. That should be me too. I'm sure I would have visitors donning pastel colored gift bags filled with tiny baby clothes and plush toys, all eager to hold River and inhale his baby-fresh scent while running their fingers gently over his feather-soft skin. I should be holding him, feeling the warmth of his small body against my chest. It's not fair.

I should release the blinds, stop looking. But it's too late.

Peyton opens the door, her hair in a messy bun with a section of loose hair curled and swept behind her ear. Her arms are full, a cotton blanket swaddling her baby as she presents him to whoever the people at the door are. She never mentioned grand-parents in the area and said Lincoln's family are all from New York. Maybe they flew in to visit.

The woman hands the gift bag to the man and reaches her hands out toward Peyton, waiting to take—I don't even know his name. She hadn't decided. It's hard not to question if Peyton and I were ever really friends now. Maybe everything that has happened in the past year is a figment of my imagination. Except this house. This house is real, and I'm sure it is a carrier of bad luck to whoever lives here—it robbed me of a precious life and left me with a gaping hole in my heart that grows larger every day. There will be nothing left of me soon. The house will get rid of us the same way it did the last owners. All of those foolish dreams I had—each one is gone. My chin trembles, warning me of another wave of uncontrollable emotions I can't seem to suppress. I suck in a deep breath, close my eyes, and grit my teeth.

Another door opens and closes, startling me to open my eyes. It was our front door. Oliver storms outside, walks down to the end of our driveway and places his hands on his hips, staring at Peyton and Lincoln's house and the grand introductions on their front porch. I should remember he's in pain too, but my tunnel vision is thick and selfish.

Oliver catches Peyton's attention and she glances at him briefly then turns around and gestures for everyone to go inside her house.

She peers back at Oliver once more, expressionless from as far as I can see, then disappears into her house and closes their front door.

Oliver can't stop her from living her life because of our issues. I appreciate the attempt to shield me from the reality of what's happening around us, but he should see what good that did for me this past week. If anything, I should pull myself together and deliver her the congratulations she deserves.

No one did this to me.

No one drugged me.

No one lied to me.

Maybe if I say that all enough times, I'll start to believe it's true.

THIRTY-FIVE

GINGER | TWO MONTHS AGO

Peyton doesn't have an honest bone in her body. Jenna deserves to know what type of person she's grown to trust, the person who she has allowed into her life. However, I think I know Jenna well enough to assume she won't believe a word I say, not if it's anything negative against Peyton. At least I know the charade can only go on for so long before Peyton is forced to confess her sins.

The bottle of Cabernet on my counter pulls me over as if it has hypnotic powers. I flick off the cork and press the opening against my lips, tipping the neck of the bottle so the liquid glides down my throat. The more I know, the harder it is to remain a prisoner of my mind. I need the thoughts to mute.

My phone buzzes on the coffee table for the fourth time in the last ten minutes. I'd like to think someone from the baby shower noticed I'd left in a rush and is wondering if I'm okay, but I doubt that to be the case. No one cares if I'm there or here. No one cares if I'm alive. "I'm not enough. Right, James?" I shout.

As usual, there's no response.

When the familiar burn coats my stomach, I place the bottle

down and fetch my phone from the living room, finding the missed calls to be from Joel. He must need something, but it's been a while since he's needed much of anything from me. He's so self-sufficient, successful, and wealthy now—what use does he have for a mother who devoted her life to him for twenty-one years?

I tap on the missed call and press the phone to my ear.

There's hardly one ring before the call connects. That's a first. "Mom," Joel says, urgency in the word that means nothing to him.

"Is everything okay?" My heart flutters, wondering what he could be calling about.

"Will you be home in an hour?"

"Yes, why? You're making me nervous. Did you find something out?"

"It's nothing to worry about, but I just want to talk in person. I'll see you soon."

Before I can ask any further questions, Joel ends the call.

I've been pacing the living room for an entire hour, watching out the window for Joel's SUV to pull into the driveway, but to my surprise, Sam's car pulls in followed by Carter's truck, and after a long minute of no one moving from their vehicles, Joel pulls up along the curb. The sets of tires crunch over the salt left on the roads from the town trucks treating the icy conditions last night. Hopefully it was our last cold snap of the season as we get closer to the middle of March. The weather always teeters this time of year between warm days and cold nights. I wait by the door, watching Michael step out from the passenger side of Sam's car. Sam, Carter, and Joel all follow without exchanging a word. The last time we were all together was Christmas when they spared two hours of their day for me.

As if this is any normal occasion, I open the door and each

of my sons step inside, giving me a flimsy hug and hello before making their way into the living room. "What is this, an intervention for being your mother?" I ask after Joel makes his way past me. "Is today my lucky day when all four of you decide you still love me?"

"Mom," Sam says, "come on, let's not get snippy."

Sam is a junior in college, obvious by his collegiate black jogging pants and gray hooded sweatshirt. He's long overdue for a haircut and I can't imagine the last time he shaved his scruffy dark beard. It seems to be a habit of his between the late winter months and early spring days. Once the weather turns a bit warmer, he'll get a haircut and a clean shave because he can't stand the feeling of sweating. Joel is the only one of the four dressed in business attire, properly groomed. Michael works from home and must not look in the mirror—I'm assuming by the splattered stain of tomato sauce all over his tan T-shirt and sweat-stained white baseball cap. Then there's Carter—my ripped jeans and tight T-shirt kid who thinks he's going to land a job modeling.

"I'm not snippy. The four of you never come by. I'm sure anyone in my situation would be wondering what purpose you have being here."

Joel and Carter take a seat on the sofa. Sam drops down in his father's recliner, and Michael sits on the edge of the coffee table, which he knows I hate.

"Taylor Drell called me last night," Joel says, leaning forward to rest his elbows on his knees. "Officer Drell." He must be clarifying in case I forgot that his friend became an officer in town.

"I know who he is."

"Our conversation was off the record, but he seemed concerned about your well-being." I wasn't expecting the conversation to turn in this direction. "He noticed the amount of security cameras you have had installed and said you looked frazzled when he came to ask you about some woman named Andrea Lester."

I lean against the hearth just beside the fireplace and fold my arms across my chest. "Frazzled?"

"That's what he said. Anyway, this woman is somehow tied to your name per an anonymous tip."

"As I told your officer friend, I don't know why I would be connected to this Andrea person. Maybe that's why I appeared frazzled. Wouldn't you be?" Is it so hard to give me the benefit of the doubt, maybe just once?

"Mom...are you Andrea Lester?" Carter asks. He might as well be pointing a finger at me with his accusatory stare. Joel shoves his elbow into Carter's arm. "None of this makes any sense. Joel found some connection between your name and hers online and it's hard to not wonder..."

"Carter—hold up," Joel says, cutting his brother off before he says more than what they must have planned.

"Excuse me? What kind of absurd question is that? I'm your mother. How could you question who I am?"

"The tip about Andrea Lester was in connection to Tommy's death. His car accident wasn't an accident. Someone tampered with the brakes in his car," Carter adds, refusing to back down despite Joel's objection. "We've never heard of this Andrea person, yet, it seems you have, and we know how you felt about Luanne. You always wanted to be closer, but she could never make time for you. That must have bothered you, I'm sure." Carter is trying some sort of reverse psychology on me, trying to get me to admit to something I had nothing to do with. I'm their mother. How could they think so little of me?

"You think I had something to do with Tommy's death, and how in the world do you figure I'm associated with this Andrea Lester person?" I have had no reason to hurt that man. There isn't one, and they know this. Sure, I wish Luanne would have wanted a friendship with me, but I respected her need for space and never pushed the boundaries, and none of that had anything to do with Tommy. It amazes me how easily anyone can become a suspect when there isn't an arrow pointing with certainty at one person. I wish I was more surprised to hear this bit of information, but with the gossip and rumors that have been floating around for months, most of us have suspected foul play. Some think Luanne had something to do with it, but I don't think she did.

Joel clears his throat and presses his fingers to his temple. "It's just hard to digest, especially without an explanation of what happened to Dad too. I mean, after twenty years, he just got up and left without a trace. He abandoned his kids after devoting his life to being a father."

As if we needed an interruption, the house phone rings from the kitchen. I could use a moment to regain my composure. "One moment, please," I tell the boys as I scurry into the kitchen to grab the phone, and answer, "Fowler Residence." Another debt collector. Of course, this call has to come now of all times. "I'm sorry, he's not in at the moment, but I can take down a message for him." Another person insisting on finding him...someone else completely unaware of the fact that I want to find him more than they do. "I wish I could say when would be a better time. I apologize for any troubles. Take care now." I hang up on the man still asking questions I can't answer, knowing the interrogation can go on for several more minutes if I don't end the call.

"What was that?" Joel asks as I return to the living room, squeezing my hand around the back of my neck to release the tension.

"Another debt collector," I say with a sigh. "It's never-ending some days."

"Still? I thought you were paying the bills?" Sam asks, dropping his head into his hands.

"Most of them, yes. Some of them, I don't have access to,

and they won't help me into the account without his permission." Nor can I afford to go through our retirement fund paying them off. I don't want to burden them with the nitty-gritty details when they are already going through so much.

"Maybe the truth could help?" Michael insists, sarcasm lacing his words.

"The truth? The truth is that he abandoned his wife of twenty-five years," I add. I'm not sure abandoned is the proper word to use but it's the only way I can think to describe his actions.

"It would be hard to believe that there is no record of Dad anywhere. It's hard to convince ourselves that we've all spent countless hours searching for him over the last couple of years, and we're still no closer to an answer," Joel mutters.

"What would you like me to do?" I ask. They're old enough to realize magic wands aren't an answer.

"Do you promise you're telling us the truth, Mom?" Michael asks, taking his hat off to run his fingers through his shaggy hair. It pains me to the pit of my stomach to hear him question me like this.

I place my hands over my heart. "Yes. I know just as much about your father's whereabouts as you all do. I'm not sure what information you're expecting to garner from me. I would have told you all had I found new information." My palms are clammy and I drop my hands to my sides then slip them into my back pants pockets.

"Okay, okay, enough of the accusations," Joel huffs. "We need to put Dad aside for a moment and discuss this Andrea person we've done some searching for." Joel takes a quick look at his brothers before continuing. "It turns out there are many Andrea Lesters and there's no way to narrow down which may be related to Tommy's accident."

"I don't think the answer to this investigation will be found online," I reply.

"Well, the issue is...one of the Andrea Lesters we found online came up with an alias of Ginger Fowler," Joel says.

My right knee gives out and I stumble to catch my balance, grabbing hold of the ledge of the fireplace for support. "Who would do such a thing?"

The boys think this answer is easy. They think I'm going to stand here and tell them: I would do such a thing. I am using a false name. It's me, Andrea Lester, who is associated with cutting the brake lines on Tommy's car for no good reason. If I could do something so awful to a neighbor, I must be the sole reason my husband has gone missing too. That's why they're all here.

"None of this makes sense, Mom. If you're in trouble somehow, you know we'll help you, but if you had something to do with Dad's disappearance...we want to know why. We deserve to know," Carter says.

I don't think one of them would help me if I was dangling by one finger off a cliff. That's how they've made me feel these past couple of years.

I take a couple of steps closer to the sofa and narrow my glare to give each one of them a stern look. "If I had any clue where your father was, I would drag his ass back here to straighten you four out. He would be disgusted with the disrespect you have shown me. Although I shouldn't be surprised, you have all neglected me the same way he did. So, shame on you, leaving me here with a broken heart and not one shoulder to lean on after spending my life giving you all everything I could."

THIRTY-SIX

JENNA | THREE WEEKS AGO

I have too many checklists, and a checklist for my checklists. This is what happens when a woman makes it past her due date, never mind a week and a half late. At the two-week mark, I'll lose control of my birthing options as the doctor said she would need to induce labor for the safety of our baby and me. I must have walked two miles a day for the last week with no signs of impending labor.

If I had known that scrubbing grout with a toothbrush while on my hands and knees in the bathroom would cause my water to break, I would have started my cleaning rampage sooner.

"Oliver!" I peer down, spotting the puddle developing around me. "My water broke." The strong scent of peppermint burns my stomach like an acid, reminding me of the early days in my pregnancy when I suffered bouts of morning sickness following every potent scent I endured.

I'm not sure where he is, but I'm glad it's after work hours and he's here somewhere in the house. With a short pause between my statement and the clomping of his bare feet against the wooden floors, he nearly skids to a stop in front of the downstairs bathroom, finding me in the awkward position I haven't moved from.

"Oh my God. Okay, okay. Stay calm."

I am calm. It's clear he's not. "I'm fine. We just need to call the midwife and my mom." The temperature in the house seems to rise even though the sun is starting to set. It was mild and partly cloudy all day but it's like a heat wave just settled over our house. "Also, could you close the windows and turn the air-conditioner to a colder setting?"

"Okay, okay...but are you in pain?"

I shake my head before analyzing what I'm feeling. "No. I don't have contractions yet."

Oliver spins around in a dizzying circle before finding his phone in the back pocket of his pants. He stares at the display for a long few seconds, then searches through his contacts.

I twist around to take my weight off my knees and ease onto the floor, leaning against the wall. I didn't think of what to do if my water broke.

Oliver races up the stairs and then back down, placing the stack of towels we set aside for this moment. I take one and slowly mop up some of the mess and take another and slide it beneath me. I rest my head back against the wall and close my eyes, convincing myself to take slow deep breaths. I want a peaceful environment and no stress. That's the point of a home birth.

The front door opens and closes several times and I'm trying to block out the commotion while we wait for the midwife and Mom to get here.

"Jenna." I hear Peyton say my name and I'm not sure why she's here, but I open my eyes to find her kneeling beside me. "Come on. I covered the floor with pillows, padding and towels. Let's get you out of the bathroom."

"Where's Oliver? What are you doing here?"

Peyton smiles at me, her cheeks glowing with excitement.

"He texted me to say your water broke and he's freaking out. He could have left the latter half out and I would have seen for myself when I walked in the front door because he's currently chasing his tail around the living room. Celeste will be here in a few minutes. She's on her way."

Peyton offers me her hand, but I push it away. "You can't help me off the ground. You'll put yourself into labor too and then we'll be in trouble." My joke doesn't sound too humorous.

As I'm pulling myself up by the base of the sink, a wave of pain strikes my core, and my stomach tightens like it's turning into steel. I'm stuck, hunching over, unable to straighten my posture because of the pain. We're both silent as I wait for the cramp-like sensation to pass. It feels like forever by the time my muscles relax. Then I can stand up straight and walk toward the living room.

"I was going to ask you if your contractions started, but it looks like—"

"That was the first one," I tell her.

Peyton holds my hand through the next three contractions before the midwife rings the doorbell. Oliver has just finished setting up all the supplies we've accumulated and seems a hair calmer when inviting Celeste in.

"My mom should be here soon," I tell Peyton.

"She will. Don't worry," she says, pressing a damp rag against my forehead.

Celeste looks different than when I first met with her. Her hair was down in long curls when she came over here a few weeks ago, and she had on a light coat of makeup. She's dressed similarly except her scrubs were a solid pastel pink last time and now the bottoms are black, and the top is tan with a puppy dog print pattern. I appreciate her confidence and the ability to take charge the moment she arrives.

It's only been a few minutes, but we're already deep into meditation through breathing exercises.

"How are you doing, Mama?" Celeste's voice is like the combination of a harp and a summer breeze.

"I'm okay," I say through an exhale. "I know I'm in good hands now, especially as the pain is growing more intense."

"Pain is to be expected, but we're going to breathe through the contractions and take it all nice and easy," she says calmly. "Oliver, let's get her some ice and cool wash cloths."

Suddenly, I can't help questioning if I was wrong about a home birth...maybe I can't handle pain like some other women can. What if I can't do this?

After hours of laboring, pressure builds in my lower abdomen and I struggle to open my eyes, finding Celeste and Oliver by my side. "I know you must be tired," Celeste says.

"I have a lot of pressure," I utter.

She smiles. "Good. That might mean it's time to push."

She and Oliver switch spots and he's by my head, holding my hand and peppering kisses along my forehead. "I'm so proud of you," he says.

With more awareness percolating, the pain I have been breathing through is becoming much fiercer and I feel like I'm losing my sense of focus. "Where's my mom?"

"It's so late at night, babe," says Oliver. "She must be asleep. I called her a few times, but she didn't pick up."

She told me she would keep her ringer on in case I went into labor in the middle of the night. "Are you sure?"

"I've left messages and sent texts too. It's okay. I'm here," he says, sounding much calmer now than he was before. "Peyton left just a bit ago to give us some privacy, but she said to call her once our little man arrived."

"Okay, Jenna, we're going to start pushing," Celeste says. She mumbles a set of instructions that come in like waves of choppy words. I remember she said my body will know what to do so I'm relying on that with how worn out I am.

I try not to scream through the pain. I grit my teeth and continue attempting my breathing exercises, but everything hurts so much that I just want to cry and say I can't do this anymore. Celeste's voice blends into a high-pitched squeal zinging between my ears. I'm not sure how much more I can take.

"Come on, babe, you can do this. You're so strong." Oliver's voice is finally clear and gives me the motivation to push through the incoming contraction. "We're about to be a family. God, I love you so much."

My breaths are out of control, and I can't seem to slow down. I clench my eyes and teeth, trying to focus on Oliver's words.

Then a faint cry breaks through the heaviness in my head but fades into the distance.

"Oliver, I need you to—" I can't hear what Celeste said to him. "Let's get the placenta delivered," I hear.

Another cry followed by silence.

"I know."

"Okay."

"Let her hold him," Oliver demands.

Warm skin presses against my chest and I fight the weakness in my head to open my eyes, spotting a head full of light brown hair. I strain more to see his beautiful face. *River.* It's the name we decided on, and he looks like a River—a beautiful and natural stream of life merging with our world. His eyes blink as he peers at me with a look of wonder and my heart bursts—a tsunami of pure infinite love, a feeling never to be matched.

River is lifted off my chest as exhaustion weighs heavily on my eyelids. My mind is now filled with the face I will dream about every night for the rest of my life. "Take him over there," Celeste says. "Just hold him."

"How do I—" Oliver mutters. "Oh my God."

The sound of a sniffle captures my attention and I strain to lift my head off the pillow, spotting Oliver spin around in a slow circle with River wrapped in a blood-covered receiving blanket. "Is that my blood?" I ask through hard gasps. Oliver clenches his eyes shut but holds River in a tight embrace. "Is he—are they okay?"

"Blood is normal. I need you to slow your breathing down, Jenna," Celeste says, pressing a wet cloth to my forehead.

How can I slow my breathing when I don't feel like I'm breathing at all?

THIRTY-SEVEN

JENNA | NOW

After rummaging through the clothes in my closet, flipping through hangers of attire I used to love, I manage to find a pair of leggings and one of Oliver's old maroon and white Lakespur University T-shirts to throw on. None of my pre-pregnancy clothes fit. Who knows if they ever will again. It's been so long since I've been in a daily routine that I'm spinning around, trying to figure out what's next.

Deodorant. I shuffle through my nightstand to find the antiperspirant, also spotting the earrings I used to wear daily. I then find a bottle of prescription pain reliever pills, a generic brand of opioids, and move my hand over the transparent orange container, pausing before lifting it out of the drawer.

I didn't put this here.

I could barely keep my eyes open, let alone find a bottle of pills alphabetically sorted in the medicine cabinet to then hide them strategically in my nightstand drawer. I've never hidden anything from Oliver, and I wouldn't have a reason to hide these because I've never wanted to take them.

Someone put these here.

Someone was drugging me.

I make my way downstairs, tying my damp hair up into a sloppy bun. *Who would do this?* Oliver is sitting like a stiff board on the couch, staring at the black screen of the television.

"There you are," he says, greeting me with a beaming smile. "Did the shower help?"

I'm not sure what kind of question that is—if he means with my crushing grief or removing the grime still stuck to me like skin from the behavioral facility.

"Not exactly."

"Can I do anything for you?"

"I'm going across the street to congratulate Peyton and Lincoln. Our loss shouldn't be their problem, and I've been missing since she gave birth."

Oliver adjusts his position to somehow straighten his shoulders even more. "Jenna, she understands and doesn't expect you to act like you aren't going through this—" He stands and moves toward the front door. "I think you should give it a bit. You just got home and I think seeing a baby might—"

"Be upsetting?" I interrupt him. "Yeah, I would say so too, but her baby isn't going anywhere, and the longer I put this off, the harder it will be, so I'd rather suck it up and act like I'm happy for her as a friend should do."

Oliver leans a hand on the front door and tips his head forward. "You mean, like...like she acted at dinner that night when she thought you might be pregnant? Remember she ran out of the house because she was so upset?" His icy stare holds me frozen. "Can you just put yourself first right now?"

I step forward, not faltering. "Oliver, move. I'm doing what I need to do."

A long moment of hesitation passes between us as we stare at each other. It's just another reminder that I suddenly feel so completely disconnected from him that I have no clue what must be going through his head at the moment. I want to convince myself that he's trying to protect me, but I also feel like he's trying to protect himself from me.

His movements are robotic, accepting my command as he steps to the side and leans on the side of the couch. "Do you want me to come with you?"

"It's up to you." I didn't ask if he's met the baby yet. I have no idea what he's been doing for the last three days of my life or even the last week, really.

"Sure," he says, opening the door. The humid air sticks to my skin, causing a slight chill to follow while passing beneath the thick, darkening clouds. The scent of rain is strong, and it won't be long until the clouds burst into fat tears.

Oliver takes my hand as we cross the street and make our way up to their front door. "They have company. Should we wait until later maybe? This feels rude."

"If she has company, she's prepared for company. It's better now than if she's in the middle of feeding the baby later."

Oliver takes in a deep breath, preparing himself for the same pain I am. There's no way around it though. I ring the bell and squeeze Oliver's hand. My heart races, my stomach aches, and my chest feels like it's caving in for every second longer we stand here staring at their front door.

I ring the bell once more. There are others here. I'm sure someone has heard the doorbell.

Five minutes pass before Oliver loosens his hand from mine. "It's obviously not a good time," he says. "Why don't we try again later when she doesn't have company?"

Oliver tugs my arm, to pull me away from the front door and down the porch steps. When we reach the bottom of her driveway, I turn back to see if she happened to come to the door. Instead, I see a hand clutching a curtain by her side window. The fabric releases and sways gently from side to side.

"She's avoiding me."

"I don't think that's the case," Oliver says, still pulling me toward our house. "Maybe she's worried you might resent her."

Lucky for Peyton, it isn't her I resent.

Oliver opens our front door and holds it so I can pass through.

"I'm going to sit out here on the porch for a while before the rainstorm rolls in." ...and stare at Peyton's house until her front door opens.

Oliver releases the door and sits in the seat across from me. "Babe, I don't want this to sound insensitive in any way, but my paternity and bereavement time is up, and I have to get back to the classroom tomorrow, but I'm worried about leaving you alone all day. I was thinking maybe your mom could come spend some time with you while I'm working. Would that be all right?"

I could go back to work too. I don't have a baby to tend to. There isn't a purpose in taking maternity leave if I'm not a mother. "I'll just go back too, keep myself busy."

A look of concern lines Oliver's face. "I spoke to your boss. He insisted you take the month at the very least. He wants you to take time to heal emotionally and physically."

"You spoke to Leonard Cole?"

"He called to see how you were doing last week, to make sure you received the gift basket the firm sent." I wasn't aware we even received gifts.

"That was kind of him." He must know I'm not in the right headspace to help anyone else since I can hardly help myself. I was sure nothing could ever distract me from work, but I was wrong.

"Your mom will be here tomorrow morning before I leave for work. I spoke to her already and asked if
she—"

"I don't think I'm ready to speak to my mom right now. The

things she said when she visited me at the facility...I can't just forget. Can you call her back and say you changed your mind?"

Oliver leans forward as if the weight of the world is resting on his back. "What did she say to upset you?"

"She asked if I killed River, or alluded to it..."

"What? You must have misunderstood her. Your mom? Jenna..." Oliver reaches for my hand, but I refuse to give in. I know what she asked me, and she asked because of whatever information she had been given—whomever that was from.

"I don't know what to think or believe right now, which is why I'd prefer to be alone."

His shoulders bow forward as if he's been sucker punched. "You know you can trust what I tell you, right?"

Just as rain drops begin to pelt against the porch awning, Oliver's eyes fill with tears and my heart breaks again. I want to say yes, but the word isn't forming on my tongue so I nod, hoping that's enough.

THIRTY-EIGHT

GINGER | THREE WEEKS AGO

The glare from the sun pouring into my living room window forms a halo over my laptop screen, making it impossible to see anything while sitting on the sofa. It's a sign to take a break from endless online searches for answers I know I won't find.

While my sons have done little to support me since their father—since James—left us, they have been around more this last month after bombarding me with accusations due to Officer Drell digging for information on an investigation that has nothing to do with me or my family. Although I think they're only here to find clues to help Officer Drell, or to simply determine why my name is somehow connected to Tommy's death. It wasn't because they were close to him, and I don't think it's because they fear for my safety living across the street, so I'm not sure what their true interest is, nor do I think they'll come clean.

To me, it's just unfathomable for something so horrific to happen so close to home, and within a couple of years of personally encountering a loss of my own.

It didn't take long for me to connect the dots on my name being an alias for Andrea Lester. It's all part of the threat—the game of power. I didn't think Andrea was capable of homicide, but I've apparently underestimated her once again. I've also spent weeks trying to determine why she would be linked to Tommy's death. I thought I could help that woman. I tried. I tried until I couldn't but it seems the only thing I managed to do was wind her up then set her free.

2019

"You're really doing this, huh?" James asks, walking into the kitchen and finding me hunched over my laptop.

"I already have my first patient session tonight. I've waited so long to be in a position where I can use my knowledge and most of my Master's degree to help people. I'm still that woman you met all those years ago who wants to make a difference in the world." My pulse speeds up and my cheeks warm at the thought of remembering who I was before I was just a mom.

James leans over my shoulder and places a kiss on my cheek. "I'm proud of you, sweetie. I think this is such a wonderful idea, and I think you're onto something great."

A notification pops up on my screen, informing me my patient is waiting, so I connect the private message chat.

Andrea Lester has joined the chat.

GFowler [psychological assistant]: *Hi there, Andrea. I'm Mrs. Fowler, one of the psychological assistants working with the Thatcher Behavioral Health community. I've reviewed your files from Dr. Garmen and am familiar with your history. As Dr. Garmen mentioned to you, I will be helping you with some cognitive coping mechanisms to guide you through some methods of self-healing. Our chat will remain private between us and Dr. Garmen as he reviews this* *to evaluate your progress. Can you confirm you are choosing to join this session at your own free will?*

Andrea begins to type immediately following my question, taking no time at all to respond.

AndreaLester [patient]: *Yes, thank you. I confirm that I'm here by my own free will. Thank you for squeezing me in tonight. I've been having a harder time than usual lately and Dr. Garmen suggested we increase our methods of therapy. So I'm hopeful for a good outcome.*

GFowler [psychological assistant]: *Wonderful, I'm glad to hear you took his suggestion. Would you be comfortable explaining the reason you have been having a difficult time lately? It's clear by your records you have been suffering for quite some time.*

AndreaLester [patient]: *I'm sure you've heard this reason many times before, but the pitfalls of social media have brought me back to the dark place I once was in. Anger has been brewing in me as I'm forced to make the decision to remove myself from an online social life to avoid triggering memories from that time in my life that I can't seem to escape from. I don't want to be a ghost on social media because I'm afraid to face my past.*

Normally, I would suggest someone like Andrea stay off of social media for the exact reasons she has explained above, but she's right—avoidance shouldn't be her punishment for what was done to her. Our pasts follow us and it's better that we learn how to cope than run away.

GFowler [psychological assistant]: *I think you're brave for wanting to take on a battle with the source of your pain. I believe I can help you do this. You see, sometimes we must stare into the face of what scares us the most until we are able to view beyond.*

AndreaLester [patient]: *That's exactly what I'm hoping you can help me do. Remove these fears once and for all.*

THIRTY-NINE

JENNA | NOW

I didn't intend to fall asleep outside on the front porch last night. My face is wet with morning dew, but a blanket covers me from the neck down. My hair is matted to my face and I'm stiff from sleeping curled up in a ball on the side of the wicker love seat. An ache in my neck makes it hard to look around, but I find Oliver conked out. He's upright with his head hanging to one side. I assume he'll be in more pain than I am when he wakes up.

The chirping birds mute my incoming thoughts for a moment. I wonder if they feel pain like people do—if they would still be singing if one of their babies fell out of their nest.

After stretching the kinks in my neck, I sit up and drop my legs off the cushion, my phone falling with them. The clank startles the birds, forcing them to flee from the surrounding trees, and wakes up Oliver. He jerks upright, grabbing the side of his neck and furrowing his eyebrows.

I reach for my phone, praying the display didn't crack. I got lucky this time. "Sorry for falling asleep out here," I say. The rainstorm didn't last long, leaving us with a pleasant warm breeze. Oliver didn't have to stay. He could have gone to bed, and I would have understood.

"I know how you love the distant rumbles of thunder—it's your white noise, and you seemed comfortable so I didn't want to wake you," he says, running his fingers through my gnarly hair.

Other than to use the bathroom a couple of times, I haven't moved from this seat since late yesterday afternoon after waiting at Peyton's door for nothing more than the silent treatment. We ordered pizza and scrolled mindlessly through our phones until I rested my head down on the throw pillow. Life feels somewhat meaningless, and I don't remember how I felt before finding out I was pregnant. It's like that road is blocked off and there's no way back.

I wipe my phone on the blanket to remove the sheen of moisture then check the time. "It's already a quarter past eight."

"The fresh air will do that," Oliver says, still stretching his neck from side to side. "I need to get ready for work in a few minutes. Your mom said she'd be here by eight thirty."

"Oliver, I said I wasn't ready to talk to her yet..." He leaves at nine, so it's more than clear he thinks I need a babysitter.

"I understand, babe, and I considered your feelings, but you shouldn't be alone right now, and I don't have any other options. You should take this time to talk to her and tell her how you feel. Maybe you can clear the air about what she meant to say, or what you misunderstood, perhaps."

A pit forms in my stomach, knowing I hardly have the energy to talk, never mind the conversation I need to have with Mom. "Okay," I say, staring at my phone. I notice a missed call from just a few minutes ago, and a voicemail from a number I don't recognize.

"Who called?" Oliver asks.

I tap over to the messages and open the transcription:

Hi Jenna, this is Dr. Kasper from Ashlyn Behavioral Health Center. I've come across some information that I'd like to speak with you about when you have a free moment today. I'll be available all morning. You can reach me at the number I've called from. This is not a wellness check or related to your admission, but it is imperative you get back to me. Talk soon.

"What's that all about?" Oliver presses for information while cleaning his glasses with the hem of his shirt.

"I'm not sure. One of the doctors from Ashlyn would like to speak with me." I don't give Oliver a moment to think about the request. I hit redial and lift the phone to my ear.

There's never been a time in my life when a doctor has answered a direct call from me, never mind on the first ring.

"Dr. Kasper speaking," she says.

"Hi, Dr. Kasper, it's Jenna Milligan, returning your call." I spot a loose thread on the woven cream-colored blanket draped across my lap and tug, watching the threads pucker around the one I'm pulling.

"Thank you for calling back so promptly. I hope you got a good night's sleep last night and are feeling okay today?"

"I did, thank you, and yes, I'm okay. Is there a problem?"

I hear her shuffling around and the sound of a door closing. "Yes, so I came across some information I think you should have." Her voice echoes now, wherever she's speaking from. "Celeste Brown is the midwife who delivered—"

"River, yes."

Oliver perks his head up, curiosity flickering through his eyes.

"I've been working with a case worker to generate some of the information you have been unsure about. Some of the details you gave were concerning and I wanted to make sure our decisions to admit you were based on accurate facts."

"I don't understand." I'm not sure if this kind of follow-up is common after a patient is released.

"Celeste Brown is not a licensed midwife, nor a certified medical examiner. In fact, she was a practicing obstetrician for several years but lost her license due to malpractice. I'm not sure if you knew to ask for proof of her medical licenses, but it's important for you to know this information."

My lungs feel like a deflating balloon, stealing all the air out of my body, and I'm not sure how to respond. "I—uh—" My gaze shifts to Oliver and the apprehension creasing along his forehead as he stares at me, waiting to find out what I'm being told.

"Jenna, if you need to come in and see me to talk, please do. You don't have to and you don't have to stay, but I want to make sure you are going to be okay."

How could I be okay? "Uh—yeah, I'll call you if I feel like I should come in. Thank you—"

"I'm sorry for what you're going through."

"I appreciate it."

"What's going on?" Oliver asks, standing from the seat.

I disconnect and grip the phone in my hand, pausing for a minute before responding. "Oh, I left my journal they had me writing in each day. She wanted to know if I wanted to hang on to it in case I feel the need to write anything down. She was also checking on me."

"You told her you didn't understand. What didn't you understand?"

Instinct pulls my stare over toward Peyton's house. "How trauma can have long-lasting side effects. I thought they let me go because they deemed me to be stable."

A grimace arcs along Oliver's lips, his eyes downcast with anguish. "The worst is over, babe. It's nice they were checking on you."

Yeah. Nice.

"Do you feel guilty for choosing a home birth over the traditional hospital route?" I ask. I would like to tell him how adamant about the decision he was. He was so adamant that he convinced me it was the perfect plan for us.

But Peyton, she's the one who found Celeste, and then she ended up having a hospital birth. She's avoiding me, and now I think I know why.

"No, absolutely not," he replies while my mind is whirling. "I think we did what we thought was best and the rest was in God's hands. We should not blame ourselves, Jenna. Please, we can't do that. We've been through enough."

We. I carried our baby around for nine months. I gave birth to him. I've been deceived by a midwife and then drugged by someone who has access to my personal belongings in my bedroom. I'm certain that's only touching the surface of what I've experienced.

"I want to have a funeral for River. Where is his body?" My heart thuds slowly between each word as if it's threatening to stall out.

Words I never thought I would have to speak to my husband.

A cloud breaks apart in the sky and the sun embodies us as if blacking out the rest of the world. "I—well, we talked about...I brought him to be cr—"

The door opens across the street, the grease on the hinges failing to do its job. I leave Oliver with his unfinished sentence, knowing I can't bear to hear what he's about to tell me I agreed to.

"Jenna, wait," he shouts after me. "I need to go get ready for work or I'll be late. Can you wait until later to visit—"

I need to do this now—with or without him.

"It was so lovely for you to have us stay the night," I hear through the blinding light as I cross the road.

"Any time, Aunt June. Take care of yourself Uncle Ricky," Peyton shouts.

By the time I step out of the glare, a look of shock pales Peyton's complexion. "Jenna," she says as if I just came back from the dead.

"Why are you avoiding me?"

"What?" she asks, slouching forward as a grimace weighs down her bottom lip. "No, I'm—you think I'm avoiding you?"

As I cross her lawn, I notice she's wearing her baby in a sling across her body and Lincoln steps up behind her, placing his protective arm around her shoulders. She covers her son's head with her hand as if she needs to protect him from something. As if she needs to protect him from me.

"Hey, Jenna," Lincoln says.

"Hi. I just wanted to congratulate you both."

Lincoln's lips twist to the side like he doesn't understand why I would want to do such a thing. Peyton's nose scrunches and her forehead dimples. "You don't have to do that..." she says.

"I need to," I say before sucking in a breath.

She bounces her knees and sways gently while cradling the bundle nestled into the sling on her torso. "Are you doing all right? How's Oliver?" she asks, looking past my shoulder toward our house.

"We've been so worried about you all," Lincoln says, swallowing so hard I can hear the struggle in his throat.

"I'll be fine, at some point. Oliver is...well, he's Oliver, trying to stand upright and remain strong for my sake, but he has to go back to work today." I'm not sure I'll ever be fine again, but I can't stand still, frozen in a moment that has changed my life. I need to move forward, and the person I am is one who congratulates her friend properly after she has a baby. I force a smile. I haven't moved my lips like this for so many days, I feel like I'm straining the muscles in my face. "What did you end up naming him?"

A knot forms in my throat, making it hard to swallow and

tears burn against the backs of my eyes. I need to hold it together—Peyton deserves that from me. I take the two steps up to her and place my hand on the back of the baby's head, relishing the fine feathery sprigs of hair.

"Dylan, Dylan Anthony Reeves," Lincoln says, pride glowing in his eyes as he peers over Peyton's shoulder, down at his son.

"We're calling him Dyl for short," Peyton adds.

Dylan stretches his arms up, his fists curled in tightly as he struggles to open his eyes from his nap. He peeks up at Peyton with his big dark eyes and leans his head back against the sling. "He's beautiful. Absolutely perfect. That chin, my goodness," I say gently sweeping my finger across the slight clef. "I'm just so happy for you two, truly. I know this is a miracle and you deserve to soak up every ounce of this blessing."

Peyton sniffles and nods. "Thank you," she whispers. "I'm so sorry for—"

"No, let's just focus on Dylan," I say.

"I'm warming a bottle, but I hope to see you guys later," Lincoln says, leaving Peyton with a kiss on the cheek.

Peyton steps in toward me and lifts her arm, wrapping it around my neck and kissing my temple. "I shouldn't have avoided you. I couldn't bear to see the pain on your face. My heart hurts for you and it's so full for me at the same time. Nothing feels right, Jenna, and the guilt—it hurts."

"No more guilt. Just happiness. He deserves that, and so do you."

Peyton pulls in a shuttering breath and presses a smile into her trembling lips. Silence breaks up the moment like a light gust of wind until the sound of tires against the pavement draws our attention to the street. "Is that your mom?" she asks, peering past me.

I hold my hand up above my eyes to shield the sun. "It must

be. Oliver thinks I need a babysitter while he's at work," I say, rolling my eyes to brush off the comment as a joke.

"He's been so worried about you, was a wreck while you were at the...the place—hospital. He's a good man. You have an amazing support system."

"The behavioral facility," I say, correcting her, trying to sound unashamed as I force an agreeable smile. He's a good man and supportive—that must be why he had me admitted for psychiatric distress after losing our baby. I hate that I feel like I was discarded and handed over to someone else while at my lowest moment.

FORTY

I'm not sure I've slept more than a dozen hours in the past week. I've filled an entire notepad with passing thoughts on how and why Andrea Lester could be associated with Luanne and poor Tommy. I've stopped trying to figure out how someone could forge an alias online because there seems to be too many opportunities. Plus, I've heard the boys talking about some *night-web* or *dark-net*, a place where hackers congregate. Evidently, anything can happen on that side of the internet. I'm going to have to file a police report before this goes any further, but I'm weighing the risks of that too.

"Motion has been detected at the front door."

After I expressed my apprehension about this situation with Andrea to the boys, Joel threw me a bone and hooked up my doorbell video camera to my kitchen speaker, so now I receive an alert every time something is happening outside. It's kept me from checking the notifications on my phone so often, but I might become conditioned to panic every time I hear this robotic woman's voice. I'm not sure any of the boys are aware of what I've truly been through with Andrea; it was something I didn't want to involve them with.

I take my phone from the coffee table and tap the matching notification on my screen, waiting for the live stream to pop up. The glare from the sun is making it hard to see much, but I can clearly hear a conversation between Peyton and another female. I could be wrong, but it sounds like Jenna.

With a peek outside of my front window, I'm able to make out the top of two heads on Peyton's front porch. The other female has dark hair like Jenna's. It must be her, which means she's home from the psychiatric facility. That was uncalled for, but Oliver was lost and took all of the suggestions he could get.

A dark blue car pulls around the corner, disappears into the glare and doesn't come out the other side. I bet that's Deborah going to stay with Jenna for the day. Oliver hasn't gone back to work, and now that Jenna seems to be home again, the poor thing, he must need to get back on track.

The sound of a door closing is followed by the sound of feet crunching along the street's gravel. "Jenna, what are you doing?"

I'm positive now that Deborah is across the street and Jenna must be walking back home from Peyton's. I don't know how she can face Peyton with a baby. My heart just breaks for what she's going through. I doubt I could even leave my bed, never mind walk across the street.

I don't have any comfort food prepared to bring over, but I also didn't know she was home. Oliver was tight-lipped about the details of her stay at the facility. He was quite the hermit during those few days. I tried to bring him a couple of meals, but they sat on the front porch because he didn't come to the door. He never took them inside.

Willow walks past me and hisses before burrowing herself beneath the curtain I'm tugging on. "I know I'm in your spot. I'll move in just a minute."

"I'll take care of her, just worry about yourself," Deborah shouts. That woman's voice sure does carry. I noticed that the day we went out for lunch. I think the entire restaurant was staring at us because they could hear every word she was saying.

I can't go over there empty-handed. I spin around, facing the kitchen, trying to come up with something I can whip up, but I spot the vase of tulips I plucked from the backyard the other day. I grab the vase with the spring bouquet and head out the front door, across the road.

While waiting for Jenna or Deborah to answer the door, I spin around, noting the glare is just as bad on this side of the street. At least Perfect Peyton won't see me over here, God forbid having a party without her. I haven't even seen her since she had the baby—or so I heard she had the baby from Tanya. I brought a casserole over there too, but no one answered and I'm not sure when they took the food inside. Not even a thank you. I regret being so nice to people sometimes.

Deborah answers the door with her hand held above her eyes. "That sun is ferocious today," she says, holding her arm out to welcome me inside. "How are you doing, dear?" She gives me a tight hug. "Thank you again for the thoughtful call last week."

"Don't mention it," I whisper. I don't want Jenna to wonder why I was calling Deborah. As a mom, I know how awful it can be to watch your child go through something so traumatic. I figured she might need a shoulder to lean on too.

"Come on in. Would you like some coffee?"

"I don't want to be a bother." I'm curiously scanning the room, not surprised to see all the baby furniture and accessories tucked away. It doesn't look like there was ever a thought about a baby here.

"Oh, nonsense. Sit down. Jenna's changing her clothes upstairs, but she'll be back down in a minute. Make yourself comfortable while I pour you a cup in the kitchen."

The moment Deborah disappears into the kitchen, a series of thuds grows louder from the top of the stairwell.

"Mom, I have the bottle," Jenna shouts from upstairs.

The bottle?

She's quick to make her way downstairs and my confusion clears up upon noticing a pill bottle rattling in a plastic bag.

"Ginger..." she says, stopping a few steps from the bottom. "I didn't know you were here."

The poor girl is so pale and the dark circles beneath her eyes tell stories of their own.

"I brought you flowers," I say, pointing to the vase of tulips I set down on the coffee table.

"Thank you. You didn't have to do that," she says, holding the pills behind her back.

"Oh, sweetie, it's nothing."

Jenna takes the last few steps and walks past me, slowly, clearly lost in thought. "Ginger, you mentioned using a doorbell camera once, didn't you?" I'm not sure I did tell her that, but I'm confident Peyton would have shared that information.

"I don't recall, but yes, I do use one. It gives me some peace of mind at night."

"Do you keep the footage?" she asks, staring across the room toward the kitchen. She hasn't made eye contact with me once.

"I do, yes." I'm not sure where she's going with this inquisition.

"How hard would it be to find some evidence that my husband is having an affair with someone?"

My body instantly turns cold. "An affair?" I choke out.

An uneasy smile tickles her lips. "Yes."

"I—gosh, I don't know. I haven't personally seen anything, but I don't watch all the footage." It would take me hours every day to go through it all, especially since I chose the full-time coverage plan. "I'm sure Oliver woul—"

Deborah turns the corner from the kitchen with two coffee cups in her hand. She eyeballs her daughter first then me, likely wondering what she has walked into.

"Mom, the midwife I had—I just found out she didn't have a medical license, that she lost it due to malpractice as an obstetrician. Isn't that odd?"

I'm staring at Jenna's profile, but I can tell she hasn't blinked since Deborah walked into the living room.

"What in the world are you talking about?" Deborah asks, her hands trembling as she places the coffees down on two coasters.

"The case worker at the Ashlyn Behavioral Health Center found out, and the doctor called to inform me this morning, which means River didn't have a medical examiner sign off on his death certificate because Celeste doesn't have the ability to do that either. If she didn't, I need to find out who did. But, despite all of this news, Oliver also somehow imagined us having a conversation where I said I wanted to have our newborn son cremated. So, do you still think I killed my son, Mom?" Jenna folds her arms tightly over her chest, her fists balled into stones. She's out of breath from talking so furiously and fast, and the firm clench of her jaw puckers the skin around her mouth.

I gasp and lift my hand up to my mouth. I shake my head and nervously glance over at Deborah, wondering if she really believes Jenna could harm her sweet little boy.

"Cremated?" Deborah asks. I don't think that would have been my first reply. "I thought—you—"

"I wouldn't cremate anyone unless it was their dying wish," Jenna says firmly.

"I know that. You've made that quite clear throughout the years, ever since Granny passed away."

"Yeah," Jenna says.

"What's Celeste's last name, if you don't mind me asking?" I'm tempting my luck just entering this conversation, but I know the midwife was Peyton's plan plotted into Jenna and Oliver's head.

"Brown. Celeste Brown."

The name sounds familiar to me and I'm not sure why. Perhaps one of the girls mentioned her at some point over the last few months, but maybe not.

I'm so hung up on every bit of what Jenna's saying, I almost forgot about her initial question regarding my video footage. "Do you think Oliver would cheat on you with the midwife?" I ask. It doesn't make sense.

Jenna's shoulders fall upon hearing my question out loud. "She's quite a bit older than he is, but something isn't right." I think she's barking up the wrong tree, but I don't want to put any other ideas into her head when I have no proof. "I bet she's the one who mixed up my pills, switching the over-the-counter pain relievers out for opioids. It was to cover her for her mistakes, to make me delusional."

While she's working herself up over possible conspiracies, I'm feeling the same since I wasn't aware of any pill swapping, but it might explain the state of delirium Jenna found herself in.

"Jenna, sweetie, I think you're taking this too far. Stillbirths occur daily," Deborah says.

"Then why did you think I might have something to do with his death?" Jenna fires back.

Deborah steps to the side and drops onto the sofa beside me like a sack of flour, hugging herself tightly. Her breaths are heavy and quick. She's going to hyperventilate. "I shouldn't have said that to you. I was angry for you—at you, I guess, at myself for not fighting you harder about being in the hospital."

"I was in a psychiatric facility, Mom. That's what you said to me and then left—you left me screaming for you like a little girl would call for her mother as she's being kidnapped. Do you have any clue what that did to me?"

Now I'm wishing I didn't come across the street. If this was the lesson I needed to learn in order to stop barging in on people, so help me God, I will never knock on another door again.

"Okay," I say, standing up. "Jenna, come here." My nerves are firing through every vein in my body as I take a hold of Jenna's arm and tug her into the kitchen. "I'm not going to defend what your mom did. I understand your anger and why you are upset. You have every right to be, but I think you're both asking the same questions about the wrong people. Do you understand?"

Jenna's eyes fill with tears and strands of her hair fall to the side of her face as the first tear falls. "No, I don't. I feel like the world is caving in on me right now. Why do I feel that way? What if—what if I did something to River and then blocked it out?"

Her questions are full of logic for a person going through a mental breakdown. "Sweetie, I studied psychology for years. What you're saying is possible, yes, it can happen, but as a bystander—" Wait. A bystander. "Why wasn't your mom here when you were in labor?"

"Oliver tried to call her, but she must have fallen asleep."

"What?" Deborah shouts from the other room, obviously listening to everything we've said.

We step back into the living room, facing an appalled look on Deborah's flush face.

"Oliver tried to call you several times," Jenna repeats.

"I didn't get one phone call, Jenna. Not one. The only call I received was from Oliver at six in the morning, telling me River was stillborn and it all happened so fast that there was nothing you could do."

Jenna stares at a spot in the middle of the living room as if she's imagining the scene laid out in front of her. "I was in labor for hours. My water broke not long after Oliver got home from work that night and when I asked about you, he said it was well into the middle of the night and you must have fallen asleep. That you must not have heard the phone ringing."

Dear God. No one has been pointing a finger at Oliver... Why would he lie though? What possible motivation could he have?

"I'm ashamed to say I was at the front door around seven that night," I say. "I saw Peyton run across the street here with a bag of supplies and then noticed a car pull into the driveway that I didn't recognize. I got worried something was wrong, so I rang the bell several times until Peyton peeked out from the top window of your door. She ignored me as if I was a stray animal on the front porch, but I thought she was just being petty and wanted to be the only person here to help you." That sounds as ridiculous as it felt that night, but I regretted coming over here, knowing Jenna was overdue and having a home birth. It was none of my business, but I made it my business like I have a bad habit of doing.

"Maybe Oliver asked Peyton to call me, and then she didn't," Deborah says. "Jealousy can bring the worst out in people sometimes."

I know that better than most. I'll spend the rest of my life running away from the cruelty of what jealousy can do to a person.

"I'm going to the pharmacy to pick up something I need," I announce. Ginger and Mom are acting like two forensic investigators with a notepad, and I don't have time for this.

"Okay," Mom says, waving her hand at me. "Wait. No. I'm supposed to be staying with you. You're not running errands." I already assumed this would be the case, and I'm sure no matter how much I argue, I won't get far so I'll have to manage with her tagging along.

"Have you questioned why Oliver insists that I need a babysitter? Do you think maybe you're being manipulated to believe I'm insane?" Mom is staring at me, her eyes bulging as if my questions couldn't make any less sense. I might as well go find a magnifying glass and start searching for clues.

"I'm going with you," she says. "I won't take no for an answer, and I'm driving."

"Fine, whatever you want to do."

"What is it that you need? Maybe I have it at my house?" Ginger offers.

"You don't," I reply. "It's personal."

"I see," Ginger says, standing up. "Well, maybe I'll take this time to finally go across the street and offer my well wishes too."

I wonder if Peyton has been avoiding her? I imagine she doesn't have any intention of inviting Ginger in to meet Dylan if she was going as far as to avoid me all this time. It's as if she's worried someone will judge her in her role of being a new mom.

I'm thankful Mom had the decency to wait in the car while I ran into the pharmacy to collect the items I needed. But now that I'm slipping back into the car, I notice her knuckles are white with her hands gripping the steering wheel. "What are you going to do with those prescription pain pills? Is that why you need to go to the pharmacy? I'm confused," she says before I can even reach for my seat belt.

"No, I just needed some melatonin—something natural, to help me sleep. It's not a big deal. I'm bringing the bottle of opioids to the police department with the hope that they will check the bottle for fingerprints."

"What good is that going to do? What if they are your fingerprints?" I used a latex glove to lift the bottle of opioid pain relievers out of my nightstand and drop it into the plastic bag. If my fingerprints are what they find, then at least I'll know I'm capable of making horrible decisions when I'm at my worst.

"I can rule myself out of the equation, and Celeste would have fingerprints registered in the database due to her former license. If someone was drugging me, I need to know."

"I agree," Mom says, backing out of the parking spot.

The shock from her response draws my gaze toward her face, seeking to confirm she is on the same page as I am, but all I see are heavy eyelids and a deep frown line.

I figured she would tell me to take a step back and consider the facts again before involving law enforcement. "You agree with me?"

"Yes, I know things have been very difficult for you, but you're my daughter, and I know how many times I have had to plead with you to take an over-the-counter pain reliever, never mind something so strong. It's just hard to think someone would trick you into taking them." Mom sighs and swallows hard then briefly places her hand on my knee.

"I don't have many other options right now."

"I know, sweetie."

I slouch into my seat and pull down the visor, flipping the top up from the mirror. I stare at my complexion and touch my fingertip to the center of my chin.

Mom glances over for a quick second then returns her focus to the road. "Are you okay?"

"Yes, my skin is dry."

"You might be dehydrated. Did you stop taking the folic acid? That could be the cause too."

I close my eyes and flip the visor back up, needing to stop the barrage of incoming questions.

The ride from the pharmacy to my house is hardly five minutes each way, but it feels like an hour when all I want to do is be alone with my thoughts. It's clear that won't be happening anytime soon when I spot Ginger trotting across the street toward us just as we pull into the driveway.

"She is incessant. Please don't invite her in again right now," I utter.

Mom doesn't argue. I'll happily tell Ginger I need some quiet if she can't take a hint. I hardly have one foot out of the car when she takes my wrist. "What are you doing?" I snap.

"I need to talk to you inside right now."

"Is everything okay, Ginger?" Mom asks, her voice hoarse with concern.

"No, not at all," she says before closing us into the house and locking the door.

. . .

After a daunting day of forming notes and a timeline to keep track of what has happened to me over the last few weeks, my mind is even more numb and exhausted now, but sleeping isn't an option. Thankfully, adrenaline is keeping me awake, my eyes fixed on the picture frame across the room, dimly lit up by the wall-plug nightlight below. It's a wedding portrait—a photo taken just after our lifelong vows were made. I've been staring at the innocent smiles on our faces for hours since we went to bed, wondering how I can be questioning so much right now.

It's just about two in the morning and I think it's late enough at night to do what I need to do. He's snoring like a lawnmower and drooling like a teething toddler. An alarm clock can hardly wake him in the morning so I shouldn't have trouble sneaking out.

I'm careful to roll off the side of the bed and tiptoe out of the bedroom, snatching my midnight-blue robe and matching slippers on the way out.

While crossing the quiet street against the tepid current of air, I take a moment to stare up at the farmer's moon with a subtle red halo highlighting the few scattered clouds within the glow. Where the moonlight fades, the stars vividly glitter into the distance. I take out a pair of latex gloves I'd hid in my pocket last night, knowing I can't leave a trace of me anywhere. The last few steps are accompanied by the sound of an owl hooting in the distance.

The side door of the attached garage uses the same key as the front door, or at least it does for my house. In Peyton's case, I doubt I need a key to the side door because she brags about never having to lock it in our safe neighborhood. I use the screen of my phone to light up a path through the junk in their garage, ensuring I don't trip over anything while I make my way toward the interior door. I hold my breath as I twist the knob, wondering if they would lock this door and not the other. I have her spare key in case she ever gets locked out, but the quieter I am, the better off I'll be.

The door is unlocked as I assumed and leads me right into the hallway between their living room and stairwell. I've always been the good girl, the rule follower, but even the innocent have a breaking point. My heart hammers like a nail being forced into a thick post of wood in the dead of night, so thunderous, I wonder if anyone else can hear what I feel. I try to swallow against the dryness in my throat, but every muscle in my body is so tight and stiff, I can hardly blink.

Dim nightlights along the wall offer me enough visibility to make it upstairs without the use of my phone display. As I step out of my slippers and pad up the stairs in my thick socks, my ankles shiver as if I'm cold and I'm begging my toes not to crack like they often do. I find relief when I spot a light carousel blinking from the last room on the right. That's not Peyton and Lincoln's bedroom. The main bedrooms are on the opposite side of the garage.

White noise grows louder the closer I get to Dylan's bedroom. My chest grows heavy, and my breaths weaken as fear fights against adrenaline.

I'm surprised he's already asleep in his own crib. I thought most parents kept their baby with them for at least the first month or so, but what do I know? I'm not a mother.

Dylan's room is carpeted, swallowing up any slight sound I could possibly make. Lavender and baby powder are the only scents to take in—a mother's dream. He's swaddled in a receiving blanket, fast asleep with a pacifier dangling from his lips. I spot the baby monitor attached to the top of his crib and reach around the back to slowly nudge the lens to the left, praying it doesn't create an alert. We ended up adding the same baby monitors to our registries, both opted for one that doesn't send alerts for motion, only choking, cries, or if the baby stops breathing. *The studies have shown an increase in anxiety for parents when they are awoken to every small noise or movement from their baby.* I'm not sure what happens if the camera moves, though.

I hold my breath for a long few seconds, waiting to hear if Peyton or Lincoln stir.

The white noise is all I can hear.

I need to get this done. I reach into my pocket...Oh my God, no. No, no, no. My hand is so unsteady, a piece of paper I need slips out of my pocket and falls beneath the crib. This can't be happening. This is why good girls shouldn't do bad things. I kneel to feel around blindly in the dark, sweeping my hand across the carpet until I find the small piece of paper, but as I'm pulling my hand back, another scrap of paper rubs against my wrist. Without knowing which is which, I take both pieces and shove them back into my pocket, before pushing myself back up to my feet.

It's now or never, Jenna. Come on, I tell myself. Just as I reach my shaking hand toward Dylan, a cell phone ring impales the white noise and silence from down the hall. *It's two in the morning.*

Shit, I need to get out of here. Panic drives through me again like that hammering nail into wood.

I scurry into the hallway and continue down the stairs, holding my breath, praying the phone keeps ringing...

I step into my slippers and the ring stops.

"What?" is all I hear by the time I reach the interior garage door. I slip through a small opening and take my chances on tripping over every gardening tool they failed to put away. I manage to make it through, only kicking one small metal item to the side. My hands are out in front of me, searching for the side door in the darkness, and I find it just as a thunderous set of footsteps sound from within the house.

"Who's there?" Lincoln shouts at the top of his lungs.

Floodlights blare from the front of the garage, and I have no way to cross the street without moving through the blazing glow so I make my way toward Ginger's house to the right. I chug through her grass and into the backyard where her sliding porch doors are.

My hands are sweating inside of the gloves and my fingers are shaking so fiercely, I have trouble searching for Ginger's contact, but I manage to find it after a minute. I lower the volume, worried about who might be listening and press the phone to my ear, pleading she picks up.

"Dear God, are you all right?" she answers.

"Can you let me in through your back door? Quick."

"Why are you outside? Did someone try to break into your house too? The police are on their way. Don't worry, but I'm coming."

"No, no, no one tried to break into our house. No police are needed. Please, just—"

A light goes on and I see her punching in numbers to the keypad of her alarm system in the hallway.

"Alarm mode: disarmed," a robotic voice announces. It's loud enough to hear through the glass.

Ginger approaches the sliding door, unlatching a top lock and a bottom lock before sliding the glass over far enough for me to shimmy inside. Before saying a word, she locks the door and pulls me toward her stairwell to shut off the light in the hallway then re-arms her house alarm.

"Alarm mode: armed."

"What in God's name are you doing at my back door at this hour?"

"I—I—" I can't catch my breath. I didn't realize I was out of breath until right at this moment.

"I just got a neighborhood alert that a camera spotted an intruder on Peyton and Lincoln's lawn. The alert said the police were called."

All I can manage to do is shake my head. I thought Ginger was the only one in proximity with a doorbell camera.

"It was me. I went into their house like I told you I was going to do earlier," I confess through a whimper.

"You did not tell me you were going to do that," she shrills. "I would have asked you if you were out of your mind."

Again, my breaths quicken, and my pulse is so fast, I feel dizzy. "I did tell you. I know I did."

Ginger squeezes my arm and rattles me. "Jenna, snap out of it. Why would you break into their house?"

"Because of what you said earlier," I say.

"I understand—it's important and something you needed to know, Jenna, but like I also said to you, this matter needs to be handled with caution or you won't stand a chance of finding out what you need. What were you doing there?"

For someone who seems to hold more secrets than anyone else in this neighborhood, she's awfully demanding of information from me now, but I'm going to need an alibi.

"I needed to know if there was something going on between Oliver and Peyton. After what you said...the pieces just started coming together. Wouldn't you need to know?"

Ginger leans back against the curled scroll of her staircase railing. "By breaking into their house in the middle of the night? What were you hoping to find? Why would you take that risk?"

Ginger holds up her weight using the railing but eases herself down onto the step. I follow and sit beside her and a piece of paper falls out of my pocket, onto Ginger's bottom step. She leans forward, picking it up before I do.

"Is this yours?" she asks, standing up to reach the light switch. The upstairs hall light illuminates and shines over the paper in her hand. It's a receipt from Boutique Baby.

Ginger points to the cardholder's name beneath the x's of the credit card number. I stare at the name as Ginger clutches her chest.

"No, no, no...how could I not know?" she cries out, her eyes widening.

"I know this name too."

It doesn't matter how much time passes. No one can ever be sure that the person they think they know isn't hiding in the darkness, lurking like a living nightmare, waiting to attack.

FORTY-TWO

GINGER | NOW

I hear the distant blare of sirens, but I know the closer they get, the more panic will ensue. No law enforcement official would use a siren in the middle of the night unless there was a reason to alert everyone. An intruder is a reason to alert people, but I don't think the intruder is who they should be worried about.

"Where does Oliver think you are?" I ask Jenna as I pace the living room like a mouse trapped in a shoebox.

Jenna is pale, her eyes are red, and she's trembling. For as well as I believe I've come to know her, I'm quite sure she's never been in this sort of trouble before. She doesn't even know what I know, and I'm not sure she understands the gravity of what she's uncovered. A familiar cold sweat skates down my arms and legs along with a wave of nausea. I can hardly get myself to focus on Jenna, and this is about her, not me. She needs me.

"I don't care where he thinks I am," she says, crumpling the receipt in her hand.

"If they come to the door and question me, I might need to tell them you're here and why," I say, trying to remain calm when my past is flashing before me, unwinding, developing, resolving, and becoming clearer by the moment.

"Um—" Jenna says, staring up toward the ceiling in thought. "Tell them you weren't feeling well and you called me to come stay with you for a bit tonight, but only if they ask. Oliver might not know I'm gone, and he would say we were asleep."

"Okay." An alibi should not be our first concern, but she doesn't know that.

"Who posted the neighborhood alert?" Jenna asks.

"Tanya. She must have had a camera installed too. I know she was having trouble with some missing package deliveries." Tanya is the least of our worries, but Jenna doesn't know that either.

"Would she have seen me come over here? Would she be able to make out who the person was?"

"Not with the floodlights Lincoln installed," I say just as the sirens echo through the house. Flashing lights dancing along my closed blinds, bleeding in through the narrow cracks. "Let's go upstairs."

I lead Jenna up to my bedroom, only lit by the glow from the television. "You sleep with the TV on too?"

I take a seat on the end of my bed, staring at the rerun of court TV. "I've never liked going to bed with the TV on, but James couldn't fall asleep without it, so it was something I learned to live with." Much like James himself.

Jenna shoves the receipt into her bathrobe pocket. "Ginger, how do you know Andrea Lester?"

I've only had a few minutes to prepare myself for this question and I'm still coming to terms with how ignorant I've been, not knowing I've been living next door to a woman who has a severe vendetta against me.

2019

My phone rests in the center of the kitchen table and I stare at it, wondering when we got to a point in time when technology became a leash. I should have gotten a separate work phone – my phone number is only supposed to be used in case of an emergency.

Fifteen text messages have come through in the last hour, but that's nothing compared to the last few weeks of bombarding messages. I've explained the definition of an emergency, but Andrea Lester has become reliant upon my advice and help, and it's gotten to the point where she can't decide about a meal without attempting to consult with me first. I have followed protocol and told her to write down all her questions for our next session, but it's like she's testing me, and I don't understand why.

I can only assume she might be crying out for attention, which leaves me with a heavy blanket of guilt. She needs more than online therapy, and I've provided her with names and numbers to call. It's become obvious that I can't give her what she needs.

"Ginger, honey, just turn the phone off and come to bed," James says, locking up the house and turning off the downstairs lights. "You can't keep giving in to her. It's unhealthy for both of you." I want nothing more than to agree with James, but what he's suggesting could be damaging.

"It could be considered abandonment to a patient if I shut my phone off," I tell him. Although, Dr. Garmen did say I need to set boundaries. I thought I had. To be honest, I'm not sure this qualifies as abandonment when Andrea has chosen to abuse the privilege of having my phone number. Then again, she is suffering and has been for years. I know very well that there is no time limit when it comes to moving on from trauma, and cognitive behavioral therapy can take time. Of course, there are also some patients who don't ever seem to get better, no matter how much therapy and counseling they receive. Andrea and I have been working together for almost four months, and though I thought there was a bit of improvement, she's taken a turn for the worse this past month. "I'll be up in a minute. I promise."

"Okay, but you need to report this incident and the others from the last few weeks to Dr. Garmen tomorrow. Ultimately, it's his decision on how he wants to handle and treat this patient."

I take my phone and scroll down through the list of her messages, asking random questions, stating facts about trauma victims, and ideas for coping mechanisms that I have already suggested. She seems to reframe a lot of my suggestions to sound as if they are her own. With the hope of one last attempt to console her today, I type out a response.

Me: *Andrea, I need to put my phone down for the night. Our next appointment will be the perfect time to go over these questions and ideas. I have a family to tend to and I can't be available at all hours of the day to talk. However, if you feel this is an emergency and need immediate care, you can call 9-1-1. Also, as another reminder, our text messages are not monitored or protected, and it's important to keep personal matters to our secure chat session.*

I watch the dots beneath my message, warning of an incoming response. The flickering ellipses act like a slow pulse on my screen for several minutes before her response displays.

Andrea Lester: *Your husband isn't ill or suffering from past traumas. He doesn't need help like I do. Plus, you said your children are grown, the youngest is never home. But me, I need you, and you aren't helping me. It's your job to help me.*

She's officially crossed a line as she has come close to doing before. I haven't mentioned anything about my private life aside from having a husband and four sons, the youngest getting ready for college. The one line of information is at the bottom of my medical biography, and it's the only personal fact I added to help patients know I'm not some online bot, but a real person with a passion to help others overcome their struggles.

> **Me:** *I understand how you feel, Andrea. Tomorrow morning, I'm going to put you in contact with Dr. Garmen to reassess your condition and assign you to a new therapist who might be a better fit for what you're looking for regarding support. I will see to this first thing in the morning, but for now, we must put this conversation on hold until then. As we've spoken about, try some of your breathing techniques and write down all of your thoughts.*

The stress of sending an unstable patient off to self-treat at this time of night makes me very nervous, but there isn't much else I can do for her. I know I've gone above and beyond to offer her support. Despite how I might feel, I'm not responsible for her actions.

> **Me:** *Again, if you feel this is an emergency, please do call 9-1-1 for immediate care.*

Today

"She was my patient when I was working as an online therapist assisting a psychiatrist." *Patient confidentiality.* Everything she told me would remain private unless she were to become a threat to someone else. "How do you know Andrea?" I return the question before saying anything more.

Jenna crosses her arms over her chest and leans back against the wall. She takes in a lungful of air and releases it slowly through pursed lips. "Andrea Lester is Oliver's ex-girlfriend. I've never met her in person or spoken to her, but she's called Oliver on many occasions, and now everything seems to make so much sense."

I lift my hand to my mouth. "I never met her in person. Which is why neither of us would recognize Peyton to be Andrea Lester."

Jenna slides down the length of the wall until she's on the ground and wraps her arms around her knees, pulling them into her chest. "It can't possibly be a coincidence that we ended up living across the street from her, right? I just don't understand why Oliver would put me through this—for what reason? I didn't force him to marry me, to choose me."

"I'm not sure I could think any of this is a coincidence either," I agree.

"Peyton's—Andrea's baby has a cleft chin, like Oliver. Do you think that could be a coincidence?" Jenna asks, touching her finger to the center of her chin as she stares through me with unblinking eyes.

I was wondering if Jenna had noticed the baby's chin too.

My doorbell rings just as I assumed it would. "We have nothing to hide, you have to come downstairs and answer the door with me." Jenna continues staring past me and I'm not sure she's listening to me or even heard the doorbell ring. "Jenna, come on. Everything will be okay." I'm lying. Nothing is going to be okay. Jenna doesn't know half of the reasons why nothing will be okay, but I can't let her take the fall for what she did. I try to pull her up to her feet, but she's like a lead weight.

The bell rings again and if I let it go much longer, they might have reason to speculate I know something. God knows, Peyton—Andrea—would throw me to the police like a piece of meat into a lion's den.

I tighten my robe and amble down the stairs alone, fumbling with the alarm system again.

"Alarm mode: disarmed."

I make my way to the front door and fuss with the deadbolt and doorknob then open the door with hesitancy, just a crack at first. "Lakespur Police. We're very sorry for disturbing you so late at night, but it's important we speak."

I open the door more and push my hair back off my forehead because I just woke up and I must be a mess. "What's—what's going on?" I press my fingers into the corners of my eyes because of how bright their lights are outside.

A young, tall officer with the build and stature of a member of the armed forces stands, somewhat robotic with one hand on his hip and the other on the radio above his shirt pocket. I don't recognize him, but it isn't often I have encounters with those who run the night-shift hours. He must be around Michael's age, and I wonder if they know each other. As my eyes adjust to the flashing lights, I spot a second officer looking through the shrubs beneath my front window, a flashlight in hand. I'm not sure anything larger than Willow would fit under there though. "There was an intruder next door and we aren't sure where this person is now. Have you witnessed anything unusual or heard anything that might help us?"

"Next door? At the Reeves residence?" I ask, pointing to Lincoln and Peyton's house.

"Yes, ma'am."

I clutch my chest and loosen my jaw to offer a look of shock. "I—my goodness. Well, thankfully my security system alarm has been on since the sun went down. I was asleep and I didn't hear anything at all. Are they all right next door? Was anything taken?"

"No, they're fine, thankfully. We have some doorbell footage from your neighbor across the street, but unfortunately the perpetrator is a blur because of the flood lights next door. If you happen to come across any evidence, please let the police department know right away, ma'am. Again, I'm sorry to disturb you so late at night. You won't mind if we check your perimeter, will you?" I'd like to tell him the other officer is already well underway in doing so, but I'd rather end this conversation.

"Of course not. In fact, I would feel much better if you do."

"Keep that alarm set. It's good you have that." The officer tips his head and backs away from the door.

"Thank you and goodnight." I close the door, secure the locks then the alarm, and head back upstairs to find Jenna.

I could have told the officer what I know about Peyton—who she really is, but there will be questions of how I came across the information and why I didn't report it to Officer Drell. I shouldn't know her as anyone other than Peyton Reeves, but Andrea Lester—an unstable woman suffering from trauma disorder—has a history of keeping her enemies close by. I know from personal experience.

FORTY-THREE

JENNA | NOW

I can't go back home, but Oliver will know I'm not there when he wakes up in the morning.

It's almost four in the morning. The police have cleared out of the neighborhood and if I don't go back home in the dark, someone will see me coming out of Ginger's house in the morning which will require another set of explanations.

I've been sitting on the floor, leaning against Ginger's bed, staring mindlessly at the TV. Ginger is still pacing. She's making me dizzy.

"I should go back home before the sun rises."

Ginger stops pacing and stares down at me with her hands on her hips. "I don't know if that's such a good idea."

"He doesn't know anything that happened tonight, I'm sure. If he thought I was missing, he would have already rung your doorbell, trust me."

"No," Ginger says, pressing her palm against her forehead. "Jenna, if Peyton is Andrea Lester and Andrea Lester is Oliver's ex-girlfriend or whatever they were—I know all about their past, what Oliver did to make Andrea the way she is now. He ruined her life."

I pull myself up along the bed, needing to be eye-level with Ginger as I connect the dots. She is blindly accusing Oliver of being the statutory rape Peyton told me about...the forced abortion. "How do you know it was Oliver?" I want to prove her wrong, more than anything. But how did we end up here, living right across the street?

"Her ex-boyfriend was a physics professor at Lakespur University who needed to keep his job when his student, Andrea, ended up pregnant from their fling. He brought her to a back-alley clinic to handle the pregnancy. He was thirty—in a position of authority. She was seventeen, just a month shy of eighteen, in her freshman year. It was a felony."

My jaw falls like a fishhook caught my lip. My stomach cramps and I fold in half, squeezing against the pain in my midsection. "No," I cry out.

Ginger scoops her arm around me and pulls me up, into her chest. My mind is racing, thousands of thoughts coming at me from every direction. The possibilities of what happened, what could have happened, the lies, the few truths, what I'm supposed to do, or how I'm supposed to...

"Wait," I gasp. "You said he brought her to a back-alley clinic where she got the abortion?"

"Yes," Ginger answers quietly. "Now I remember where I had heard the name Celeste Brown before."

I shake my head and ball up my fists, pressing them into the sides of my face. "Don't say it, please," I sob. "Please."

"It was three years ago that I read that name in Andrea's file, but as soon as you mentioned Celeste Brown, it felt like I had seen the name just yesterday. I just couldn't remember where..."

The weight of my despair pulls me back down to the ground, slipping out of Ginger's arms. "I must go to the police. She killed my baby, and she drugged me."

"If you're not up to it, I can call your mom and tell her

what's going on. Then, I'll take you to the police department so she can meet you there."

The kindness Ginger is showing me, mixed with the pain reeling through me, coils me into a ball, wishing I could make everything stop.

Oliver knows my father abandoned me. He promised me he could never do such an awful thing to his child. I didn't stop to ask if he would do it to his wife. Maybe he's only with me because I'm a child law attorney...if I ever found out the truth about his past, he probably thought I could protect him and keep him from losing his job. Everything has been a lie and I have nothing to show for it, other than the world soon finding out how terrible of an attorney I must be if I was living with a sexual predator, one responsible for statutory rape, and I had no idea. He's stolen my life from me, just like he did to Andrea, and I was just a puzzle piece of Andrea's revenge plan.

"She's beside herself. It's been two hours and she's still on the floor of my bedroom curled into a ball. She cried herself to sleep so I decided to wait a bit before calling you, hoping to spare you from a middle of the night heart attack call." Ginger is louder than she must realize and I'm not sure I agreed to her calling Mom for me, but I don't have the energy to tell her. "How long do you need? I'll bring her to the police station as soon as you're ready."

Ginger walks toward me and crouches down to her knees, sweeping her hand over my cheek. *I'm awake.* I just don't want to be.

"We should get going. Your mom said she'd meet us at the police station in a half hour." I'm not even sure what time it is. My phone is still in my pocket, but the battery might be dead, or Oliver could be asleep still. Once he realizes I'm not there, I don't know what he'll do but I don't want to be here when he does find out.

I push myself up, feeling the blood rushing to my head.

"Do you want some tea or coffee before we go?"

I shake my head, feeling like there's water sloshing around between my ears. It doesn't take me long to assess my appearance, the robe, a Lakespur University T-shirt that I'd burn if I had something else clean to wear, my black sweatpants, and fuzzy dark blue slippers. I empty my robe pocket, moving the contents into the loose pocket on the side of my sweatpants. "I'll leave the robe here," I utter.

"I'm not sure what size shoe you are, but I have a pair of running shoes in a size seven if you want to wear those. You look to be about the same size as me."

"I'm sure they'll fit. Thank you."

It doesn't take us long to slip into Ginger's car, which she thankfully secures in her garage unlike the rest of us. "If you just slouch down, no one will notice you in the car as we make our way off the street," she says. I want to say to her that it seems like she's done this before. She has solutions for everything, and I feel like I'm lost in the middle of the woods, without survival skills.

I didn't check my phone before dropping it into my pocket, but I slip it out once we're on the main road outside the neighborhood. The battery is dead and that gives me a slight sense of relief.

"The police might not listen to a word I say, you know. If anyone finds out I was just admitted to the Ashlyn Behavioral Health Center, they'll chalk up my story to nonsense."

"No, I don't think that'll be the case," Ginger says.

She's probably just saying that to ease my nerves, but not much can help with that now. Ginger continues talking and I'm not sure I've heard one word she's said in the last few minutes. Even as we pass a political rally with shouting protestors all stabbing picket signs into the air as we enter downtown, it can't distract me from the barrage of darkening thoughts swarming through my mind.

Mom is already parked and waiting for us. I just want to jump out of Ginger's car and run into her arms, wishing her embrace could fix me like it used to when I was a kid.

No words are exchanged as we all step out of the cars and I fall into Mom, burying my face in her shoulder. "I told you I will always take care of you, and I don't care if you're in your thirties or fifties, I will always be here," she whispers in my ear. Tears burn the backs of my eyes again but I need to keep it together so I can file this report calmly.

The three of us walk through the first set of glass doors of the police station and wait for the woman behind the front desk to release the locks on the second set of doors. The buzzer sounds like the abrupt alert of a wrong answer on a gameshow.

I wish this was a gameshow, winning everything one minute and going home with nothing the next. That seems to sum up my life now.

"How can I help you?" the woman says, taking a moment to study each one of us.

"My daughter needs to file a police report and needs advice on how to handle a domestic situation," Mom says.

The woman behind the desk must think I'm incapable of speaking for myself so I step forward. "Why don't we start with your name, birthday, and address," she says, holding her focus on me. I find her name badge between taking in her questions and forming the answers. Pamela.

"Jenna Milligan, February eighth, nineteen-eighty-seven, two-forty-two Sapphire Road, here in Lakespur."

"Okay, perfect," she says, typing my information into her computer. "What's going on?"

I take a moment to collect my thoughts, knowing there are just too many to assemble in a way that will make sense. "I have reason to assume my husband is responsible for an unreported crime involving my neighbor who I believe to be Andrea Lester but goes by the name Peyton Reeves—Reeves is her married name. I recently gave birth at home after being convinced to do so by Andrea and my husband, and Andrea introduced me to an unlicensed midwife. My child was stillborn, though I still question the validity of that, because I can't remember much of anything, from minutes after the birth until nearly a week later because drugs were found in my system, and I don't think I took them on my own—I wouldn't. I've never taken or used drugs. I was brought to Ashlyn Behavioral Health Center because of my delirium and found out there that my baby was dead. Andrea also had a baby around the same time and her child has genetic features—a cleft chin—like my husband. I'm not sure what to think, but I'm questioning everything that has happened to me, and I am in the right frame of mind, despite what my husband wanted me to think." I'm out of breath as I finish my explanation because my heart is racing so hard. The little air I have left in my lungs leaves me needing to gasp.

Pamela seems to have kept up with me, typing out every word I spoke. "Okay, so you have reason to believe your husband has had extra marital affairs with Andrea Lester and believe they had something to do with the death of your child due to the uncertified midwife?"

"Yes, ma'am." She summarized my story so simply as if it isn't as hard to believe as I thought.

"Do you know the name of the midwife who delivered your baby?" Pamela asks.

"Celeste Brown."

"I'm going to go speak with one of our officers on duty and fill him in. He'll be out to speak with you shortly. You can have a seat in the lobby just behind you."

The chairs remind me of the ones in the lobby of Ashlyn

Behavioral Health Center and I feel like I'm going back in time, to when everything was foggy and unclear.

"They're going to need some form of proof," Ginger says, placing her hands down flat on her lap.

"I have a bottle of pills at home that may or may not have my fingerprints on them along with someone else's."

Ginger doesn't respond and Mom just takes my hand within hers.

The kerplunk of iron locks unhinging echoes between the walls as an officer stalks through the secure doors to the side of the front desk. His tall, brute figure in uniform makes me feel small within this tight space. "Folks, good morning," he greets us. "I'm officer—Mrs. Fowler, I wasn't expecting to see you out here this morning. How are you?"

"Officer Drell," Ginger says. "It's so good to see you again. I'm well, and I heard you were finally able to catch up with Joel for a bit?"

"Yes, ma'am. It was nice to spend some time with him. It's been too long."

Ginger knows this officer and I'm not sure if that's going to help or hurt my situation.

Officer Drell clears his throat and redirects his attention to me. "Pamela filled me in on your statement." He glances back to Ginger. "I see we've located Andrea Lester."

"What do you mean?" I ask.

"Why don't you come back into a room where we can speak privately. All three of you can come."

We give each other a fleeting glance but follow the officer through a set of secured doors and then into a small, empty, white-washed room with only a faux wooden table and four white plastic chairs.

We all take a seat, each of us just as stiff as the other. Ginger drops her head as Officer Drell peers over at her first before speaking. "I truly didn't know I was living next door to her," she says. "She goes by the name of Peyton Reeves."

Officer Drell narrows his eyes at Ginger as if he's trying to read between her words. "You said you didn't know of any Andrea Lester, didn't you?" An ache swells through my forehead and temples as I stare at Ginger, wondering what Officer Drell is talking about. Is this not the first he's spoken to her about Andrea?

"I did," Ginger says, shame lacing her words. "I had an Andrea Lester as a patient once, it was confidential, and when you were asking, I didn't think it was possible you were asking about the same Andrea Lester because it had been years since I had treated her, and she wasn't from the area."

Officer Drell appears uncomfortable as he tugs his belt up beneath the slight bulge of his belly. "Okay," he says with a sigh. "How did you come across the information that the woman living next door is Andrea Lester rather than Peyton Reeves?"

My stomach is burning from running on fuel, nerves, and apprehension. If I admit to breaking into Peyton's house, I could end up in jail for breaking and entering. Withholding the truth could also result in the same.

"I was friendly with her and found a credit card receipt in her house with the name Andrea Lester," I say. "I wasn't aware she was a former patient of Ginger's, but I recognized the name because my husband used to date someone by that name. The coincidence was a little much, and given everything that has happened to me in the last month—"

"Do you have the receipt on you?" Officer Drell asks.

I reach into the pocket of my sweatpants, feeling around for a piece of paper until I realize I must not have taken it from my robe pocket. "No, I don't. I don't know how I managed to forget it, but I can get it to you."

He nods as if trying to understand why I would come here so unprepared.

"Do you have any other evidence to give your story more validation?"

"I don't believe my son's death certificate is valid," I say, pulling at hairs now.

"So, you think Andrea Lester had something to do with that?"

What other answer am I supposed to give him other than, "Yes."

"Unfortunately, what you have here today isn't enough for me to acquire a warrant to dig much further. Certainly, I can make a visit to Peyton Reeves' residence and question her about Andrea Lester, but I won't have much reason to question her if she denies knowing anything. In fact, from the reports I received this morning, it looks like that residence had an intruder last night. Do you know anything about this?"

"No," Ginger answers before I can consider the thought of lying, but if it's proven later that it was me and I don't speak up now, no one will believe a word I'm saying going forward. I know how this works. Once a reputation is tarnished, there's no going back.

My knees bounce uncontrollably as a cold sweat washes across my face. An internal battle is making me feel like there is a spotlight burning over me. "I—" I try to speak, but only air escapes. I clear my throat and close my eyes. "I do," I say. "It was me, but I don't consider myself an intruder. Peyton, or Andrea—whoever she is, gave me a spare key. She said I was welcome over anytime without question. So, I went last night to collect an over-the-counter DNA sample of their son, but I didn't end up getting it."

Officer Drell's eyes widen, and he pushes his chair back away from the table to lean forward. "Mrs. Milligan, just because you were given prior authorization to enter their residence whenever necessary, it doesn't necessarily deem your entry to be without force or intent. Officers were called to the scene to locate a so-called intruder."

"I'm aware. I'm an attorney, officer. I also know the Reeves weren't the ones to call dispatch though."

Officer Drell leans back into his chair and crosses his hands over his lap. "I don't know what's with that street, but there is always something going on there. First, James goes missing, then Tommy dies from a premeditated car accident, and now this... Where is the baby's body?"

A sob erupts from the bottom of my stomach, and I can't stop my tears no matter how hard I try. "My husband said I agreed to cremate him, and I didn't. I don't even know where—" Mom wraps her arm around me as I break down again.

"Okay, okay. If any of you have any proof or evidence that could possibly assist us to look into this, please bring it to us as soon as you can."

"I do have something," Ginger says, pursing her lips together as if she were sucking a lemon. Her red-webbed vein eyes widen as if shocked by the sour taste in her mouth.

My eyes widen and my jaw drops. The room seems to be closing in around me as I wonder if the entire world is keeping secrets from me. Officer Drell is staring at her, unblinking, and seemingly holding his breath as I am. "I spent a couple of hours early this morning going through archived footage from my doorbell camera. I'm willing to hand it over if you think it might be helpful. I watched through clips on the day Jenna went into labor and there's some nighttime footage I can't make out. There was also some footage from the day of Tommy's accident, but it was also early in the morning when it was dark, so it's hard to make out."

I clench my hand around my throat, pressing my fingernails into my flesh.

Officer Drell's brows arch. "I can look. There isn't a whole lot we can do to enhance doorbell footage, but maybe if we tweak the settings and brighten the image up a bit, we'll see something."

"I wish I had more to give you," Ginger says.

"We're going to have more questions for you, Mrs. Milligan, but I'm going to need to sort this report out first to figure out where to start. We need to find out what morgue or facility your baby was taken to, and we'll move forward from there." Morgue. The hairs on the back of my neck stand erect and I squeeze my arms around my torso. "Since you have a reason to believe your husband might be involved in this case, I advise you to find somewhere else to stay for the time being."

Despite everything, it's hard to fathom that we're talking about Oliver in the same breath as discussing the morgue where River might have been taken.

Oliver has been a wonderful husband. I thought we had shared so much happiness. I don't understand how someone can fake that or hide such a terrible past. He's a beloved professor at the university.

"Thank you, officer," I say, standing from the table first.

Mom and Ginger follow and Officer Drell leads us back out into the lobby. "We'll talk soon," he says.

Once it's just the three of us again, I stare out through the glass doors and shake my head. "I should go home before he worries about where I am."

"Jenna, no, no, that's absurd. You'll come home with me," Mom says. "Oliver could be a felon."

"I agree with your mother. Do not go back into that house," Ginger follows.

"Oliver should be more afraid of me right now."

FORTY-FOUR

ANDREA | LAST YEAR

"Write in your notebook, it will help. It's the best kind of therapy." I keep putting this off.

How often do therapists, shrinks, and counselors say the same thing to the wrong people? In the past, I've written hundreds of pages of notes, and nothing helps. Words can't erase the past. Maybe some inspirational words could help Luanne though.

The darkening stormy sky outside offers a sharp reflection along the window above the sink in Luanne's kitchen, and I admire my flawless skin, the shine of my lustrous hair, and the toned physique everyone thinks I easily maintain. I've cleaned at least twelve casserole dishes in the last half hour and my fingers are beginning to prune, but I promised to help Luanne with everything I could. *The poor thing. I'm sure all she wants to do is grieve alone, but her house is packed with family, friends, and others she probably hasn't seen in years. It's so unfortunate that a funeral seems to be the most common time to have a reunion.*

I'm not sure when I became this person—someone who plays the part of a kind, genuine person. It was a transformation that took time. All good things are worth the wait, and now the outside of my body is a glamorous fortress to conceal the hideous mess that lives inside of me. I'm like a beautiful scarlet-red poisonous apple—deceiving, alluring, and captivating.

At seventeen, we think we know everything. Breaking the rules is okay if it's harmless. I couldn't have been placed in a more boring class my freshman year of college. Physics. I barely made it out of high school biology with a decent grade, but with a major in forensics, the class wasn't an option. I had to find a way to become one with the information if I was going to pass.

I wondered if the young professor with a perfect smile, rain-cloud blue eyes that shimmered beneath the fluorescent lights, and dimples deep enough to pinch, would assist me in garnering a greater understanding of the material I was struggling to wrap my head around. The laws of motion were summarized into one sentence each, but I understood them as something else. *An object can't be moved unless an external force takes effect*: beguiling eye contact, a teasing smile, the need for extra help, offering attention worth taking, and compliments worthy of receiving. Never tell a soul in exchange for breaking this one law, disrupting the basic theory of physics.

The lesson in the end was: laws aren't meant to be broken, and when they are, someone always pays a consequence. I was Professor Milligan's consequence and in return, my future went up in flames.

An unwanted pregnancy, an unwanted abortion, and unwanted infertility—the deeper the problem grew, an equally troubling outcome would follow. It seems, the harder I try to fix my life, the worse it becomes. How foolish I was to think I didn't need to learn the laws of physics.

It's been hard to understand how someone in Oliver's situation could freely, seemingly without a worry in the world, advertise their life on social media. Even ten years after our three-month brief, clandestine relationship that was dictated by an ultimatum between job security or a future with me, I still sometimes wonder if he regrets his choice and thinks about me when curating his posts—what could have been. Maybe he feels the need to prove his strength in forgetting about the past, closing a door on me as if I was a nagging field mouse waiting at his back door. His point has been made...Oliver Milligan can keep his head above water without having what he claimed to truly want—me. Maybe he thinks that's what I would have wanted for him—his happiness.

According to social media, Oliver has tenure at Lakespur University—a nice insurance policy to keep his job, a beautiful new wife, Jenna, who's a child-law attorney, someone to protect him if I were to ever rattle his cage, and now the darling couple is looking for their forever home, and if anyone knows of a good realtor, send the information his way.

Jenna's the one with the public social profile, and she has been posting about the desire to buy a house in a young housing development.

I felt the same way about this beautiful community when I moved here to be closer to a long-lost friend a couple of years ago. It's perfect for first time home buyers who are looking to plant their roots. Lots of kids fill the streets, block parties that never go out of style, neighbors watch out for one another like family, casserole dishes are always being traded back and forth to the point where no one knows whose dish belongs to whom— the exchange is just another gateway into a good conversation with one another. People would do anything to live in this neighborhood, but no one has publicly listed a house here in over two years.

I place the last dish on the drying rack and shake the water off my hands while scanning Luanne's kitchen to see if there's anything left to put away for now. Bouquets of flowers and baskets bundled with varieties of fruits line the countertops as well as the oversized granite-top island. I stroll along each side, stealing a glimpse at each sympathy card. One bouquet of flowers has a blank sympathy card, an easy mistake to make when trying to focus on the kind gesture. I snag the card and rummage through the nearest drawer where Luanne keeps a stack of stationery and pens.

I tap the end of the pen against my chin as I conjure the message I want to write.

An accident is only an accident if no one confesses to an ulterior motive. No, no, too obvious.

May today's pain be tomorrow's sorrow... no, that's depressing.

I know:

We send our deepest condolences
The darkest of nights might seem blue
But the sun will again rise

I pull the cap off the back of the pen and slip it over the tip, staring at the lettering I altered to keep the card anonymous since I don't know who was nice enough to bring these beautiful flowers. A bouquet without a note seems worthless, so I'm just helping whoever forgot this detail. I replace the card within the bracket and return the pen to the drawer.

While staring at the words for a long moment, I wonder if it's missing something.

"I heard Luanne was trying to acquire life insurance just two weeks ago. Isn't that suspic—" The hushed whispers stop abruptly upon turning the corner to find they aren't alone in the kitchen. "Oh, Peyton! We didn't know you were in here. We were just stopping in to see if anything needed to be tidied up before we left." Marybeth and Tanya, the gossip queens. I'll do them a favor and pretend I didn't hear them talking about Luanne in her house at her husband's funeral. The nerve.

"Everything is all clean in here, but that's sweet of you to check," I tell them, crossing my hands over my chest.

"Wonderful," Marybeth says. "I have two soccer practices and a violin lesson to get to this afternoon, so I need to scramble anyway."

"Same," Tanya follows. Her kids don't play soccer, but I understand what she means.

"Have a good day, ladies. Thanks for all your help today." They didn't help, but it's like thanking the person who let a door go in your face. If you thank them anyway and add a little warmth to the words, it takes them a moment to understand why someone would be so gracious after they were a thoughtless jerk. Sometimes, sarcasm can be an art form.

They both struggle to smile and twist on their heels, leaving the kitchen as quickly as they arrived, but a bit quieter.

How could they blame Luanne? There isn't a sweeter person on this street. She didn't deserve for this to happen. Which is why no one would ever suspect she could be responsible somehow.

I relocate the pen in the drawer and slip the anonymous sympathy card back out. I know what I left off the end:

Unless it's you...
the cause of his demise.

I consider signing the card with Marybeth and Tanya's names, but I won't go that far. Not today. I tuck the pen away once more and move the flowers to the other side of the kitchen, placing them between a few others before returning to the living room where Luanne is sitting on her ottoman, freeing up the rest of the furniture for guests. She's lost in her thoughts, staring through her surroundings as if they're on the other side of a glass window.

I place my hand on her shoulder first, hoping not to startle her from her daze. "Sweetheart, everything is cleaned up and put away," I say. "I've separated the leftovers from the catering platters and placed half of the containers in the refrigerator and the other half in the freezer to defrost when you're ready. What else can I do before I let you get some rest tonight?"

Luanne's eyes are heavy, and she has little energy to even talk. I can't blame her, of course. The thought of my life spiraling out of control within a matter of days is hard to manage. She lifts her hand and places her warm palm on my cheek. "You are my angel. I'm not sure how I would have made it through this week without you."

"Tommy is your angel," I say, taking her hand and giving it a squeeze. "I'm just the courier."

Her grimace arches deeper and tears flood her eyes. "He is, isn't he?"

"He always will be. We both know he's in a better place now. We just have to wait our turn to find out all the wonderful things that come after this life."

"Peyton," Luanne says between sniffles. "I need to sell the house, and quickly. Just between us, Tommy didn't have life insurance, and I have no way to afford to live here. Do you know of any realtors?" I want to tell her she shouldn't be saying such a thing to anyone right now, but it's a little late for that.

I sit down beside her on the ottoman as the mourners draped in black circle around the living room sharing stories in whispers. Luanne was preparing food in the kitchen at the last block party when Tommy proudly admitted to all of us that he didn't believe in the scam of life insurance, but I think it's best if that is unbeknownst to her. I know he wouldn't have wanted this for Luanne. "I have a friend who specializes in private sales, which saves you from having to list the house and pay double realtor fees. She's on the ball and makes sales with a snap of her finger. Do you want me to talk to her?"

Luanne straightens her posture as if a weight has been lifted from her shoulders. "You would do that for me?"

"Consider it done," I say, blotting her cheek with a tissue again. She shouldn't have put on mascara today.

"I owe you my life, Peyton. I'll never forget what you've done for me in my time of need." *You're not the one who owes me your life, but you are a hurdle in my way.*

"I'll see if I can contact her tonight. Don't worry about anything. You've got this, and I've got you." Luanne wraps her arms around my neck and squeezes.

I don't understand why people feel it's necessary to loiter after a funeral. It was clear Luanne wanted to be alone, but it took three hours for her house to finally clear out. Only then I could I finally leave.

"I'm home, hun," Lincoln says, walking through the front door. "How was the service?"

"So, so sad. I just got home too. I stayed to help clean up after everyone left. My heart just breaks for her every time I see her poor face. I told her you send your love. She knew you couldn't get time off from work and she understood."

"I'll stop by there tomorrow to see if there's anything she needs done around the house. I know Tommy took care of everything. I can't imagine she's having an easy time picking up even some of these pieces."

I shiver at the thought. "Life is cruel, just cruel."

Lincoln hangs up his coat and places his briefcase down then comes over to give me a kiss on the cheek before heading upstairs to shower off the day.

"I'll start dinner in just a few minutes," I say. "How does chicken piccata sound?"

"Like you're the perfect wife," he coos with an endearing smile.

Once he's upstairs, I log in to my laptop and navigate to my newly created inbox for katherine.eloise@ke_realty.com. As I start an email, a grin forms along my lips. It's been a long time coming, but all good things are worth the wait.

To: Oliver Milligan [olivermill@lakespurmail.com]

Subject: Private Sale Listing in Desired Neighborhood on Sapphire Street

Dear Mr. Milligan,

I found your request on privatehomesaleslakespur.com, asking to be notified with any upcoming private listings in your desired neighborhoods. I have a listing at 242 Sapphire Street in Lakespur with an unbeatable asking price, also negotiable. The listing will remain private for the next few days, but we guarantee many offers will come in once public. The current owners are in a need of a quick sale and are only looking for serious buyers. I can offer you a photo of the property's exterior, but due to the seller's needs, we don't have interior photos at this time and likely won't until the listing becomes public.

You are entitled to a home inspection to protect you as buyers, but the house is selling "as-is". If you are interested in placing an offer for this property, please let me know as soon as possible. There are a few other interested parties also motivated to put an offer on this property.

Thank you for signing up to receive alerts on private listings in Lakespur. I look forward to hearing from you soon.

Sincerely,
Katherine Eloise
Realtor/CEO
K.E. Realty

It will be nice to have some fresh blood on this street.

FORTY-FIVE

JENNA | NOW

It's mind boggling how easy it is to recollect certain moments in life, especially while staring out of a car window with nothing but the blurry view of thick spruce trees. Mom seems to be visiting her own demons while white-knuckling the steering wheel, gritting her teeth along with her unblinking stare. We might be sharing the same worst memory, the one that stands out like a dead patch of grass in the center of a brilliantly green garden. The day Dad came home from work, packed his hard-shell, scratched up suitcase with everything from his drawers, and snapped the locks shut. I was too young to understand that some people don't have the ability to feel empathy. My tears and pleas as I squealed, "Daddy, don't go," were nothing more than a buzz from a swarming bee in his ear. If he could swat me away, he would have. He promised Mom he would be a loving husband, provide for her and their child. Mom was a nurse before they met, but it didn't take long to persuade her to be a housewife and a stay-at-home-mom. He had her right where he wanted her—needing him to live, to eat, for shelter, and warmth. That's what he wanted until he found something new.

He left us without a penny, an asset, or way to find him.

After being out of work for years, Mom couldn't easily find a new job while taking care of me on her own.

We struggled, got evicted from our apartment, went without meals when we couldn't find space in a halfway house, and all along, Mom knew if she had the money, she could get herself an attorney and collect back pay for all the child support Dad walked away from. It was an endless cycle, like a hamster running in a wheel, faster, and faster, foolishly thinking it's getting somewhere. Mom cried herself to sleep so many nights, but only the nights she was sure I had fallen asleep first. I wanted to help us, but I couldn't until I was old enough to stay alone while she worked. Eventually, I could get a job too, and then some day, I would become the attorney she would need to get back everything that was owed to her. I did that.

I didn't see this sharp turn coming in my life, though. I thought I had seen it all. After everything we had been through, I thought I could read a person and know whether they are good or bad, but I was wrong.

"I wish you would reconsider," Mom says now, glancing at me briefly before returning her focus to the road. She places her hand on my lap and I'm sure she wishes she could physically hold me here, but she can't.

"If Oliver has spent the last however many years of life hiding a crime to protect his job and reputation, and then decided he was going to ruin my life, he's the one you should be worrying about."

"You're angry and people can do terrible, unthinkable things when provoked. Jenna, I think you need to breathe before walking into that house."

"I won't kill his baby, don't worry." The words come out on their own accord, like a cold fog from my mouth on a brittle, frigid day. There's no way to contain the numbing storm raging inside of me.

Mom presses on the brakes in front of my house, her foot is

like a brick and we both jerk forward upon coming to a stop. She's staring straight ahead.

"I get my strength from you, Mom," I say, pinching a slight smile to the corner of my lips, reminding her of the woman I still am.

She nods and her jaw muscles tighten as she presses her lips together. "I know," Mom replies in a whisper.

I open the door and storm up the center of the lawn, making my presence known with the clunk of my footsteps against the hollow wood of the front porch. I let myself in, finding Oliver standing in front of the couch, staring out the bay window with his phone clutched in his hand. His cheeks are red, his glasses are lens-down on the coffee table, and he's not ready for work, where he should have been a half hour ago.

"Where the hell have you been? Your phone is off. You were gone when I woke up. Are you trying to give me a goddamn heart attack?" The questions shoot out of him like rounds of a machine gun.

"I had to run some errands."

"At seven this morning?"

I shrug. "Can I see your phone? Mine's dead."

"Why?" *First sign of apprehension.*

"I have to make a phone call and my—phone—is—dead." I lunge toward him and swipe the device out of his hand.

"Jenna, what's gotten into you?" Oliver's eyes widen and the peachy hue of his complexion drains to a satin-white with a slight sheen like the wainscoting of our stupidly perfect dining room. His theatrical expression matches that of someone being held up at gunpoint. Even his hands shoot up in the air in surrender. The deflection is bemusing.

"Hold on," I say, holding a finger up while I scroll through his contacts. Ah. Here, I tap on Andrew's number and then the speaker button. The phone rings twice and the call connects.

"Who are you calling?" Oliver asks.

I hold the phone up for a quick second so he can see I've tapped Andrew's number. "Just And—"

The call connects and I'm greeted by a, "Oh...hey there. Is everything okay? Did someone try to break into your house last night too?"

With a forced look of shock and a slight gasp, I respond, "Peyton?" before glancing down at the display on his phone, doing my best to keep my voice even. "I'm so sorry. I thought this was Andrew, a guy Oliver works with. I must have dialed the wrong number."

The silence is as piercing as the after-effect of an explosion.

"Oh," she says.

"Wait, did you just say someone tried to break into your house last night?"

The blood drains from Oliver's face and I imagine Peyton must look the same. "Uh—yeah, it was so weird. They didn't take anything, but it scared us."

"Thank God no one was hurt," I say. "No, no one tried to break into our house last night, but maybe we slept through it. The doors were locked so—"

"I tried calling you, but your phone keeps going right to voicemail."

"I forgot to charge my phone. Hey, let me give you a call back after I get in touch with Andrew."

"Sure. No problem," she says with hesitance.

I end the call and drop Oliver's phone onto the couch.

"Jenna, you need to take a breath or something. You're beet red. What is going on right now?" I can't believe what he's saying after I just proved Andrew is Peyton.

"Don't worry about my breathing. Tell me about Andrea Lester, or Peyton, as we call her. When did you first meet? Was it two years before we met like you said, or was it about...ten years ago, perhaps?"

Oliver holds his hand up and points at me. "Don't pull your attorney shit on me, Jenna. I'm not on trial here."

"You're still going to answer my questions," I hiss. "Where did you bring River's body? Did you bring him there still wrapped in the bloody blanket you were holding him in minutes after he was born? I'm going to need the name and location of the morgue or cremation facility—whatever it was you said I agreed to while I was drugged up on opioids."

Oliver runs his hands through his hair, and the gloss of sweat from his forehead picks up a glare from the window. "I-I have the information upstairs. I'll grab it for you. I'll grab it."

"The ashes too, please. It's been almost a month. Cremation usually doesn't take more than two weeks. I want to have a funeral for him, like I said."

"I don't have his ashes, Jenna."

"Then the morgue will have them, right?"

Oliver shoves his hands against his hips and bows his head, letting out a heavy breath. "Okay, I'm going to have to call the Ashlyn Behavioral Health Center back and tell them you're on another downward slope."

"Or..." I annunciate with cynicism, "what if...*I* call Ashlyn Behavioral Health Center and tell them my husband, a physics professor at Lakespur University, committed statutory rape ten years ago when he was thirty with a seventeen-year-old student named Andrea Lester, got her pregnant, and forced her to get a back-alley abortion." I point out the window toward Peyton's house, mouthing, "It's her." Oliver clutches his chest as if this is a real shocker to him. "But now, Andrea, who calls herself Peyton, found him, and has decided it's time to play a game of revenge. Here's the kicker though...he thinks he's going to get away with it. I mean, have you ever heard of something so outlandish? I'm pretty sure he needs some serious intervention."

"You sound psychotic," Oliver says, gritting his teeth, his

pale cheeks brightening along with the rise of his blood pressure.

"Do I?" I laugh.

"Who told you all of this? Was it Ginger? The crazy lady across the street who killed her husband?"

Ginger didn't kill her husband. He left them. That woman couldn't hurt a fly. "You don't know what you're talking about."

"But I do, and I know that's who has been filling your head with all this shit. So, you're taking the word of a murderer, and have gone and created this ludicrous narrative about a girl who you were calling your best friend just a week ago, and your husband who you vowed to spend the rest of your life with. You don't see anything wrong with this?"

"Get me the information for the morgue so I can locate our son's ashes."

"What if I don't have the information?" he asks, toying with me.

"You just said you do, and if you don't comply, I'll have the police help me. This won't be hard to do seeing as the death report, if there is one, was based on misrepresentation and inaccuracies. This would be an unfortunate situation for the morgue or private cremation company you hired, as I'm sure you can understand. Celeste wasn't a licensed medical professional. In fact, she's better known for botched abortions and losing her medical license. I'm sure you didn't know that, though. Andrea wouldn't let you in on that secret of hers."

"What—what are you talking about?" Oliver is grasping at his chest, tugging at the fabric of his T-shirt, maybe wishing he could tear his skin off because of how vile he must feel in it. "I thought you loved me. Why are you attacking me and accusing me of all this heinous stuff? I couldn't imagine doing anything you have accused me of doing. I couldn't even think up a story like this, yet, you have, and you make it look so damn easy. How?"

"It's called doing my due diligence, something you hadn't quite figured out how to do yet." I scratch the back of my neck, pinging my stare back and forth between the view outside the window and Oliver's scowl. "You know what's even crazier than everything I just told you? Peyton told me...this isn't hearsay... that she had an abortion at seventeen and it unfortunately left her sterile, but then...as the universe set out to grant wishes, Peyton received a miracle. I mean...that stuff totally happens sometimes, but it happened at the very same time I became one percent of the population who somehow conceived while taking a birth control pill, regularly, at the same time every day—so, you got your wish too. What are the odds, Oliver?" I take a step closer to him. I could blow on him and he'd probably fall over right now. I've never hated another human being so much in my life. "Here's a hint...the odds are much less than one percent."

FORTY-SIX

GINGER | TWO YEARS AGO

If I can just get the thought out of my head, everything would be fine. It's ridiculous to think James would have an affair. We've been married almost twenty-five years and have four wonderful sons together. No one would throw that all away for some floozy next door. She's young and dumb and he's middle-age and oblivious, but maybe she can't ask her husband to fix all the stupid crap that keeps breaking in her house. James works too, but we're supposed to feel sorry for her that Lincoln works sixty hours a week.

It's just a thought, a nasty thought that has taken up space in my head. There is no truth to the thought, and I will not feed it anymore.

Maybe I need new mantras.

I glance up at the clock on the wall, seeing James will be home in about five minutes. I wanted to surprise him with shepherd's pie, his favorite meal. Maybe it'll help us clear the air since we've been arguing so much this week. I don't want to give him a reason to go running off to another woman.

With my mitts on, I open the oven and pull the casserole dish out. At least if the boys come home any time before midnight, they'll have something to eat too. I don't remember the last time we all sat down at the table together. Lately it's just been James and me, like the old days when we were first married. I'll put on some jazz tonight and we can just relax.

As soon as I get the casserole set down on a hotplate, the doorbell rings. I can already guess who it will be.

I peek out the side window and confirm it's Perfect Peyton. I'm guessing tonight she'll need a cup of flour. Last night it was a cup of milk, and the night before was an egg.

"Hi, Peyton," I say upon opening the door.

"Hi, Ginger. I know you're probably getting sick of me coming over." Yes. I am. For several reasons.

"I should help you make a grocery list before you go next week. What do you think?" I suggest, laughing to soften the statement.

"I would love that. I'm such a space cadet sometimes. I can't seem to remember anything, and even when I make a list, I either lose it on the way to the store or leave it in the car and don't realize it until I'm well into the middle aisle."

"Maybe you could type the list into your phone?"

"Maybe," she says, tilting her head to the side as if she needs to consider the thought. "James isn't home yet, huh?"

"He should be home any minute now," I drawl.

"That must be why it smells so good here."

"What is it I can help you with, dear?"

"Could I have just one more egg? I'm so sorry. I'll buy you a carton next week to make up for what I've borrowed this week."

"Of course, and you don't need to buy me eggs in return. It's fine."

I turn away from the door and make my way toward the kitchen. As I'm reaching to open the fridge door handle, I see movement out of the corner of my eye and I'm bewildered to see that Peyton has decided to follow me into the house.

"I love your kitchen. It's so homey, and what scent is that candle I smell?"

"Pine," I answer curtly. Anyone would know the smell is pine.

"Hey, have you ever had any roach issues in your house?" she asks, her eyes scanning the area.

"A few times," I say. "They seem to sneak in through the garage."

"Yeah, James said the same last week when he was fixing that wonky fuse I've been having trouble with. I kept hearing little scratching sounds, and it was keeping me up at night. The thought of these critters getting into my room gives me the creeps. Anyway, he said he had a bottle of pesticide I could borrow. You wouldn't happen to know where it is, would you?"

"Your house is just full of problems lately, isn't it?" It couldn't possibly be that you just need my husband's attention...

I turn back for the kitchen, knowing James keeps that stuff under the kitchen sink. It's set in way back but I see the orange bottle and put it up on the countertop.

Peyton is still looking around the area between the dining room and kitchen as if she's trying to find something. "Also... don't kill me," she groans. "This is embarrassing...but, do you also have a spare roll of toilet paper too?"

She's got to be kidding me. When will I learn how to say no? "Sure, I just have to grab a roll from the storage unit in the garage. Give me one minute." I amble out to the garage, breaking into the storage bins in the back corner. I just stocked my bathrooms this morning and I'm not restocking them for her.

It takes me longer than a minute to remove one single roll from the bulk packaging and I'm silently cursing Peyton out each time I lose a grip on the plastic wrapping.

Just as I secure the storage container and head back inside, I spot James pulling into the driveway.

"Here you are," I say.

"Thank you so, so much." Peyton's high-set ponytail bops from side to side with every word she says and every step she takes. "Oh, and James is home. Perfect timing. That fuse blew in my bathroom upstairs again and Lincoln won't be home for another couple of hours. Do you think he could fix it for me really quick?"

I eyeball the shepherd's pie I just took out of the oven. "You know, I just took our dinner out. Maybe when we're done with dinner, if Lincoln still isn't home, I can send James over to help. Is that okay?" Perhaps, use the bathroom on your first floor instead for the next two hours.

"Sure, that would be great. Thanks," she says, her voice high pitched and whiny.

James walks in through the front door, grunting as usual when he comes home after a long day at the office. "Hi, honey."

"Well, hello to you too, James," Peyton says, following a chuckle. My God. It's no wonder I'm suffering from paranoia. She doesn't even hide her behavior from me.

"Oh, hi, Peyton, how are things?" he asks with a hesitant raised brow as he pinches the back of his neck.

"Great except for a blown fuse," she says with a sigh.

"Again? I think you may need to get an electrician in there to look at the wiring."

"I know. I know. I keep telling Lincoln this, but he's just always too busy."

"Surely, you can manage to find one on your own," I suggest.

Peyton laughs as if I just told her the funniest joke she's ever heard. "Oh gosh, knowing me, I'd end up hiring an ax-murderer or something and I'd be home alone when he came over."

"He or she," I correct her.

"Well, you know what I mean."

"Anyway, if you can spare any time to help a girl out," Peyton says, pressing her palms together as if she needs to pray for a middle-aged man to come rescue her, "I'd be forever grateful."

"Ah," James says, glancing over at me, knowing how many conversations have revolved around Peyton's incessant needs from us both, but mostly him, as of lately.

"After dinner, dear."

"Yeah, if Lincoln isn't home by the time we're done with dinner, I'll come take a look at the fuse. Okay?"

"Sure, that would be great. Thank you." Peyton bounces on her toes and waves with just her fingers as she struts out of the house in yoga pants that leave nothing to the imagination.

James seems to have gotten my hints seeing as he doesn't turn around to watch her walk out the door this time.

"I'm not going to say a word. I just wanted to make you your favorite meal so we could have a nice dinner tonight," I tell him.

"Shepherd's pie?" he questions with a chipper smile.

"Yes, sir."

"Oh, you do still love me," he says with laughter before placing a kiss on my cheek.

"Of course, I do. I just don't like her." I turn back to the kitchen so I can dish the food out. "Sit down and relax. Could I pour you a whiskey?"

"Please, please. Thank you, dear."

I scurry to get everything out to the table, noticing Peyton didn't take the bottle of pesticide and I never gave her the egg she needed to borrow, which means she'll be back.

I'm not answering the door while we're eating. I need to draw a line somewhere. Already, our food has been sitting out for a good ten minutes. With the lights dim and a stillness within the house, the free-flowing blend of rich tones flow from the old radio in the kitchen. The serpentine harmonies between the brass, percussion, and piano remind me of our younger days when we would sit at a cocktail table in a smoky jazz bar, reveling in the ambiance until the lights came on after midnight.

"You even put on jazz? Is there a special occasion?" We didn't need a special occasion to listen to our favorite music when we were young.

I shrug. "Not really." Other than trying to distract you from the needy twit next door.

We both spoon in the last few mouthfuls of the pie and I finish my wine and James empties his glass of whiskey. There's no rush tonight, I lit a couple of candles, and the music tops off the perfect ambiance. I could sit like this for hours, just me and the man I love. "One more year and we'll be empty nesters. We can finally do all that traveling we've been talking about for so long," I say.

I glance over at James, wondering if the thought makes him as happy as it does me. "Yeah," he says, placing his hand on his chest. He lifts his glass tumbler and waves the rim beneath his nose.

"Is everything okay?" He drinks that whiskey every night.

"I don't know. Maybe the whiskey didn't agree with one of the ingredients in the pie. Did you use anything new tonight?"

"No, of course not. It's the same way I always make it for you."

James's face becomes pale and sweat glosses between his brows. He rests his elbows down on the tabletop and drops his head against his fists. "Something isn't agreeing with me. I think I'm going to be—"

James barely makes it off his seat when he falls to his knees to release the bile his body is purging. "James, oh no. Sweetie," I say, dropping down beside him to rub his back.

When the purge seems to end, I help him back up to his feet. "What did you have for lunch?"

"I don't—just a sandwich from the cafeteria." I walk him over to the couch and fluff the throw pillows so he can lie down.

He has one hand on his chest, the other on his stomach and he's wincing. "Should I call for an ambulance?"

"No, no, please don't. I'm sure it's from lunch. I just—do we have any antacid I can take or ginger ale?"

"Let me check." I run up the stairs to check the bathroom in our bedroom, knowing he keeps a stash of antacids up there, but there's no bottle. Maybe there are some downstairs, but Peyton had asked me for them several times this month and God knows, I'm out of them now that I need them.

The bathroom medicine cabinet downstairs has nothing either as I feared, and there's no ginger ale left either.

"I don't have either. I can run to the store quickly and grab some or I can take you to the hospital?"

"Yeah, could you just go get something at the store? I'm sure it'll help. You know how my stomach acts up all the time anyway. I'm sure I'll be fine."

"Of course. Just stay put and I'll be back as quick as I can. Call me if you need me, okay?"

"I'll be fine, honey."

I lean over him and kiss his forehead.

It isn't until I've burnt rubber backing out of the driveway and turned two street corners that I realize I didn't notice if he had his phone near him. He can never seem to find it after he gets home from work even though it's always in the same place on the kitchen counter. The aroma of dinner is his biggest distraction and the reason he places his phone down, forgetting about everything other than what he'll be filling his stomach with. Of course, he might not have put his phone down tonight if he'd known he'd soon end up sick to his stomach.

FORTY-SEVEN

TWO YEARS AGO

I walk back into the house, finding James draped across the sofa, his body convulsing. "Oh my God, are you okay?" No response. His eyes are rolling back into his head and he's so pale. "James?"

With a quick touch to his face, I find his skin to be clammy. "What in the world is going on?" I dash for the kitchen to get a wet compress, but just as I run a rag beneath the faucet, a thud echoes between the walls. "James!" I run back, finding him sprawled out on the floor next to the coffee table. I drop to my knees and place the compress on his head. "Do you think some of that pesticide ended up in your drink?" Life is just so funny sometimes. One second, you're eating dinner and the next thing...well, here we are. I press my fingers to the artery, finding no pulse. *Just as I hoped.*

"Oh God. You poor man. Everyone loves you so much. This is going to destroy us all. Did you even try to call 9-1-1?" I ask, knowing he won't respond.

I scan the room to see if there is any hint of his phone nearby, but it's in his coat pocket. He didn't call for help.

"I'm glad you didn't call 9-1-1. That would have made this

so much harder after what you've been through tonight. No one needs to be a suspect here. It was an accident, clearly."

In a pit of desperation comes adrenaline, a form of strength we don't know we're capable of until we're in the moment.

James is gone.

He passed away from natural causes.

He passed away from unnatural causes.

He's left his family, alone, forever.

I trail up the stairs toward the linen closet in the bedroom hallway. How awful to think that these comforter size vacuum seal bags would go to waste when they're such a space saver? What an odd gift this was.

I take two from the neatly folded pile and bring them downstairs then pull the vacuum out from the hall closet and roll it behind me back out into the garage. My hands are swimming around inside of the yellow rubber gloves and I hope I'm able to get a strong enough grip on the plastic to pull them up and over poor James's body.

I struggle to lift each limb, never realizing how heavy dead weight can be, but I curl him into the fetal position—although, sharply in half would be better—like a piece of paper that needs to fit in an envelope.

I guess this is another checkmark on my list of lifelong accomplishments—execute an insurmountable challenge. This checkmark could make me out to be such a monster, but I doubt I'll regret this. I wouldn't want to spend the rest of my life in a prison cell.

The vacuum hose is in place around the circular seal, and I suction the air out of the second bag, ensuring his body is compact and confined within the two thick plastic layers. I try to push his body toward the garage door, but he's heavy and the plastic isn't helping as much as I hoped it would.

Vegetable oil. That'll do the trick, and there's plenty of it. A quick trip to the kitchen to grab the bottle and rub the oil down the side along his back. I wedge my feet into his side and yank James onto his back. *Lubed up and ready to go now.* With a grip at the bottom of the bag, I pull him backward toward the door, finally getting him out onto the cement floor in the garage.

I should have been more prepared for such a strenuous workout.

Next, I circle around the garage, studying each corner, so neatly organized with James's tools and materials for home repair and yard work. He likes to keep busy. I notice a box of large industrial trash bags he must have bought when he was repairing the back sundeck last summer. I had never seen such a thick trash bag and I asked him what its purpose was. He said they were indestructible, top of the line, and could hold just about anything. Well...now, it will be used as his final resting place.

I lower the trash bin onto its side, the ninety-six gallon one. I need to be sure not to overfill it because the trash truck won't take this size bin if it's over three hundred pounds, per the town's bylaws. Thankfully, James can't be more than two-fifty. With the trash bin squared into the corner of two walls, I'm able to slide his body into the bin, thankful the vacuum seal is holding the folded shape. I close the lid but shudder when realizing I need to lift the bin upright still.

Again, I scan my surroundings, only lit by the three dangling work lights. I pace over to the workbench, spotting the red car jack beneath.

"You never know when you might need to change a tire in an emergency. Just pay attention so I can show you how to jack up the car. Anyone can do it. It's simple, really."

The car jack is heavy, but not as heavy as the trash bin, so I settle it down just in front of the top lid since it's angled off the ground a few inches. It's enough space to get this moving in the right direction.

It takes me a few minutes to get the crank moving, but the bin is moving off the ground on an angle. I'm not sure how much farther I can lift it before I must do the rest of the heavy lifting, but I need some more height.

"Mom?"

I choke on the air that escapes my lungs.

"Where are you? Dad?"

I leave the jack in place and straighten my posture before returning inside the house. Carter has come home from wherever he was all night, most likely his girlfriend's house where he spends so much of his time lately. I reach the open doorway between the garage and the house, finding him staring right at me.

"Peyton, hey, what are you doing in our garage? Do you know where my parents are?" Carter asks, scratching the back of his head with a look of confusion.

Your father is dead, in the trash bin, and your mother just received a text message from his phone saying he called for an ambulance and to meet him at the hospital. You, though, I wasn't expecting to walk in right now.

"I—uh, well, tomorrow is trash day. I saw them pull out of the driveway just a bit ago. It looks like they were in a rush to get somewhere, and I noticed your dad hadn't put the trash out like he usually does when he gets home from work. I thought I'd give them a hand since they always do so much for me," I reply, wiping my glove-clad arm across my forehead, spotting a puddle of bile Ginger seems to have left behind.

Carter shakes his head. "In a rush? I wonder where they were off to. They didn't say anything to me."

I try to laugh, and smile, but I'm so stiff from all the heavy lifting today—I mean, not as stiff as James, but still. If he sees the vomit, he's going to ask questions I can't answer. "You never know when it comes to your mom. When she gets an idea in her head, sometimes she just likes to jump on it, right?"

James's phone vibrates in my back pocket for the tenth time in the last few minutes. Ginger keeps calling over and over, understandably so, but if James was in an ambulance, he wouldn't be able to answer his phone. Surely, she must realize this.

"Yeah, she can be spontaneous sometimes. My dad never seems to mind and usually just goes along with whatever crazy idea she's come up with." Carter raises a brow and shifts his weight from foot to foot. It's obvious this encounter has become awkward. "Well, I can get the trash out to the curb since I'm here."

Shit. No, not part of this plan. I didn't think he'd even show up. According to Ginger, all he does is spend time at his girl-friend's house and hardly ever comes home. "No, no, I was just about done with the trash. I can get it."

Carter shakes his head. "Oh...okay, well I was just stopping by to check in on them, but I'm heading back to my girl's house for the night. So, if you're sure about the trash, I'm going to head back out."

"Totally. I got this. Go. Be young and have fun. Just, not too much fun, not until you're of a legal age," I joke. Maybe someone could have hammered that advice into my head. I likely wouldn't be shoving a body into a trash barrel right now.

"Will do," he says, tipping his head before turning to leave. "Hey...do you smell that? I think there's something greasy on the floor." He pushes the toe of his shoe around the remnants of oil.

"No, I don't," I say, defensively. "I bet your mom was polishing the floors before she left. The woman doesn't stop cleaning." I doubt Carter would know the difference between floor cleaner and oil. I don't think Ginger has ever let any of them cook or clean a day in their life. There are so many other things she could devote her time to.

"Oh, okay, probably," he says with a chuckle. "I'll see you around then. Thanks for helping them out. I appreciate it."

"Anytime."

I wait for Carter's headlights to be out of sight before returning to the garage. The uptick in my pulse gives me another burst of energy to crack the jack a bit more until I can pull from the corner to kick the bottom forward onto its wheels. Sweat is soaking through my clothes by the time the bin is upright, and I've almost forgotten what I'm working so hard on to accomplish.

The garage door button glows on the side wall and I hit the button, watching the dark street reveal slowly beneath the opening.

I've taken heavy trash bins down the driveway many times. I can handle this.

It's an unsteady mission, and I have to stop and take several breaks between the garage door and the bottom of the driveway. Just after I manage to get the bin in place, I return to the house to empty the kitchen trash receptacles so I can add some extra bags to top off the pile above James—just an extra measure of safety.

With one last trip back into the house, I close the garage door, grab a wad of paper towels and a degreasing cleaning spray from the cabinet beneath the sink, and wipe up the streak of oil left behind. I don't want Ginger to fall when she eventually gets home. That would be too much to handle in one day. I peel off her yellow rubber gloves and toss them onto the counter next to the whiskey bottle. I wonder if anyone will find those with her sweat marks inside.

As I cross the lawn toward my house, I peel off my protective layer of latex gloves and shove them into my pocket then glance over to the trash bins at the end of their driveway. *I'll keep an eye on you tonight, James. I promise.*

FORTY-EIGHT

JENNA | NOW

The anger inside of me is raging through my body like a grease fire. "Can we just calm down for a minute and talk about this?" Oliver asks, still standing like I'm about to physically assault him. I'd like to, but I would never lay a finger on him.

"Were you cheating on me? Yes, or no?" I ask, demanding an answer.

"No," he says without blinking. "I have never cheated on you."

"Why is this all happening, Oliver? Why do we live across the street from your ex-girlfriend?" There are so many pieces to this puzzle. The level of deceit to create such an intricate web of lies is unfathomable to me.

"I didn't do this," he says. "She's crazy. Andrea or Peyton, whatever the hell she is going by now. She's crazy, Jenna."

"How did we end up living across the street from her?" I ask again, grinding my teeth so hard my jaw aches.

"I swear to you, I don't know. I noticed her on the front porch the day we walked into the house for the first time, and I thought I was seeing things, but I wasn't."

"So, you didn't think to tell me?"

Oliver grasps at his hair, tugging as if he wants to pull each strand out of his head. "I did think to tell you, but then I didn't because I knew it would ruin our marriage."

"Looks like it was a lose-lose situation," I tell him.

"I'm so sorry, babe," he says, pressing his hands together in prayer. "I swear to you, I never meant for any of this to happen. I love you. I just wanted to spend my life with you and—"

"After you ruined Andrea's life at seventeen?" I question him.

"We all do stupid things when we're young. I didn't think I'd still be paying a consequence for that ten years later."

"You weren't young. You were thirty-one. You knew better, especially as a professor."

Oliver scoffs before responding. "Wow. Isn't it you who said: 'Forty-one is the new thirty-one, which makes...thirty-one the new twenty-one?'" He truly has a response to everything. It's like he's convinced himself that anything can be chalked up to an accident, even when it ruined another person's life.

The yelp of a siren startles me as it seems to appear out of nowhere. More sirens join in, creating a bleeding resonance of alarms soaring in our direction. Tires screech to a halt and I fearfully peek out the front window, spotting four cruisers parked across the street.

"What's going on?" Oliver asks, running to the front door.

I don't know. They didn't seem too motivated to help when I was at the station earlier.

Oliver runs outside and I follow, curious to see what's happening. We watch as three officers approach the front of the house across the street and one rages his fist against the front door across from us. A fourth speaks into his cruiser radio from outside the vehicle parked along the curb and two others are in the street, seemingly on guard. Lincoln appears in the opening, startled, and out of breath.

"We're looking for Andrea Lester. Is she here now?" the shorter of the three officers speaks up.

Lincoln's jaw falls and he nods with such subtlety, it's hard to know for sure if he was saying yes. Three police officers push through the door as Lincoln is forced to step to the side. Three remain outside in front of the door.

"What's going on?" Lincoln asks.

Minutes pass and I'm not sure if I've taken a breath when Ginger steps out of her house with a pair of sunglasses on, casually staring next door as if she knew this was going to happen.

Two police officers escort Peyton out of the house, her hands cuffed behind her back. "Lincoln, the baby!" she screams out. "Go get him." Peyton fights against the officer's grip as if she stands a chance of breaking away from them. "You have no right to arrest me. I've never done anything wrong, not even gotten a speeding ticket. You are making a serious mistake." She whips her head around, finding people from the neighborhood watching the scene go down. "Who did this to me?"

"You did this to yourself," Ginger replies, her voice calm and monotone.

"No!" Peyton screams. "He did this." Her gaze cuts like a knife over to Oliver. "You! This is all your fault. You ruined my life when I was just seventeen. Does anyone even realize this? You're an upstanding physics professor who everyone admires so much, except no one knows who you truly are. Even your wife. He screwed me when I was seventeen. He was thirty-one and my damn professor." She laughs like this moment is humorous. "But it was all good fun until I got pregnant. Then he forced me to abort the baby. He forced me. He said I had no choice in the matter and brought me down to this godawful clinic. You ruined my life and then went on acting like you still deserve to have everything you could ever want and desire. You owed me. You know you did." Spit is flying from her mouth as the officers struggle to bring her closer to one of the cruisers. I press the palm of my hand over my mouth, trying to hide the sight of my fallen jaw. I must look like a frantic animal pinned within a pair of headlights on a dark road at night.

"You have already stated that you understand your rights and that anything you say, can, and will be used against you in a court of law, Mrs. Reeves," one of the officers says to her.

"I don't care. That man across the street should be the one in handcuffs. He committed a felony and got away with it because I couldn't afford a lawyer at seventeen. No one helped me or told me what my rights were until it was too late, but now I know it isn't too late."

"Save it for court, Mrs. Reeves," another officer says.

"Everything that has happened around here in this neighborhood is because of you. Everything, Oliver. You're the only one to blame."

I'm not surprised at Oliver's silence. There's nothing he can say. It will only make this situation worse for him.

Lincoln comes out the front door, holding Dylan in his arms, clearly bewildered by what's happening. How far into the dark could someone be when living with a pathological liar? Love is blind, but she had me fooled too.

Peyton gives Ginger a once over before her head is shoved forward as she's jolted into the back of the cruiser. "You were a lousy therapist. It's no wonder you didn't earn your degree."

I'm the only one Peyton doesn't say a word to. I'd like to think she feels an ounce of remorse for what she's done to me, but someone like her must not feel much at all.

The cruiser containing Peyton and two of the officers takes off, leaving the other four behind. They come over to speak to us and my heart tumbles in my chest, wondering what they're about to say.

"With regard to your past with Andrea Lester, you should consider finding yourself an attorney, Mr. Milligan. Everything

Andrea Lester has just said is on record." Oliver glances over at me, disappointment shadowing his face.

"I guess this is what we call irony," I tell him.

"Jenna," he mutters, my name sounding like a plea.

The heaviness of realization penetrates my chest like a lead pipe, and I wonder if he knows me well enough to sense my agony. I refuse to let a tear fall even though I feel like each bone in my body is shattering into dust. I'm not sure how I'm still standing.

"We'll be performing a DNA test on the child as proof for the court, but you are also under arrest, Mr. Milligan, for being an accomplice to kidnapping," the officer says.

"Kidnapping?" I ask.

I stare past the officer, across the street, watching one of the other officers take Dylan out of Lincoln's arms. Lincoln falls to his knees, sobbing, pleading for this—whatever this is—not to be true.

"We have footage of Mr. Milligan escorting a baby across the street from your house in the middle of the night on April 5th. The DNA test will confirm our suspicions, but there's a possibility that your baby might—"

"Might what?" I shout, my voice crackling through the rising phlegm in my throat.

"Might not be dead."

I'm in the middle of two worlds colliding together and I'm not sure I know how to comprehend what this all means. Are they suggesting that Peyton—Andrea's—baby Dylan isn't Dylan, isn't their child, but rather— "I don't understand," I croak out.

No one responds.

The air in my lungs is trapped, suffocating me. With tunnel vision, I'm left with a blurry haze swirling around me as I scratch my nails against the flesh on my chest to remind myself that I'm present, awake, experiencing this moment. My throat tightens and I dart my gaze in every possible direction, searching for clarity that everyone else seems to have but me. There's so much happening at once, including Oliver receiving his verbal Miranda Rights while an officer walks toward me with Dylan in his arms.

Ginger is running toward me. "Are you saying this child is River?" Ginger shouts.

The officers appear confused. "Between the footage we have received, no record of birth for Dylan Reeves, or hospital record for Andrea Lester or Peyton Reeves, as well as no certified record of death to be found for the Milligan baby, we'd like to bring Jenna and the baby down to the hospital for an expedited DNA test. This child needs to be with his biological parent." I watch the officer place the baby in the back of a cruiser. "We have a car seat and you can sit with him in the back."

My lungs burn from holding in the guttural cry demanding to be released, but I'm still in a state of shock, afraid to tell myself that innocent baby is my River. "Okay," I say, the word hardly audible.

"May I follow her to the hospital, officer?" Ginger asks.

"Of course."

"I'll call her mother, as well. Jenna, I'll be right behind you," Ginger calls after me as I walk in a stumbling trance toward the same car they put...River. It must be River. The world couldn't be so cruel to take my baby away from me twice, could it?

FORTY-NINE

GINGER | NOW

Only a month has passed since Andrea was arraigned, but while she awaits trial, she's serving time without the option of bail.

I mulled over the thought of paying her a visit and made the decision to do so once I found out I'm one of Andrea's approved visitors. I'm not surprised to be on her shortlist. All she's ever wanted is for me to give her my full attention.

She doesn't care how many lives she ruins, so long as it benefits her in some way. This behavior roots from somewhere much darker than the relationship she had with Oliver ten years ago, and the topic isn't something we reached in the times we spoke. Each session was about her hatred for the man who destroyed her future and who continued to get away with it day after day.

The security clinks and clanks of the doors make my heart jump in my chest each time I walk through another metal door until I reach a wall of thick windows, sectioned off by narrow partitions with a phone and a chair on either side. On the opposite side, prisoners in orange jumpsuits wait for their visitors.

My nerves fray as I sit in the blue plastic chair and lift the black phone to my ear.

"I didn't think you would ever come visit," Andrea says, leaning in toward the plexiglass. I've never seen Andrea like this: dark circles beneath her eyes, no makeup, limp blonde lashes, ruddy chapped cheeks, and grease coating the roots of her hair. The pumpkin orange color of her jumpsuit does not complement her, especially without the fake tan she used to maintain year-round. By the lifeless look in her stare, I assume she hasn't slept much in weeks. I can't help but wonder if she considered the possibility of being caught for the crimes she's committed. Then again, does any criminal?

"Why did you cut the brake lines on Tommy's car?" I say. Andrea isn't worthy of a hello. I have questions and need answers. She's already facing a life sentence in prison, so she has nothing to lose by giving me the truth.

She shrugs. "How else could I get Oliver and Jenna to move in across the street? Tommy's the one who was bragging about not having life insurance. It's like he wanted—"

"Stop," I tell her, seething into the phone.

"Why?" she replies. "At least I sent flowers to Luanne unlike you. You didn't even show up at the poor man's funeral." The smirk on Andrea's face makes me glad there is glass separating us. I'm not sure I would be able to keep myself from lunging at her. The rage fills my body with fiery heat and my heart thuds to the same heavy clomp of the prison guard's boots as he paces back and forth behind the visitors. There isn't a hint of remorse in her eyes.

I clench my fists around the phone's handset, hearing a slight crack within the mechanics beneath the rubber coating. I grit my teeth and mutter, "No one told me about the funeral, because I was being eyeballed for his death on top of my husband's disappearance."

Andrea shakes her head, her greasy blonde ponytail swinging side to side. "Ginger, Ginger, Ginger, you yourself told me that in order to fix the pain in my life, I would need to remove the obstacles first. So that's what I did, and I had to go about it the right way, obviously—well until Jenna screwed up my life even more."

I ball my fists up on my lap. "Stop blaming everyone else for what you did. There are no logical reasons for the crimes you have committed." I try to keep my voice down, so I don't draw too much attention to our conversation. I'm not done talking, and I don't plan to come back here again.

"That's not true. I had logical reasons," Andrea says, folding her arms down on the shallow counter in front of her. "Long before I even met Tommy, I had made the decision to follow your advice. You inspired me to take control over what influenced my life. Of course, that's the only bit of advice I had to take with me since you gave up on me. You," she snickers, "you were my therapist and wouldn't give me the time of day because you were just..." a sigh forces a wave of static through the phone, "so busy being a perfect homemaker to your lovely family." Her voice rises in pitch as if she's trying to mimic the way I sound. "I thought maybe if I moved closer, you'd change your mind about me and realize I just truly needed someone to talk to. I wasn't trying to abuse your time or take advantage of your patience. I was lonely and needed someone—anyone, Ginger. That's all I needed."

Andrea's chin quivers and I wonder if it's an act. I question if I gave up on her too easily, whether this all could have been avoided if I had given her more time. "That isn't all you needed," I utter, unsure of myself now.

She grapples her cuffed hands around her ponytail and tugs. "God, Ginger," she grumbles, "you were the first person to show me understanding for what I had been through. I knew if I could have just one person understand the pain I was living with, maybe I could have a chance at the life I desired."

"You didn't need validation from anyone but yourself," I

say, repeating words I know I told her years ago. Obviously, it didn't mean much to her then and it likely means less now.

Andrea inhales sharply and releases her grip from her hair, placing her hands down against her lap. "I even changed my name to see if I could get you to like me without all the preconceived notions you had for me. If you chose to be my friend, I wouldn't have to fight for your time. You'd want to be around me, and I could then convince myself I wasn't this monster—the psychopath you made me out to be."

Every word that comes out of her mouth is more ridiculous than the one before. I don't need to tell her that people don't commonly trick others into becoming their friend for selfish reasons, never mind move in next door. "A friendship is based on honesty," I tell her. It's something a mother would tell her young child. "Oh, and I never thought you were a psychopath."

"Well, it doesn't matter anyhow," she says. "As it turns out, you hated Peyton even more than me, which made it clear what the root of our problem was." I'm dumbstruck, my jaw falls open, and I can't imagine what reason she made up. "James was obviously the problem there." Her eyes narrow and she shakes her head with a cold, direct stare. "My God, you spent all day cooking that man's meals, cleaning the house, preparing for him to come home from work as if you were awaiting the arrival of some king. No one does that crap anymore. We don't live in the 1950s. It was overkill and we both know you could have spared a few of those moments to share a cup of tea with a friendly neighbor on occasion." She leaves out the fact that I have four sons, and last year, one of them was still living at home. When she moved in, three were still living with me. I was taking care of everyone in my house, not just James. But it's not worth reminding her of the truth or arguing. She sees what she wants to see.

"You can't blame everyone for your own downfalls," I tell her, seething inside from her belligerent insults.

"Ginger, the bottom line is...when you want something you can't have, you don't just sit around waiting for it to drop on your lap. You go get it, right? That's what you told me, remember? You know, just like when you saw me, a very pregnant Peyton, drinking out of a tequila bottle during Jenna's baby shower? I wanted it so I took it. God, I just couldn't stop myself, and oddly, despite your worldly advice, you didn't try to stop me either. You just ran home to avoid the reality of facing another imperfect person, didn't you? That's what you do, though, you give bad advice and then can't live with the consequence. James would understand what I mean, wouldn't he?"

Her questions and statements are erratic and dizzying, but like a bolt of lightning, I'm struck with a blinding epiphany. *James was obviously the problem*, she said. "Where is he, Andrea?" I growl, my mouth filling with saliva like an angered dog. "Where is my husband?" Not one hospital in this state had a record of him. People don't just disappear, but people do blame the significant other when no one else is left to question about a disappearance. I don't even have an alibi. I also don't have proof to blame Andrea for James's disappearance, but how could I think anything different at this point? He was sick when I left the house to get him medication that night, and then he told me he was going to the hospital, but he obviously didn't. I've spent the last two years trying to figure out if James hated me so much, he made up an elaborate story to simply get away from me.

Andrea smirks. "All I did was take out your trash for you that night. No one was home to do it and I know James was a stickler for making sure the bins were out. How does that translate into me knowing where your husband went?"

"His car was left behind. He didn't run away on foot or escape from a hospital."

Andrea shrugs again. "I'm not sure what to tell you, but I

think it's unfortunate that people think you have something to do with his disappearance."

I whip my head around, looking to see who might be listening. Although I'm sure our conversation is monitored. "Why would you say something like that? I love my husband. I would never hurt him. You're the one who made everyone think I might have done something to him, including my children. How many lives can you possibly ruin before you feel an ounce of remorse for what you've done?"

Andrea leans back in her chair and stretches her neck from side to side. "Ginger, the one thing you failed to do in our therapy sessions was help me understand why I was so desperate to take a chance with a man who held a position of power, a professor who seemed to enjoy giving me a little extra attention. Why did I let my resentment for Celeste, the former doctor who ruined my body and life, silently control me? You never asked me the question of whether I sought retribution. I wanted to talk about it, but I couldn't figure out how to bring up the subject on my own. Even now, I'm wondering if I'll ever be able to forgive these people who have pushed me to the place I now exist." Andrea's gaze pings off each wall surrounding her as if she's reminding herself of where we are. "If you had asked the right questions, you might have given me better advice. You might have at least told me not to involve Oliver's innocent wife or use her for collateral damage. Poor Jenna," she snickers and scratches her ear against her shoulder. "But that's all water under the bridge now. Some of us were just never meant to catch a break in life. My life sentence will likely be here, and yours...well, you will have to live the rest of your life, wondering what really happened to James. But if you find him...you can keep him."

FIFTY

ANDREA | NOW

After six weeks of living in this rat-infested hellhole, I've yet to receive a date for my trial. The attorney appointed to me upon arraignment said it could be a while before we hear anything more—just another case of no one having time to listen to me. The irony of pleading for someone's attention, anyone's attention, my entire life to now being forced to meet with a correctional counselor to talk through my troubles is like tearing open a wound to see how long it takes me to bleed out.

The woman sitting across from me is new, which means she'll know half of my story and need me to fill in the blanks like I've done three other times with the counselors coming and going.

We sit here in silence in this puny brick-clad room that smells like stale body odor. She's been writing down notes on her yellow legal pad since she sat down, uninterested in making eye contact. So far, the only thing I know about her is that she has thin black hair, tied into a low ponytail. Her cherry-red blouse is bunched at the buttons and her handwriting is illegible, at least from trying to read it upside down.

"Andrea, I'm Diane, one of the psychologists here, and I'll

be taking over for—" she pauses and flips through her notepad, "Bethany who you spoke to last. I'm going to review the notes I have here, and you can correct me if anything is misstated, okay?"

Just as the rest of them, she shows no emotion or will to connect as most therapists do. I wonder if it's the way they are trained to treat prisoners or if I've just had bad luck. It could be the fact that the guards think I need to be handcuffed and have my ankles shackled. "Sure," I mimic her disposition, wishing I could lean back into my chair the way she is in hers. My shoulders are pulled back and it's impossible to sit in any other way than hunched forward in this bucket chair.

"This isn't your first offense or charge. You were arrested in 2013 for causing a motor vehicle accident while under the influence, and you had four temporary restraining orders held against you between 2014 and 2016. Is that correct?"

"I had two glasses of wine and skidded on a patch of ice into another vehicle. It would have happened if I hadn't had a drink that night too. As for the restraining orders, I must have missed the parenting lesson about reading mixed signals in relationships."

Diane clears her throat and taps the top of her pen against her notepad. "While I wouldn't typically bring up past marks on your criminal record, I think it's worth mentioning the issue surrounding stalking and harassment, especially with Celeste Brown and Ginger Fowler being two of the four, both medically connected to you."

"What does that have to do with the current charges?" My question will bring me up to date on her knowledge. I know well enough not to give more information than what's already been said.

Diane's lips pull into a straight line and the creases between her eyebrows deepen. "Everything, Mrs. Reeves. To start, Celeste Brown has also received a prison sentence for practicing without a license among other false allegations following the birth of a child, a plan carried out in response to a threat of you harming her family."

I've already been notified that her phone recorded that unfortunate conversation between the two of us, so this isn't a surprise.

"She should have reported me to the police. She didn't have to follow my orders. Therefore, some might argue that her actions aren't my responsibility." If she reported me to the police, I would have told them all about the illegally run abortion clinic she had open for five years, and she knew that. It was best to follow my plan. Although now I wonder which crime would have caused her a longer sentence.

"What about Ginger?" she asks with a sigh as she checks the time on her watch. "Is there anything regarding your relationship with her that you would like to discuss?"

I shake my head. "No. She was inept at counseling people. It seems to be a common trend, don't you think?" I ask, tilting my head to the side.

Diane is unaffected by my jab as she looks up to stare me straight in the eyes. "Very well. We'll come back to that, but for now I'd like to ask you a few questions about the years prior to your first arrest." Diane clasps her hands together, the pen still pinched between her thumb and forefinger. "You see, many times, we find that our troubles in adulthood stem from incidents that occurred during our childhood. I'm curious about the life you had while growing up?"

I often wonder what happens when these therapists can't put any pieces together in the puzzle they assume exists and then have to mark their notes as inconclusive. "I had a normal childhood. My parents are still married, still live in the same house, and still have the same careers they've always had."

"What are your parents' professions?" she continues,

releasing her intertwined fingers to start a new note. Her pen tip bleeds a blue mark at the start of a new line on her pad.

"They're both corporate executives for a pharmaceutical company in the city capital, Dover. My mom is in finance and my dad is in sales," I say with a shrug.

"Those are some long hours in the office I bet," Diane says. "They must not have been around a whole lot with them both having such demanding jobs."

"Yeah, I guess. Why does that matter?" My parents were never home. I learned to cook my meals at ten and once I was able to feed myself, I became just like the fallen Christmas ornament that collected dust behind the sofa. It seems I was only thought of once a year when I was supposed to make the family look complete at their company's year-end banquet. Their choices are theirs and someday they'll realize they wasted more time working than appreciating other parts of life, but that's their problem, not mine.

"It's helpful information to know," she says. "Also, do you recall when you were initially diagnosed with BPD—borderline personality disorder"—

Her question stuns me and burns a hole in my stomach as it hasn't been brought up in the time I've been imprisoned here. I thought those medical records disappeared when I stopped treatment. "Do you?" I ask, peering over at her notes. It's clear she knows everything she needs to know so why bother rehashing every low point in my life until now?

"Yes, it says here you were fifteen and keyed someone's car because they wouldn't give you a ride home the day before. Charges weren't pressed in exchange for an agreement that you would seek counseling. At which time, you did, and were then diagnosed with BPD. It appears you were being treated with prescribed drugs for a year but then abruptly ended sessions with your provider."

"What is the point to all of this?" The metal cuffs are

digging into my right wrist bone, causing a bruise, and I'm becoming more irritable every moment longer I'm forced to sit here.

"BPD is a serious psychological illness that can require continuous care and treatment." She flips to another page in her notepad and drags the tip of her pen down the length of the page. "An unlawful sexual encounter between a student and professor, extreme efforts to avoid being abandoned by loved ones, a lack of empathy or concern, extreme anger and harmful behaviors toward others..." She's checking off each box on her diagnosis list.

"Well, problem solved. I'm locked up now, right?"

"Mrs. Reeves, our intention is to help and guide you toward a healthier mind, and I'm not sure a correctional facility is the best place to do so. I'm going to recommend a transfer to a psychiatric unit so you can receive proper guidance and care while serving your time."

A change of scenery and a little more attention is all I've ever wanted. "That sounds wonderful."

FIFTY-ONE

JENNA | NOW

For half of my adult life, the slight dimple on my chin had made me so self-conscious. I tried to cover it with different types of makeup and contouring so no one would focus their attention on what I thought was an imperfection on my face.

But over the last eight months of falling more and more in love with this little face, I adore tracing the little indentation on River's chin, knowing it was the mark that led me to the truth. If both parents have a dominant gene—a cleft or dimple in their chin, it's almost guaranteed their child will have one too.

"Mama loves you so much," I whisper to him. He smiles then giggles, staring up at me like I'm the most important person on earth.

Before the DNA test came back, I began to question science, wondering if inheriting genes wasn't as accurate as what I had learned. The answer that seemed so straightforward got washed away like sand in the tide. I even wondered if I did have a mental breakdown and, in all that time in between, I was just balancing on a tightrope that was threatening to snap. All these thoughts went through my mind over and over again until I was told my baby was alive and ready to go home with me.

"Mrs. Milligan," Officer Drell addresses me while knocking lightly on the door of the small hospital waiting room I've been pacing around for the last couple of hours since we arrived by a police escort.

"I didn't know you were here," I say, a bit relieved to see a familiar face, even if it wasn't from the best of meetings. I didn't recognize any of the four officers who showed up between my house and Andrea's.

"There was a shift switch and when I found out what had gone down today, I wanted to come down here to check on you and see what was going on with the DNA results."

Mom and Ginger come stand at either side of me. "Do you know anything?" Ginger asks.

Officer Drell pulls a piece of paper out of his back pocket. "I do."

My heart is in my throat, pulsating throughout every inch of my body. I squeeze my arms around my chest, wishing I was in control of the constriction. A cold sweat zings down my spine and I need to take a seat before my knees give out.

"Jenna, are you—what's happening?" Mom asks frantically, grabbing my arm.

"I'm fine. I just need to know—" Black spots flicker in front of me and Mom pulls me back to sit down on the chair. Officer Drell kneels in front of me, and Ginger has her hands clasped over her mouth, her eyes wide with wonder.

"The baby is your son. We're a hundred percent confident that he belongs to you and Oliver."

A surge of sobs breaks through the weak dam keeping me together today and I can hardly hold myself upright on the chair. Officer Drell places his hand on my knee and Mom and Ginger each have one on my arms. "The doctors are finishing up with the *routine check-up and we'll have a birth certificate for you to fill out shortly."*

After another moment of chasing my breaths, I'm able to compose myself enough to see Officer Drell clearly as a tear rolls down his cheek. "I'm so sorry for what you've been through. No one should ever have to go through something so terrible."

"My story has a happy ending thanks to your help," I mutter. "I will forever be grateful."

"I always knew you were a good egg, Taylor," Ginger says, squeezing his arm.

"Thank you for bringing our baby back," Mom says, choking on her words. "Jenna, I am so sorry for ever questioning you, for not seeing the reality of what was happening sooner. I should have protected you somehow—it's my job and I let you down."

"No," I sniffle. "It was my turn to do the protecting for my child. You taught me everything there is to know about loving a child and how to be an amazing, strong mother so I can be the same now..." I gasp for air, "for River."

The waiting room door opens again, and a nurse is cradling my River in her arms. "Mrs. Milligan, I think this beautiful little boy is ready to go home with you. We just have some paperwork for you to fill out and you'll be on your way."

The moment River is placed into my quivering arms, a sense of belonging, completion, wholeness overcomes me and immediately, I know he is mine and I am his.

Peyton stole River with the assistance of Oliver who "supposedly" owed her a life he had forced her to give up. Oliver confessed all that was left to admit when he was tried in court. This man who would slam on his brakes while going at the speed limit because a police officer was on the horizon, a person who pays their taxes three months early every year, keeps every receipt, dots every i, crosses every t, says sorry for the things he didn't do, wasn't going for a good Samaritan award. He was desperately trying to avoid being caught for his mistakes. Ultimately, he was willing to sacrifice his wife and his own flesh and blood to save himself. The man I loved is nothing more than a stranger. I'm not sure if I choose to believe whether he ever really loved me. The convenience of my position as a child-law attorney still feels too coincidental. He'll be serving fifteen years for statutory rape, an additional ten years for assisted kidnapping, and another ten for drugging his wife and tampering with her prescribed medications.

Everything that happened felt like a giant life test, testing me to the absolute limit, and there was only one option for me... fight until I win. Becoming a partner in Breakers and Cole wasn't my end goal when handling my personal traumas, but it became such a substantial, local story that Mr. Cole proudly offered me the "well deserved and earned" position when I'm ready to return to work after my maternity leave. I'm surer now than ever that every choice we make in life has a reason, one we may not understand until it turns our lives upside down.

"Who's ready for some strained peas?" Lincoln coos at River, lifting him out of my arms to place him down in his highchair.

"D-d-d-a-d-a," River babbles and blows a long, wet raspberry at Lincoln's face. Bubbles form over River's puckered cupid-bow lips, causing us to both laugh as we always do when he spits at us. His toothy grin warms my heart and I wonder how any mother could not spend every free moment staring at what they've created. His beautiful blue eyes could light up a dark room. He might have gotten those pretty eyes from Oliver, but when I look at him, I only see River. His hair is the same shade of brown as mine, growing into mild waves, and his nose turns up just a bit like mine does too. He's perfect.

"That's exactly what I was thinking," Lincoln replies. "After you finish your peas, we'll go for a walk and then we'll watch some football, and—"

"He might need a nap at some point too," I add in, smirking at the man I have the most unusual connection with.

Lincoln fell apart after the police showed up at his door that day. Most of us wondered whether he knew what Andrea was planning and executing, but he admitted to working too much to notice anything was askew. His emotions after losing who he thought was his son, were raw and unmistakable to me. He was in the same crushing pain I experienced when I thought River had died.

Lincoln couldn't comprehend how Peyton hid the truth so well from him, especially with what we found to be a latex belly she used to fool everyone, including him, who couldn't ever seem to feel the kicks she boasted about. The only secret of hers he knew was that her first name was Andrea and her middle name was Peyton. From the first day they met, she told Lincoln she hated her first name and wanted to go by Peyton.

I couldn't bear the thought of putting Lincoln through the heartbreak and devastating loss of a child, so we've decided to raise him together under one roof as two strong parents who will hold up a bridge above their River. I'm quite sure Lincoln has bridged a hole in my heart too. There's something to be said about life unfolding in unusual ways, and there's also something to be said about the undeniable spark between the two of us. For now, our warm stolen moments between feedings, diapers, and playtime are our little secret. Someday, we'll let everyone else in on the wonderment of life's unexpected plans.

I tend to the dishes while Lincoln feeds River, staring out the window into the backyard, where a silvery coating of frost blankets everything, including the baby swing Lincoln attached to the thick old branch protruding from the oak tree that offers just enough shade to have picnics, read books, and cool off on hot summer days. It's just a tree but I didn't know it would be my favorite part of this house until I brought River home.

"Oh, did you watch the news earlier?" Lincoln asks.

"No, I didn't have a chance this morning. Why?"

"I guess there were human remains found at the landfill in Lakespur. Forensic scientists are analyzing what was found. But how do you think a body would end up in a landfill like that?"

"I assume, a lot of premeditated planning. That's terrible," I say, reaching for the remote, curious to hear the full report. "You know, maybe Ginger would know..."

FIFTY-TWO

GINGER | NOW

Patience isn't a virtue, it's a vice that can cause sleepless nights, delusions, accusations, self-doubt, and heartache. Three years, one month, two weeks, and four days have gone by as I remained patient, hoping James would someday walk back in through the front door, pleading for forgiveness for the mistake he made in walking out on me. Hope can be an awful thing.

The sky is filled with dark clouds and rain cries down onto the tops of our black umbrellas as we stand in front of the final resting place for James, in a cemetery close to our home. I try to steady my hand, holding the paper out in front me with the words I wanted to share today.

"James was an upstanding man and I feel an overwhelming sense of guilt to have ever thought differently. As you know, I thought he walked out on his family. There are moments, now knowing the truth, that I wish he had just walked out on his family. At least he'd still be alive," I say, feeling the arms of my sons huddle over me while we look out toward our small gathering of family and friends who showed up to pay their respects to James today. Our bond is stronger than ever and though apologies were passed around, I didn't need anything more from them than what they're giving me right now.

"We love you, Mom. We'll always take care of you," Joel says in my ear.

"Always," the other three repeat.

It wasn't long after Andrea was arrested that I knew for sure she had something to do with James's disappearance. The one conversation I had with her during our visit at the prison said it all. She covered her tracks, but it was only a temporary fix.

The boys pile in, one at a time, each a slightly different shade of ghostly white. "What did you find out?" Carter asks, the four of them circling me in the living room.

"I went to visit Andrea at—"

"Mom, what?" Joel snaps. "Why—what were you thinking?"

"Quiet," I reply, my eyes wide, giving him a look that tells him to knock it off because I'm still his mother. "I had some questions to ask her."

"About Jenna's baby?" Sam asks.

"No, about your father. Son, please. Andrea was a patient of mine when I was working from home as an assistant to a psychiatrist. She came to us without a history or medical files, and a lot of what she talked about was only half truthful. She became obsessed with our conversations and began calling and texting me dozens of times each day. I was forced to end the therapy sessions with her. That's when Andrea became Peyton and moved in next door. She had a vendetta for anyone who abandoned her, or so she would describe the situation. Today, she told me your father was the problem all along. I was more concerned with taking care of him than helping her."

"She killed him, didn't she?" Joel asks, his eyes wide and unblinking as he wraps his hand around his throat.

Hearing the words come out of his mouth is like a knife to my heart. The thoughts have been swarming my mind, but I hadn't said it out loud. The spoken words make it sound real.

I shrug and pull in a sharp breath. "I still don't know any more than you do."

"Oh my God," *Carter says, slapping his hand against his mouth then dragging it down to his neck.*

"What is it?" *I ask him, running out of air with the end of my question.*

Carter takes a step back and falls into the couch. "The night Dad disappeared I came home before going out for the night. Peyton was in the garage. She said you two had gone out or something and Dad had forgotten to take the trash out, so she was just helping after all the times you both helped her. Then I left."

"Why haven't you said something?" *I shout at him, not intending to displace my anger, but how could he forget to mention something so important?* "She was in our house? What time was this, Carter?"

"I guess I didn't think much of it at the time," *Carter continues.* "I assumed you were out to dinner."

"What time did you come home that night?" *I ask again, annunciating all my words.*

"I-I-I don't know, maybe between six thirty and seven."

"Your father and I ate dinner around five thirty. I must have left the house around six to go to the pharmacy. I left him on the sofa."

"He wasn't here," *Carter says, the words struggling to form on his tongue.* "You said Dad got sick after dinner, so I just thought you had gone out like Peyton said and this all happened after you got home from dinner."

"Why was she taking the goddamn trash out?" *Michael shouts.* "Why?" *I don't know who he's demanding answers from but we're all very worked up.*

Joel begins to pace, running his hands down the side of his face. Sam drops down next to Carter on the sofa, and Michael unblinkingly stares out the window toward the end of the driveway.

"I need to make a phone call," Joel says. "I'll be right back."

With more information than we originally had when he disappeared, the investigation took a different route. It was almost seven months later by the time Officer Drell showed up at the front door. Our meetings were becoming so frequent, it was hard to guess what new information he'd be arriving with. He invited himself into the house and sat down with me in the living room. It took him a few minutes to tell me a body was found at the waste land and the dental records matched James's.

I was the one still living, but the previous twenty-five years of my life flashed before my eyes. It was my fault. I left Peyton alone in my house while I went out to the garage to find spare rolls of toilet paper. It was just enough time for her to pour something into the whiskey glass I'd prepared for James with our dinner. Only Andrea has the precise details of what followed, but by the presentation of his bones upon recovery, it appears he was put through a trash compactor, and the only way that could have happened is if he was picked up with the trash. The thought of what his body went through makes me want to put Andrea's body into a trash compactor. She deserves to suffer, and I'm not sure prison will be punishment enough.

Andrea couldn't take care of her husband or her house, and that's why she got caught.

People might only think of me as a homemaker most days, and while I'm much more than that, no one will ever question how well I know how to clean up a mess. I'm confident no one will find a fingerprint smudge on my records.

A LETTER FROM SHARI

Dear reader,

I'm absolutely over the moon that you've chosen to read *The Homemaker*. If you enjoyed it and want to keep up to date with all my latest releases, just sign up at the following link. Your email address will never be shared, and you can unsubscribe at any time.

www.bookouture.com/shari-j-ryan

Your interest in *The Homemaker* means so much to me. With all the books out there, I'm humbled and flattered to know you chose to spend your free time with one of my books. Nothing makes me happier than being able to share a new book with readers.

I loved every minute of crafting this story. To dive into the world of psychological thrillers has been a rewarding experience as I've been able to flex my creativity in new directions with unique characters and twists that have had me at the edge of my seat.

I genuinely hope you enjoyed reading the novel, and if so, I would be grateful if you could write a review. Since the feedback from readers benefits me as a writer, I would love to know what you think, and it makes such a difference helping new readers to discover one of my books for the first time.

There's no greater pleasure than hearing from my readers –

you can get in touch on my Facebook page, through Twitter, Goodreads, or my website.

Thank you for reading!

Shari

www.sharijryan.com

facebook.com/authorsharijryan
twitter.com/sharijryan
instagram.com/authorsharijryan

ACKNOWLEDGMENTS

Writing *The Homemaker* was a riveting experience. With each page I wrote, I became more invested and excited to sink my teeth into the world of psychological thrillers.

I'm so appreciative of Bookouture for offering me this chance to spread my wings. Your kindness and commitment has been invaluable to me throughout the past few years of my publishing journey. Also, I would like to thank Christina, my editor. Working together has enabled me to benefit from your expertise and talent. It's been an honor to collaborate with such a savvy and detail-oriented editor who has helped me learn and grow. And to Lucy, thank you for carrying the publication of *The Homemaker* forward without a hitch.

Linda, your unwavering positivity and belief in me has brought me so much comfort and joy over the years. I cannot express enough how much I value our friendship.

Tracey, Gabby, Elaine, and Heather—my long-time confidants, thank you for always offering your time, support, and friendship. Without you, I can't imagine where I would be today.

To all the ARC readers, bloggers, influencers, and readers who are a part of this incredible community: thank you for your positive energy and influence.

A special thanks to a few of my neighbors/friends: Kelly, thank you for sharing your excitement with me for this book, and I'm sorry for ruining a twist by wearing a certain name tag one night. Erin, if it wasn't for your suggestion to consider this genre, I might still be aimlessly staring out the window. Carla, thank you for hashing out ideas and how-tos on important subject matters that shouldn't be typed into a search engine.

Lori, the greatest little sister in the universe. Thank you for always being my #1 reader and my very best friend in the whole universe. Love you!

My family—Mom, Dad, Mark, and Ev, thanks for always believing in me and supporting my wild dreams. You all mean the world to me.

Bryce and Brayden—my wonderful boys—thank you for always believing in me. My wish for you both is to find a career that brings you the same amount of happiness someday. I love you more than words!

Josh, to have your support is everything to me. Through thick and thin of every book I write, you continue to cheer me on regardless of the unfamiliar names I continue to talk to you about as if they are real people in my life. I love you!